Middletide

Middletide

A Novel

Sarah Crouch

ATRIA BOOKS

NEW YORK LONDON TORONTO SYDNEY NEW DELHI

An Imprint of Simon & Schuster, LLC
1230 Avenue of the Americas
New York, NY 10020

First Atria Books hardcover edition June 2024

ATRIA BOOKS and colophon are trademarks of Simon & Schuster, LLC

Simon & Schuster: Celebrating 100 Years of Publishing in 2024

Interior design by Kyoko Watanabe

Manufactured in the United States of America

ISBN 9781668035092

For my mother, Laurie,
who loved my stories long before they made any sense

Author's Note

While *Middletide* is a work of fiction, inspiration for the Squalomah people and the Sacred Mountain Reservation was drawn from the author's personal experiences with the Indigenous people of Lummi and Navajo Nations.

The author wishes to emphasize that the Squalomah culture is fictional and, while inspired by Indigenous cultures, does not represent a real Indigenous Nation. All aspects of reservation life were written from a place of deep respect and with the desire to explore the unique connections between U.S. reservations and the citizen towns that they touch.

Prologue

Gray foam slapped the bow of the Crestliner as it zipped north across the still waters of Puget Sound. A fisherman by the name of Mike Ginter sat behind the windshield, bobbing up and down with the tiny boat, his eyes glued to the wall of evergreens that flanked the shoreline ahead. He was searching for the dying pine, the one with bleached branches poking through the top like exposed bones.

It was early Sunday morning, and by the looks of it he had beaten Wes to their favorite fishing spot for once. Mike cut the engine and the Crestliner slid through the hidden entrance to the cove as silently as a paper boat. As far as he knew, he and Wes were the only fishermen in town who knew about it. Between the dead pine and the one to its right was a small inlet accessible only at high tide and so narrow that he had to crouch down behind the windshield as the sweeping lower boughs scratched the sides of the low boat on the way in.

Fed by a small stream that ran through the Leith property, the hidden lake was full of fresh water that attracted the fattest trout anywhere near Point Orchards. Mike and Wes had sworn on their friendship to keep the place a secret, though not a weekend went by without someone at the marina eyeing their catch and pressing them for information.

Mike's Crestliner popped through the pines and he yanked off his hat, slapping it down on the bench beside him. He'd been fully prepared

1

to rub in Wes's tardiness, but there was his friend's boat, already docked on the far side of the lake and rocking as gently as a cradle. Mike swore as he reached for the set of aluminum oars beneath the bench. He rowed forward, his paddles sending the perfectly mirrored evergreens on the surface dancing in the soft ripples. He and Wes never risked motors here; both to prevent alerting fishermen out on the sound and to hide the fact that they were technically trespassing on Elijah Leith's property.

Mike rowed a diagonal path across the water toward his friend. Wes stood like a soldier at attention in his boat, his back to Mike, his eyes fixed on the trees. There was no shoreline here. The dark forest marched right up to the water's edge and the firs hung out over it, casting black shadows in a wavering ring around the lake.

"It's seven-forty," Mike called as he drew close, "the sun has officially been up for one minute, what's a guy gotta do to beat you out here?"

Wes didn't turn at the sound of Mike's voice, or laugh at his joke, or even acknowledge his presence. Mike dug his right oar into the water, slowing the boat and pulling even with Wes's small craft.

"You know, one of these mornings Irene's gonna . . ."

Mike's voice fell away as he stared at his friend. Wes's face was as expressionless as stone. If the man hadn't been standing on two feet, Mike might have thought he was dead.

"Look," Wes said in a voice so quiet it neared reverence.

Mike's eyes left his friend's face and followed his gaze to the trees.

There, in the shadow of a giant hemlock was a woman, hanging by her neck from a lower branch. The tips of her bare feet brushed the damp earth, and her arms dangled limply at her sides.

Her back was to them, but there was no mistaking who she was. No one else in Point Orchards had hair like that, perfect, corn silk–blond hair that fell in a sleek wave all the way to her lower back. Hair that Mike Ginter and every other man in town admired when they stepped into her office. Hair that his wife said was impractical for a doctor. A breeze stirred and her body twisted slowly on the rope. Mike looked away. He didn't want to see her face.

Two minutes after nine in the morning, Sheriff Jim Godbout tied the silver police skiff to a felled log onshore. His young deputy Jeremy was already circling the tree where Dr. Erin Landry hung, running his eyes up and down her body.

"There's a note," Jeremy called as Jim approached. The deputy slid a folded piece of paper from the pocket of Erin's fleece jacket, careful to avoid touching the cold hand that guarded it. He passed it to the sheriff, and Jim unfolded it, scanning it quickly. When he reached the end, he read it again, this time lingering over the words. He sighed deeply as he refolded the note and tucked it into his pocket. When he lifted his face to meet his deputy's eyes, he looked every bit as old as his sixty-eight years.

"Well?" Jeremy pressed.

"Let's get her down," the sheriff said sadly.

Jeremy used a branch at shoulder height to pull himself up into the tree and clambered through the boughs to the branch where the rope was tied off.

"She must've climbed up, tied the rope, and jumped," he called down, his fingers making slow work of the frozen knot.

The sheriff wrapped his arms around Erin's waist as the rope slid free. Her body folded over his shoulder, and he laid her gently on the ground beside a cluster of frost-tinted ferns. Twice he tried to close her eyes, but they stayed stubbornly open.

Jeremy jumped down through the boughs and landed with a grunt. Together, the two men stared down at the thirty-five-year-old doctor, who was every bit as beautiful in death as she had been in life.

"I just can't figure why," Jim said, shaking his head.

"You mean why she did it?"

"No, I mean, why here? The trees in this town outnumber the people a thousand to one. Why this tree way out in back of the Leith place? She could have done it anywhere. Out here her body might not have been found for weeks, months even, if Wes and Mike hadn't come fishing."

The sheriff crouched down and placed his hand on the forest floor beside Erin's head. He pinched a bit of damp earth between his finger and thumb and studied it. These woods still unnerved him after twenty-five years. They weren't the golden woods of his youth in the

Blue Ridge. Appalachian forests were straightforward and predictable. They abided by the seasons, budding green and lush as spring slid into summer, turning orange and yellow with the fall, and dropping their leaves compliantly at winter's bid, spending the rest of the year standing naked and straight as matchsticks on the hills. There, every step was announced by the crunch of dead leaves and the snapping of twigs. Those were noisy, airy forests that provided constant birdsong and cicadas for company. These Washington woods were different. They refused to change for the calendar and seemed designed for silence. Padded moss and thick layers of dead pine muffled footfalls and soaked up voices the way the rich, dark earth absorbed rain. The sheriff wiped his fingers on his pants. Behind him, water lapped gently at the dark bank, soft and soothing as a mother with her baby.

"Maybe she wanted the last thing she saw to be this pretty little lake in the woods," Jeremy suggested.

"In the middle of the night? She would barely have seen a thing."

The deputy shrugged. "Beats me."

Jim propped his hands on his knees and pushed himself to his feet. "Don't know that I blame her."

"What do you mean?"

"It was a few years ago, I don't think you were up here yet when it happened, but her little girl passed away." The sheriff pulled the note from his pocket and handed it to the deputy. "I guess she blamed herself this whole time. Got tired of living with the guilt. Can't imagine."

Jeremy read the note for himself.

I tried to make a life without Anna. It's not possible.
She's gone and it's my fault.
I can't live another day on earth without her. I just can't.
To whoever finds me, I'm sorry.

—Erin

"Should I head over to her office for a handwriting sample? That's protocol."

The sheriff hesitated. "It sure seems like a straightforward suicide, but yeah, I guess we'd better."

"Open-and-shut," the deputy agreed as he folded the note. "She must've sailed out here sometime in the night with the rope and done it."

A moment of silence passed between the two men as Jim looked around, searching.

"Where's her boat?" he asked, nodding to the lake. "If she got here by boat, where is it?"

The deputy's eyes circled the water as he thought.

"Isn't there a trail through the woods? It wouldn't be more than a mile if she parked on the road. Maybe she left her car out there and hiked back here."

Jim's gaze traveled down Erin's fully clothed body to the bare feet with only a trace of dirt where her toes had touched the ground.

"Without shoes?"

Jim wanted to be wrong, but a painful twist deep in his belly told him otherwise. Two and a half decades of service in Point Orchards and not once, not one blessed time, had anyone had the nerve to be murdered. He was eight months from retirement, and now this. He puzzled over it for another minute, but there was no way around the logic. Try as he might, he just couldn't explain away the pair of bare feet in front of him.

Jim turned and placed a hand on Jeremy's shoulder.

"Let's get her into town, I've got a call to make."

1

Elijah chased Nakita's laugh down the trail.

He was fast, but she was faster. He drove down the pace, almost sprinting, but all he caught were brief glimpses of long hair as it whipped around tight corners and flashed between tree trunks just ahead.

She knew this trail as well as he did now. They'd been running it all summer. It was the pretense, the excuse they'd given their parents; Nakita needed to train for her senior year of cross-country, and since Elijah had been captain of the team the year before, he would put in the miles with her over the summer before he left for college.

Every day since school let out, at the precise moment the minute hand on the kitchen clock slid from eleven-fifty-nine to noon, Nakita's firm knock sounded on the front door. Elijah sometimes had to remind himself not to fly to the door and throw it open in excitement after the long morning hours he'd waited to see her.

After a quick drink from the hose out back, they jogged side by side past the woodshed and behind the chicken coop, where a break in the fence opened into the forest beyond. That was their starting line, the beginning of the trail loop where they'd now put in hundreds of miles of training. There were plenty of other places in Point Orchards to run, but this trail guaranteed seclusion. Out here, they were totally and completely alone.

"Which way?" she shouted over her shoulder, barely out of breath as she reached the fork in the trail. The left turn would take them back to his house by way of a mossy mile loop through the forest; the right turn was barely an animal trail, overgrown with stinging nettles that would slap and blister their shins. That one would take them toward the sound, to the secret lake they'd first visited weeks before.

"You know which way," he called, slowing to a walk, his hands folded behind his head as he sucked in August air swollen with the sweetness of dead pine. A bright shaft of sunlight had broken through the firs overhead and illuminated Nakita's glistening body like a spotlight. She smiled, her black eyes sparkling with the same excitement that stirred in Elijah, and took off like a rabbit down the narrow trail to the right, hopping over thick patches of nettles and Queen Anne's lace in her bare feet.

The quick pace didn't feel so taxing when Elijah thought about what was just a few minutes ahead of them, and he quickly pulled even with Nakita, laughing as he darted around her.

"Hey!" She grabbed a handful of his tank top, but he tugged free and charged ahead, right through a thick patch of nettles. He ignored the sharp stinging on his lower legs as he weaved through the woods. In a way, he liked the feeling; convincing the brain to ignore discomfort was half the battle in the sport of cross-country, and he had plenty of thoughts to distract him at the moment. He caught a glimpse of shimmering blue-green through the evergreens and sprinted toward it, racing under the last of the trees and slowing to a halt right at the water's edge.

Nakita popped through the woods behind him, her chest heaving as she stopped short and caught her breath. Elijah locked eyes with her and she dropped her gaze, suddenly shy as she stood facing him beside the lake.

"I love that you run with your hair down," he said, stepping toward her and sliding his fingers through it, gently detangling small knots that the wind had tied. "You seem as free as a kid, like running is still just a game to you."

Nakita closed her eyes and tilted her head back into his hands.

"My nani said the Squalomah word for running means 'dancing

with Mother Earth.'" She shook her hair free and began braiding it loosely with deft fingers. "It's not like that for you?" she asked.

"Not really. Not anymore. It's the means to an end. I got what I wanted, the scholarship will get me out of here."

Nakita shook her head. "Let's not. Not today. We still have a week. Let's pretend we can stretch these last few days out forever."

Elijah grinned as he pulled his shirt over his head and kicked off his shoes, scooped up Nakita, and ran toward the water with her arms tight around his neck. She shrieked as he jumped in and the cool, clear water swallowed them both.

The lake washed away nettles, sweat, and inhibitions, and when they broke the surface, Nakita laughed and pressed her lips to his.

"You know," he said, kissing her mouth, her cheek, her nose, "this might be my favorite place in the whole world."

"Then stay," she whispered, burying her face in his neck.

He held her for a long minute, memorizing the feeling of wet hair plastered across his bare chest. He'd save this moment, every bit of it, in that special place she lived inside his mind. The heat of her sun-warmed skin, the salt on her lips, the rhythm of her beating heart so close to his own; he'd close his eyes and relive every last detail when he was in the sky, headed south on his first airplane ride this time next week.

"You hungry?" he asked and she nodded.

Elijah carried Nakita through the waist-deep water to where the small stream fed into the lake. He set her down on a mossy log, and she leaned forward to dangle her fingers in the creek, a glossy ribbon of light and shadow that snaked through the dark woods, gurgling cheerfully on its way around slate-gray stones that sprouted ferns like hair. Nakita sat admiring it while Elijah gathered overripe blackberries from the thornbushes behind her.

His hands dripped with purple juice when he called her name, beckoning her to a massive hemlock tree beside the lake. They sat and ate the sweet berries with their backs against the sturdy trunk, the gentle sound of lapping water filling the silence.

Elijah stood and reached into the pocket of his shorts, withdrawing a small jackknife. Flicking it open, he stood and faced the hemlock.

Nakita watched the blade in his hand as it twisted, gouging the thick bark.

"Nobody's gonna see whatever you're carving," she said practically.

"The birds will," he replied. "Maybe a deer or two."

Nakita turned her eyes to the lake. A heron on the far shore bobbed for a fish, quick as lightning, then took slow, luxurious flight with its lunch still wriggling in its beak.

Elijah hummed a casual tune above her.

"I just can't believe this time next week you'll be gone."

Elijah risked a glance at Nakita and found her eyes downcast with regret for having spoken the words out loud. They hung in the air like fog, tainting the sweetness of the silence.

For several minutes, the only sounds were the babble of the creek and the etching of his knife. Tiny bits of dust and wood fluttered down and landed on Nakita's shoulder.

"Try to put yourself in my shoes, just for a second, okay?" Elijah blew the last of the dust away and sat back down beside her. "Think of all the things I'll be able to do and see in a city, things I could never do here. It's not that there's anything wrong with Point Orchards, or any small town really, I just don't think anyone can truly find themselves in a place like this the way they could in a city like San Francisco."

"What are you hoping to find?" she asked.

"I don't know. Inspiration. Brand-new inspiration, the kind you can only find in a city."

Nakita looked around, her eyes landing on an ancient trunk nearby. It was half-decayed, with three young trees growing on top of it, old and new growth, the twisted roots of the younger trees weaving through thick patches of white lichen and pockets of decomposing bark to anchor themselves in the earth below. She nodded to it.

"See that log? That's a city. You could spend years learning its roads and houses, studying how one generation built a life on top of the last. You could find yourself there, while you count the hundreds of creatures that call that log home. And I bet, if you were willing to be quiet and just sit with it long enough to listen, it would probably tell you its stories."

Elijah jumped to his feet and stared down at her, his eyes as vividly blue and animated as the lake behind him. "That's the thing, Nakita, I don't want to listen to stories. I want to *tell* them. I want to write stories that tens of thousands of people read. Hundreds of thousands. I honestly believe I have it in me to be a great writer, but not if I stay here." Nakita remained silent, her eyes tracking him as he paced back and forth in front of the tree.

"I haven't seen enough," he claimed. "I haven't *lived* enough. Writers write what they know, and I just don't think anyone wants to read a story about someone who stays in the same small town their whole life. I owe it to myself to experience *something*, don't I?"

Nakita's black eyes flashed with indignation as she stood to face him. "And this isn't something? What is this, Elijah? What are we even doing here?"

Elijah's face softened. He took a step toward her and wrapped his hands around her waist.

"Look, it's not that I don't . . . that I don't want to be with you. But there's a life waiting for me in San Francisco, a very different life than the one I'd have if I stayed here."

Nakita remained silent and Elijah let out a frustrated sigh.

"Look, I don't know how to make you understand. You were raised with this idea that the land you were brought up on was sacred, like it was where your people were meant to be. I just don't feel that way about this town. I've been itching to leave for as long as I can remember." His gaze faltered and he stared down at his feet. "You'd probably understand if you were stuck in that cabin day after day after day with my dad."

Somewhere in the center of the lake, a trout jumped, startling them both. When Elijah turned back to Nakita, he found her jaw set and shoulders squared.

"Elijah, do you love me?" she asked boldly.

He blinked at her, this beautiful sixteen-year-old girl he'd only truly *known* since she and a few others from the reservation had joined the high school team at the beginning of the season. Once he'd opened his mind to the possibility of being with her, she had come flooding in, consuming every corner of his waking thoughts and most of his dreams as well. He had never known anyone like her. They came from different worlds. Even so, spending the summer together had been like reuniting two halves of a torn photograph, every edge aligning perfectly.

"Yes," he said, surprising himself.

"Then go," she said firmly. "Do what you need to do in San Francisco, live the life you want to live for a few years, then come back."

He closed the distance between them, folding her in his arms and pressing her head to his chest.

"I will," he promised. "Tell you what, what's today, the twenty-second? Let's make a pact right now that on August 22, exactly four years from now, let's meet at this tree. I'll have just finished college, and no matter where I am in the world, no matter where you are, or where life has taken us, we'll meet right here."

Nakita twisted her head to kiss the palm of his hand.

"Okay," she whispered.

Elijah pulled back and lifted her face to his.

"I mean it," he said, searching her eyes with a fierceness she'd never seen in him. "I'll come back for you, Nakita."

She nodded. "I'll be here."

2

Nakita scooped lard out of the tin with her bare fingers. She plopped it into the little well she'd made in a mound of flour and poured a cup of warm water over it before digging in with practiced twists and turns, rotating the bowl as she formed a rough dough. The floor groaned behind her and she paused.

"Good morning, Nani," she said without turning around. "You're up early."

Nakita didn't have to look over her shoulder to know that her grandmother was standing in the kitchen doorway, watching her knead. She felt the stare of disapproval like a branding iron on her back.

She rounded the dough into three balls and placed them on the cracked Formica before swiveling with a sigh. "Just say it."

"Does Kailen know where you're going?"

Nakita turned back to the counter. Another handful of lard went into the skillet already warming on the stove. It melted outward, bubbling at the edges.

"I haven't promised him anything."

The thin floor creaked again as Nani took a step into the kitchen.

"That's not what I asked," she said.

When Nakita didn't answer, Nani came forward and placed arthritic hands on her granddaughter's shoulders.

13

"Nakita, I only want to keep you from the pain you're inviting into your heart today."

"It would hurt more if I didn't go and I found out later that he showed up," Nakita said softly.

The gnarled hands left Nakita's back and began to flatten the balls of dough on the counter into thick circles. Nakita knew this was her grandmother's way of accepting her plan for the day, though the bridge between acceptance and approval was often a long one for Nani to cross.

The first slab of dough hit the fat in the pan with a loud sizzle, and Nakita left her grandmother to attend to the bread while she packed a small canvas sack with two apples and a strip of dried trout wrapped in paper. Two pieces of the hot fry bread followed, and she covered the third in honey before tearing it in half and handing the larger piece to Nani.

Grandmother and granddaughter carried their breakfast through the front door to where two rocking chairs rested side by side in a sunrise shadow that bowed across the porch, sagging with the aluminum roof that cast it. They ate in companionable silence, but Nani wasn't letting Nakita off the hook without a fight.

"If you would just talk to Kailen—"

"Nani, please," Nakita said shortly, turning pleading eyes to her grandmother. "Kailen's a good man, but he's young. I'm young. We have years yet to decide if we want to be together."

"He's already decided, Nakita. He'll give you a good life, if you let him."

Nakita took a bite of her bread and stared across the dirt road to the dawn-tinted river on the other side. It streaked soundlessly west behind the pines, two canoes lying overturned on its bank. The first was her father's: rustic, perfunctory, and cracking with age. The second was a gift that Kailen had given her family earlier in the summer, sleek and crafted with skill far beyond his twenty-four years. Nakita couldn't shake the feeling that it was a bribe.

"Do you remember when I was a little girl, the time you caught me on the roof holding two fistfuls of crow feathers?"

Nani unleashed a rattling laugh that turned into a cough. "Sweet girl, you thought you could fly right up past the trees if you flapped your little wings hard enough."

"You made me come down," Nakita recalled. "I asked if you were going to tell mama, and you said telling her would do no good, she would only worry."

Nani nodded.

"This is just like that," Nakita insisted. "Telling Kailen would only cause problems." She finished her bread and licked a drop of honey from her thumb.

"That may be," Nani said, rising from her chair, her eyes lingering on Nakita's face. "But Elijah has been gone for a long time, he may not even remember the promise he made. I hope you'll be safely off the roof without any harm done by the time the sun sets tonight."

Nakita sat alone on the porch a little longer, watching the river flow past the canoes.

Before she left, she rummaged through the old case of cheap makeup she'd gotten for her fourteenth birthday. Half of it was dried up and unusable, but she managed to coax a bit of black mascara out of the tube and enough gloss to stain her lips the deep hue of black cherries. Nani brushed her hair until it gleamed, and Nakita let it fall loosely over the straps of her black tank top instead of pulling it back into its usual braid.

She made herself wait until the sun had risen a full hand's width above the eastern mountains before setting off for the lake, her canvas bag slung over her shoulder.

The Leith cabin was still dark-windowed when she reached it an hour later, and Nakita felt ashamed as she crept toward the back fence, keeping to the shadows like a thief. She doubted Mr. Leith would prevent her from walking through his property to the lake, but she didn't want to explain why she was here. She'd seen him several times in town since Elijah left. It was impossible not to when she'd spent the last two years bagging the groceries of everyone who lived in Point Orchards. Every time he came through her line he was friendly, but she never asked him if he'd been in touch with Elijah and he never offered. Month after month, the cans of beer she scanned for him seemed to multiply on the counter. Why wouldn't he drink? He lived alone in a cabin in the woods; he probably missed Elijah as much as she did.

Nakita slipped behind the reeking chicken coop and through the fence. A lone hen had nested just inside the forest. Startled by unexpected footfall, it squawked noisily and exploded into the air in a flurry of feathers. Nakita swatted at it, peering anxiously over her shoulder at the back windows of the cabin before starting down the path.

The four years since she'd last run this trail with Elijah were written on the land. The already narrow path was squeezed even tighter by thick ferns and creeping Oregon grapes. A few winters' worth of felled trees had left new hurdles for her to clamber over on her way to the lake. There was no one around to saw through their middles. Elijah was the one who had maintained the trail every spring, his young muscles straining against the undergrowth as he moved foot by foot around the loop, clearing a manicured corridor with his father's machete. Left untouched for four years, the forest seemed determined to slowly erase all evidence of his labor. Soon, there would be no proof that he had ever lived here at all.

Nakita missed the fork in the trail and had to turn back looking for it. The thin path through the nettles was now a mere indent in the greenery. The stinging plants stood straight and tall, none bent or broken. She was the first one to walk through them today. They bit at her skin, raising tiny blisters that she ignored as she pushed forward toward the lake that glittered temptingly behind the trees.

She reached the tree just as the light on the water completed its transition from limpid morning sunshine to the golden glare of midday. She dropped her canvas sack with a sigh and reached out to touch the trunk.

Nakita closed her eyes, and in an instant she was sixteen again, wrapped in Elijah's arms as he carried her through the water. She could taste the sweetness of blackberries on his lips. She could see the sincerity in his ocean-colored eyes when he'd promised he would come back for her. When he'd promised *today*.

Nakita sank to the ground and rested her head against the tree. She sat unmoving through the morning hours, her body still as her mind reeled. Every sound sent her eyes flying to the dark hollow she'd emerged from, hoping despite every ounce of her common sense that she'd see Elijah's lean figure emerging from the trail, changed and yet unchanged, true to his word despite his years of absence.

Her backside grew stiff and numb as the sun traced a slow, wavering line across the water. A few hundred feet away, a young male deer grazed a lazy circle around the lake and Nakita reached into her bag for an apple. She ate half and held the rest in her hand, waiting. When the wind lifted the hairs on her arm, Nakita held out the apple, letting its scent carry to the young buck. One cautious step at a time, he approached her. Nakita kept her eyes on his for long minutes, her breath even and slow.

"There you go," she whispered as he stretched his neck tentatively toward the broken fruit and lifted it from her fingers. Nakita fed him her second apple and stroked his flank lightly as he passed by, returning to his foraging around the lake.

The air above the water shimmered with heat. Nakita stripped down to her underwear and waded in, letting the cool water support her as she floated on her back, the broken wisps of clouds sailing toward the sound reflected in her dark eyes. She drifted to the center of the lake and kicked her legs in the silky water, turning in a slow circle. Somewhere beneath her a school of trout scattered. Nakita felt their movement and remembered the strip of dried fish in her sack. Hunger drove her back to the tree, where she dressed, weaved her hair into a damp braid and ate the trout with a piece of bread.

The shadows on the far side of the lake began to bulge as the sun tilted toward the western horizon, and Nakita's thoughts drifted from Elijah to Kailen. Nani was right; Kailen would give her a good life if she let him. He was handsome and loyal, dependable as the tide. More than that, he was one of her people. That was important, far more important than a brief summer of passion that burned hot for a season but left her with an empty ache when it was gone.

Nakita tracked the billowing clouds that gathered behind the trees, their underbellies blushing salmon and opal with the setting sun. She drew her knees up and leaned her head on them. It hadn't hurt as much as she had thought it would. Deep down, she had prepared for disappointment. Truly, she wouldn't have known what to do or say if Elijah *had* miraculously stepped through the woods and back into her life. Still, she'd come. She'd come because long ago her father had caught her lying, and she'd never forgotten the look of disappointment on his face when he told her she owed the same loyalty to her word that a wolf owed to her pups. When push came to shove, her word was all she had.

The last of the light left the clouds and Nakita rose to her feet, her pledge fulfilled. She had wasted too much of her youth on a summer love to whom she owed nothing.

Nakita walked home in the moonlight. When she reached the first house just over the border of the reservation, she smiled at the lamplight pouring through Nani's upstairs bedroom window.

"It's okay, Nani," she whispered as the light blinked off. "I didn't fly, but I'm safe now."

3

Sheriff Godbout took the long way to work, heat blasting as he drove seven miles an hour below the speed limit. The remote, two-lane road he traveled on quietly circled the small town, meandering through pretty orchards and past the marina. This route took him right by Doc Landry's house, and Jim craned his neck to stare at it as the cruiser rolled past. It was a pretty, Easter-green two-story tucked back from the road in a little grove of arborvitae.

In a few weeks' time there would be a FOR SALE sign out front and some out-of-towner would snap it up. Maybe a young family with kids or some Seattle hotshot looking for a summer home near the water. Strange thing, the life cycle of a house. At the end of it, Erin would have been nothing but a blip in the house's long history. Moving into the place with her good-looking husband and a baby on the way, she'd probably danced around in the living room, talking with her husband about the years ahead, about building a treehouse for their kid, remodeling the kitchen, maybe cutting down the arborvitae and planting roses instead. Who would've thought that in just a few short years, both mother and child would be dead and the husband long gone. The house was ready for its next optimistic young couple.

It would probably be up to the bank to sell it since Erin had no next of kin. She and her husband had divorced shortly after the death of their daughter, and last Jim heard, the man had taken up tropical residence in Costa Rica. Or was it Puerto Rico? At any rate, Jim was relieved to be driving past the quaint little house and not pulling into the driveway to tell Erin's "survived by" the bad news.

Worst part of the job by a long shot. Whenever anyone in Point Orchards was killed by anything more than natural causes, the weight of informing their loved ones fell squarely on Jim's slumped shoulders. Over the years there had been a handful of fatal car accidents, a drowning now and again, a teenage cliff-jump gone bad, and once he'd had to report the grisly misfortune of a hunting accident between two young men on the reservation. The Squalomah didn't fund a police department, and since most of the reservation fell on this side of the county line, Jim found himself traveling over the border into the population of Native Americans for emergencies from time to time.

The marina rose into view up ahead. Two dozen or so white pleasure crafts sat side by side in the thin morning fog, neat as a row of iced pastries. The more industrial gray-and-brown fishing boats behind them formed two jagged lines like teeth in a rotting mouth. Several were missing, their captains already hard at work dredging the sound for seafood.

Across the street from the marina sat the Blue Goose Café. The sheriff swung the cruiser into an empty parking space and tucked his wallet into his back pocket. The Blue Goose was owned and operated by a veteran's widow named Della who maintained a generous "uniforms eat free" policy in honor of her late husband.

A few tiny white flakes landed on the sheriff's shoulders as he zipped up his jacket. The storm was early, forecasted to start in the late afternoon, with five inches called for overnight and plenty more in the morning. Point Orchards always took a beating from winter storms that rolled in off the Pacific. The town was a summer haven for tourists from Seattle, a quaint little village on the water that offered a forested retreat from the sun on rare July and August weekends when the heat grew intense, but the rest of the year it could best be described as tempestuous.

Thick, gray clouds over the Pacific were pushed inland by the wind and squeezed dry by the mountains to the east before they drifted over, white and fluffy, to the drier towns on the other side. They dumped their contents—rain, snow, and sleet, often all three on the same day—squarely on the town of Point Orchards. It was almost as though whoever founded the town had decided to place it at the foot of the mountains as an elaborate, hundred-year-long practical joke, treating its citizens to weeks at a time of relentless precipitation.

Inside the café, the smell of bacon and coffee greeted Jim like an old friend. He touched a finger to his hat and Della waved him over to sit at the bar.

"It's true, right?" she asked, placing a mug in front of him and filling it with steaming hot coffee.

"Della," he said, shaking his head, "you know good and well I can't talk about it."

Della leaned forward and propped her elbows on the counter. "Sarah came in here for lunch yesterday and said Mike got back home from fishing all frazzled. She said Wes and him found Doc Landry out there in the woods. We all feel just awful about it."

Jim took a long sip of his coffee. The Point Orchards gossip hotline was clearly up and running. How long had it taken word to spread once Mike and Wes had walked in the door and told their wives? An hour. Maybe two.

"Can I get an omelet with ham and mushrooms?" he asked, and Della took the hint, bustling back to the kitchen.

"Gimme a holler when the joe's empty," she called, leaving the pot behind.

A moment later, a hand landed on Jim's shoulder and he turned to find Jeremy sliding onto the stool beside him.

"Coroner's headed up at noon," the deputy said by way of greeting.

"Good." Jim nodded.

"I wanna be in there when he does the autopsy," Jeremy said, pouring himself a cup of coffee.

Jim side-eyed him as he tore the lids off four creamers and dumped them in one at a time.

"No, you don't. Trust me," he said, taking a long sip from his mug.

"Yes, I do," Jeremy insisted. "I want to be in there when he figures out whether or not she did it herself."

A metal bowl hit the floor in the kitchen, and Jim leaned forward to rub his temples with his fingers.

"Clam it, will ya?" he said in a low voice. "We've got enough to deal with without every busybody in town showing up at the office to play private eye."

Jim glanced through the windowed kitchen doors and found Della cracking eggs with her head tilted conspicuously toward them. He drained the last of his coffee and slid the mug across the counter.

"Lost my appetite, Della," he called to the kitchen as he eased his weight off the bar stool and headed for the door, ignoring his sinking suspicion that the gossip hotline was about to light up again.

———

The coroner arrived on time and followed the sheriff and his deputy to the Point Orchards Mortuary. He asked them for privacy while he conducted the autopsy, a request which Jim, at least, was pleased to accommodate. He'd observed exactly one autopsy in his career and that had been enough. Nothing put a man off his supper like the cracking of lifeless ribs under a bone saw.

The clock above the glass door ticked slowly around the three o'clock hour, and Jim sat with his back to Jeremy, who was pacing back and forth in the small waiting room outside the refrigerated morgue. Fat drops of water fell from a sagging tile in the corner of the small office, and Jim watched them land one at a time in an ever-widening circle of dampness on the carpet. There would be mold underneath if someone didn't take care of it before long.

"Will you take a dang seat, son?" he asked for the third time.

Jeremy sat for all of forty-five seconds before jumping up to pace again.

"I should be in there right now. This is *my* case." Jeremy threw up his hands.

"Our case," the sheriff corrected him.

"You know what I mean," Jeremy said irritably, turning on his heel and striding across the room again.

"I guess the man is used to working with folks who give him a certain level of peace and quiet," Jim said, chuckling at his own joke.

Four in the afternoon came and went. Jeremy finally stopped pacing and planted himself in front of the window instead, peering through the blinds at the snow gathering on the sloped parking lot.

As the afternoon hours dragged on, the pit in Jim's stomach tightened. This was not a "no news is good news" situation.

At a quarter to five, the heavy door that sealed off the morgue opened with a loud groan and the coroner stepped out.

"Well," he said, peeling off his gloves, "whoever wanted that woman's murder to look like a suicide did a pretty bad job of it."

"I knew it!" Jeremy shouted, practically giddy. Both Jim and the coroner shot him a look of pure disdain.

"I knew it," he repeated, only slightly more subdued.

Jim turned back to the coroner. "Let's have it," he said.

"I'll get the photos printed up for you, but there's everything you'd expect to see in a hanging homicide. Her body was fairly clean, no external abrasions, but there were a couple of discernible signs that tell me it wasn't self-inflicted."

"Were there any, uh, signs of . . ." Jim's voice fell away, but the coroner caught his meaning.

"No, no, nothing like that."

"So, cause of death?"

"Asphyxiation. There's a possibility she was strangled with the rope first before she was hung, but there's no way to be sure now. There was a typical "hangman's fracture," though." He reached up to place a finger at the base of his skull. "The neck was broken here, so she wasn't strung up gently. For that reason, I'd lean toward hanging as the cause of death rather than strangulation first."

"What else?" Jim asked.

"Well, the real kicker is the blood under her fingernails. Not much, just a little under the right middle and ring finger, but there's only one reason I can think of why it would be there. Those are the fingers that would catch skin if you lashed out to scratch an attacker. I've seen it before."

A ripple of goosebumps broke out across Jim's shoulders as the coroner continued to talk.

"The criminology lab in Seattle has been right up there with the new DNA technology. I'd say it's worth sending the blood out to see what they can tell you about it."

"Yeah, yeah, I read about that," Jeremy said, snapping his fingers. "A few years back they were able to overturn a conviction and prove some guy was innocent because they pulled someone else's DNA off the victim. Man, what'll they come up with next?"

The coroner promised a detailed write-up as the sheriff and deputy walked him to the door.

It was official. God hadn't seen fit to grant Jim a peaceful last year. He thanked the coroner, shook his hand, and wished him safe travels back to Seattle through the storm. As the man drove slowly away in his maroon sedan, his taillights swallowed by swirling flakes of snow, Jim knew with sinking certainty that he was heading into a storm of his own.

4

Elijah covered his mouth and nose with his shirt and kicked the door as hard as he could. It broke at the hinges and flew into the cabin, landing in a cloud of dust. Coughing, he stepped over it and took a long look around the kitchen. He barely recognized the room. Dust was everywhere, coating the counters, floor, and furniture, and a thick curtain of cobwebs stretched corner to corner on every window, making it impossible to see out. It had been fifteen years since he'd last set foot inside these walls, but the place was in even worse shape than he had thought it would be.

"Dad," he breathed, shaking his head.

The dust and spiders were excusable; the cabin had sat empty since his father died three years before. But the other stuff, the broken furniture, cracked dishes still stacked in the sink, and piles of empty beer cans in the corners gave him a stomach-churning look into the life his father had led in the years before his death.

Elijah was tempted to tell himself he would have come back if he'd known, if he'd had any idea how poor his father's quality of life had been at the end, but it would be a lie. He wouldn't have come back, not when he had been so busy in his pursuit of his impossible dream, the one that remained eternally around the next corner throughout his entire twenties, every bit as genuine as a mirage.

Elijah hoisted the door off the floor and propped it on his shoulder, attempting to hang it back on its hinges. He quickly gave up and chucked it straight out onto the porch, where it splintered into pieces. Coming up the driveway, he had remembered the rusty house key under the ceramic lawn jockey beside the well, but neither key nor jockey remained, leaving him no choice but to force entry into the cabin that now belonged to him, the one possession his father had in this world worth leaving to someone else.

Elijah flicked the light switch up and down to no avail and added *set up utilities* to his long mental list of things to do. He tried the faucet in the kitchen and it sputtered loudly, spitting out a few mouthfuls of rusty water. The faucet in the hall bathroom did the same. He'd have to manually pull some water from the well before the electric pump was up and running again.

Elijah grabbed his two suitcases off the front porch and carried them to his room. He passed the master suite that had been his parents', breathing a sigh of relief to find the door closed. Someday, he'd tackle whatever was behind that door. Someday, he might even move his stuff in there for the convenience of having a bathroom right off the bedroom, but not today. He unpacked the suitcase that held his clothes, but left the other zipped tight and threw it under the bed. That was for another day, too. He moved through the house, prying open windows as he went. It had rained all night, and the spring air was fresh with the smell of damp earth, perfect for airing out the musty cabin.

Elijah opened the small linen closet at the end of the hall, looking for something to wipe down the cobwebs. It was amazing, the sharpness of the memories that forgotten things could trigger. The small stack of folded towels in the closet sent him instantly back almost thirty years to where he sat on the living room floor with his mother as she said, "hot dog, hamburger, third, third," over and over, folding each towel in half the long way, then in half the short way and into thirds. She handed him the stack of towels and he ran on toddler legs to place them in the tiny closet, then back to his mother, who scooped him up and told him what a good helper he was.

Elijah walked back to the kitchen with a yellow washcloth in hand

and swiped it across the filthy windowsill. Completely ruined. It would take a hundred washcloths and several days to remove all the grime in the house. Frustrated, Elijah tossed the rag onto the dusty counter. He needed some air.

A light mist was falling as he took off through the backyard, stripping off his shirt and leaving it draped over the deck railing. Though he was wearing jeans, the impulse to run was irresistible, and he broke into a jog when he reached the empty chicken coop.

The forest trail was completely overgrown. Not runnable. His pants snagged on thorny plants and brushed the rain off of ferns, soaking him below the knee with cold water that ran down into his socks as he stutter-stepped forward. He climbed slowly over a gargantuan trunk blocking the trail. It would've been a lot easier on spry, eighteen-year-old legs than thirty-three-year-old limbs now rusty with disuse. Less than half a mile into the woods he gave up and turned around to walk slowly home.

Something quick and feathered darted across his path, and Elijah blinked at the brush where it had vanished. A moment later another one, sleek and golden, followed it, pausing on the trail just long enough for Elijah to get a good look. He laughed in utter disbelief.

A younger, wilder generation of chickens had somehow survived the fat domestic hens of his youth. His dad must've gotten a rooster at some point and nature did the rest. It was like the time he had eaten a store-bought apple and planted the seeds with his mother. Every year, the apples that the tree produced were a bit tangier, their flesh crisper, a little more veined with the wildness of the land. Elijah jogged back to the deck and snatched up the big wicker basket that his father had used for gathering kindling. He took it out to the woods and began lifting ferns and parting patches of long grass with his fingers.

Bingo.

He reached into the nest and picked up a pale blue egg no bigger than a golf ball. Five more minutes of hunting provided him with a second egg, this one a warm brown color and a bit larger. Elijah carried the basket into the backyard and set it at his feet as he scanned the property. What else? What was ripe in May? It was too early for the sweet cherries that June would bring, and months and months too early for the plums and apples that would hang from the trees out front by the road, trees that were now shedding the last of their pink and white spring blossoms.

Elijah ducked under the tin awning of the woodshed and grabbed a couple of logs from the dwindling supply. There was a time he and his father had kept this shed full to the brim with half a dozen chest-high rows of neat logs that they'd chopped themselves. Hundreds of pieces of wood left to age and dry for the winters ahead. He could picture his dad now, standing at the end of each row as Elijah moved along with a hatchet, tapping the logs that stuck out until each row was perfectly faced, a thing of symmetry and pride. Now, a mere forty or so logs remained in a scattered pile around the old chopping block, the handle of a forgotten axe sticking out at an angle, right where his father had left it, head buried in the stump.

Behind the woodshed, two blueberry bushes stood side by side and Elijah inspected them closely. Tiny green berries were budding on the thin branches, but it would be at least another month until they were edible.

Elijah walked along the fence, past the ancient compost heap his mother had insisted his father start when he was little. His eyes hunted the greenery behind the wooden boards for color. A pink berry poked its head out from under a wide leaf and Elijah plucked it, holding it up in the light. It was a salmonberry. Of course, the woods would be full of them this time of year. If he was lucky, he could gather enough to push off the obligatory first grocery trip into town for an extra day or two. The longer his return to Point Orchards stayed a secret, the better. Besides, money was something he didn't have in excess at the moment. In fact, every last dollar to his name was bundled in a single wad of twenties in the suitcase under his bed. A pathetically small bundle at that. Maybe enough to pay for a year's worth of utilities and scant groceries. Maybe. Sooner or later he'd have to face the reality of getting a job in town. But that was another thing on his list best left for a different day.

Elijah carried the basket back into the house and set it beside the woodstove. He found a lighter in the kitchen and was surprised that it sparked instantly to life when he rolled his thumb over the starter. The tin bucket next to the woodstove was usually full of rolled-up newspapers, but it was overturned and completely empty. Elijah looked around the small living room for paper to crumple. Sudden inspiration struck and he bolted for his bedroom.

Pulling the suitcase out from under the bed, he unzipped the front pouch and pulled out a book. *His* book. He tore the pages as he went, balling them tightly in his fist as he walked down the hall. He knelt before the woodstove and lit one, tossing it inside. It burned brightly in the empty belly of the stove. Elijah crumpled page after page of his own words and fed them to the fire. He'd spent ten years of his life pouring his heart and soul onto these pages for absolutely nothing. His book, his young life's work, had sold an abysmal forty-eight copies. *Forty-eight.* No one would miss it. Not the agent he'd worked so hard to impress and who stopped taking his calls after the book failed to land with a major publisher. Not the writing group he'd worked with after college, who had convinced him to publish it with a small publishing house that had never produced a well-known novel. Not the handful of girlfriends he'd had throughout his twenties, none of whom even bothered to read it.

Hot anger rose in his throat, and before Elijah knew it, he was hurling the balls of paper as hard as he could into the woodstove. The heat of the blaze singed his hands and face as he ripped fistfuls of pages out at a time, no longer bothering to ball them up as he flung them into the fire. In less than two minutes, all that was left of his book was the flimsy blue-and-green cover.

Before the sensible part of his brain could stop him, Elijah shot to his feet and lashed out at the stove, kicking its cast-iron side as hard as he could while unleashing a primal scream of frustration and anguish that seemed torn from the very soles of his feet.

Toes throbbing, Elijah sank back down before the fireplace, depleted.

He reached for the logs and placed them on top of the burning paper, praying they'd catch before his book was nothing more than ashes.

There was a relatively clean frying pan in one of the kitchen drawers, and Elijah cracked both eggs into it and set it on top of the stove.

Another memory resurfaced. This one from when he was fourteen and his father, after downing two six-packs of beer without assistance, challenged Elijah to lay his hand on top of the woodstove for as long as he could while the fire inside slowly heated it. Elijah had challenged back, telling his dad he could keep his hand on longer than the old man could. Facing each other, they had placed their hands on the cast iron. Long minutes passed as the stove grew warm and then hot and then far too hot. Elijah's fingertips were beginning to blister and every alarm bell in his brain was begging him to pull his hand from the stove, but his father still stood coolly on the other side, staring down his nose at his son. Elijah broke first, yanking his hand from the heat and running for the cold water of the kitchen sink. He never turned around to see if his dad's hand had blistered, too. He was too ashamed.

Elijah reached for the cover of his book and placed it on top of the burning logs. The orange flames consumed it slowly, edges first, until all he could see were the ten letters of the title as the fire ate them from the outside in.

MIDDLETIDE

The word shrank to nothing.

Elijah sat back on his heels and closed the glass door. He should probably feel worse after destroying the only copy he had left of his book, but he felt better. Much better.

The eggs were burned, yolks cooked to orange chalk. Elijah sat at the kitchen table and ate them out of the pan. He covered the empty hole where the front door had been with a sheet and went to bed.

He'd figure it all out, tomorrow.

5

The sun slid between two clouds, catching the axe head for a split second and lighting it up like silver in its arc through the air. It landed in the center of the log with a satisfying *thwack*, splitting it neatly in two. Elijah kicked the pieces off the stump into the growing pile behind it and picked up another log.

He swung again, cracking the log halfway through. The blade was lodged in a thick knot. Elijah wrenched the handle back and forth until it sprang free. He swung again, bringing the axe down with a grunt and breaking the log cleanly. The two halves joined the pile behind the stump, and he stooped to grab another, stopping short at the sound of gravel crunching under tires.

Elijah jogged to the back deck and grabbed his shirt off the railing. He pulled it over his head as he stepped into the house, his heart racing. Who on earth would be coming to see him? He certainly hadn't sent out housewarming invitations.

So far, he had ventured into town just three times, and each time he'd worn a Giants cap pulled low over his eyes, keeping his chin tucked as he gathered cleaning essentials and a few basic staples for the kitchen. He had seen a few familiar faces in the aisles of the grocery store: a male teacher from his middle school days whose sandy hair was now lined with gray; a woman who had been friends with his mom, at least fifty

31

pounds heavier than when he'd last seen her; and a couple of classmates
who hadn't left Point Orchards and looked pretty much the same. He'd
gone out of his way to avoid recognition, successfully he'd thought.
Until now.

Elijah reached the front door, pieced back together with wood glue
and duct tape, and grabbed the doorknob. For a moment, a pair of
sparkling black eyes flashed through his mind. Their clarity, sharp and
searing, sent Elijah's heart slamming into his ribs. He shook the image
away. It couldn't be.

He opened the door and stepped onto the porch to find a tan Toyota
pickup parked in the driveway. The door swung open and a heavy man
in his mid-sixties stepped out. A broad smile broke across Elijah's face.

"Chitto!" Elijah leapt down the porch stairs and embraced his
father's closest friend.

"Let me look at you," Chitto said, running his eyes over Elijah as
though assessing him for change. Possibly damage.

Elijah stepped back to perform his own appraisal. Other than the
lines that sat a bit deeper in the contours of Chitto's rough face and
the heightened ratio of gray to black in his braid, he looked exactly the
same. Elijah wondered how different he looked to the man who had
watched him grow up. He was still lean, but his shoulders had broad-
ened and the first traces of lines now creased the brow that hooded his
bright blue eyes. The dark hair he'd allowed to curl past his ears in high
school was kept shorter now and complemented by ample stubble on
his face, stubble that was more a nod to laziness than fashion.

"How'd you know I was here?"

Chitto looked past Elijah to the cabin. "I've been keeping an eye on
the place since your pops passed. Every now and then I drive by to make
sure it's still standing. Here, brought you something."

Elijah's eyes widened at the pristine new Black and Decker tool kit
Chitto pulled from the truck.

"Thanks!" he said appreciatively as Chitto placed the box in his arms.

"Figured you could use a new set while you wrestle this place back to
life. I'm sure your dad's old tools are rusting out back in the shed." His
deeply lined eyes moved back to Elijah's face. "Sure was surprised to see

that motorcycle here. I figured it was you. He always said you'd come back someday. Wish it'd been before he died."

Elijah nodded, pushing back against the wave of guilt by changing the subject.

"How're things with you? Is the garage still up and running?"

"Sure is. It's been tough, handling all the work myself since your dad got sick, but I'm managing. If you're looking for a job, though, I could use you."

"I might be later on," Elijah said. "I'm still trying to get my bearings and figure out how to keep this place running. I've got enough to make ends meet for a while, though."

"Let's see what you've done with it," Chitto said, clapping a hand on Elijah's shoulder and steering him toward the porch.

"Don't expect much," Elijah warned, secretly thrilled to show some-one, anyone, the effort he'd put into getting the cabin in working order again.

"What's with the . . ." Chitto gestured to the long strips of duct tape on the front door. "You know what? I don't wanna know."

Elijah laughed and led him inside.

Chitto whistled long and low. "Heck of a lot cleaner than last time I was here."

"Yeah, anyone can clean, but check this out," Elijah laid the tool kit on the counter and led Chitto to the large pantry behind the kitchen. The small window cut into the room had several pots on its sill. "I found a bunch of tiny seeds in a bag in the kitchen and planted them. My mom had herbs in here when I was little, I remember her pulling the leaves off and throwing them into soups and stuff. Not sure what this one is."

"Thyme," Chitto said, inspecting the small sprouts.

"And come here, look at this."

On the other side of the room were floor-to-ceiling shelves, all empty except for three glass jars of what looked like runny tomato soup.

"What is it?" Chitto asked.

"Thimbleberry jam. There were so many thimbleberries out in the woods I didn't want them to go to waste, so I boiled them down with a little sugar and made jam. I've got blueberries and raspberries in the fridge for my next two batches. It feels good, putting a couple of jars on these shelves. Makes me think of Mom. Man, she had this pantry completely stocked with jams and pickled vegetables. She even canned chicken stew when the hens stopped laying. You know, I think I could eventually live off this property with almost no outside help if I tried hard enough."

Chitto was looking at him with laughing eyes. "That's exactly what your parents wanted. They came out here from the city and built this place to homestead. It was your mom's dream, to have a self-sustaining piece of land. She wasn't Squalomah, but she might as well have been. She had some of the magic in her."

Elijah nodded. "I guess I took that for granted growing up. I had no idea how much work went into keeping this place going."

"What else?" Chitto asked with an encouraging smile.

Elijah led him to the backyard and showed him the large rectangle of dirt he'd taken the hoe to, churning the earth into submission where his mother's vegetable garden had been. A few tiny shoots were growing and the rest of the seeds were in the ground, but so far, all Elijah had to show for his labor were the callusing blisters on his hands.

"You'll need some chicken wire to keep the deer and rabbits out," Chitto said.

"Good idea," Elijah agreed. "There might be a little around here somewhere."

"Will you look at that." Chitto nodded at the neat row of firewood in the woodshed and the tall pile waiting to be stacked.

Elijah shrugged. "Most of that's from a tree that went down behind the fence. Cheaper than buying it. Plus, I already know how to cut and stack wood. It's been a while, but Dad had me chop a row every summer. Like riding a bike." He swung his arm in a slow windmill motion. "Not as easy on the body as it used to be though. My shoulders are killing me. Once they settle down, I'll take the bow out to the woods and see if I can hit anything. Haven't had meat in a few weeks."

Chitto turned to Elijah, dark eyes searching his face.

"Son, you can't hide out here forever," he said softly.

"What do you mean?"

"I don't know what pushed you back here with your tail between your legs, but whatever it is, folks will welcome you back with open arms, no questions asked. You're still a part of this town. Why not come on out to the fireworks in a couple days? They shoot 'em off down at the marina now. It's real pretty over the water."

Elijah was quiet for a few moments. "I'll think about it."

"You do that. Think about that job at the garage, too, I could use the extra hands."

Elijah walked Chitto back to his truck and waved him down the driveway. Long after the pickup disappeared around the wooded bend, he stood staring at the road, lost in thought. Chitto was right. He could sustain his body on food from the land, but could he sustain his mind with just his father's collection of Louis L'Amour books for company? With no one to talk to, no one to connect with, he'd probably end up just like his dad, pouring alcohol into the void in a vain attempt to fill it.

Elijah made his way back to the sloping shed beside the chicken coop. Inside, he stepped over rakes and old bags of soil to where a pile of roofing shingles sat gathering dust. He filled his arms with as many as he could hold and carried them across the yard to the rung ladder he'd propped against the cabin. He made it up to the roof with the shingles pinched beneath his arms and followed a few minutes later with a hammer in his hand and a mouthful of nails.

The last of the morning's clouds lifted, leaving the early-afternoon sun to sizzle against Elijah's bare back as he brought the hammer down again and again, patching holes in the thinning roof. He was tired of catching drops of water in metal pots every time it rained. There were three spots in his bedroom alone that leaked, and the tin pots pinged relentlessly throughout the night.

Elijah crawled back and forth in careful sections across the roof, feeling with his fingers for any give in the shingles, a sure indication of rot or mold. There were bald patches where flaking layers of the roof had been swept clean off in the wind and Elijah could see through to the rafters below. Twice he went back to the shed for another armful of shingles and by the time he climbed down in the purple dusk, his entire body ached and was feverish with sunburn.

He warmed a can of chili on the woodstove and ate it on the front porch in the company of crickets. Darkness fell quickly around the cabin, and the woods stood tall and black behind it. Elijah reminded himself for the thousandth time that he was alone but not lonely, his motto of late. They had been easier words to believe before today, before seeing his first friendly face in weeks. Walking around the house with Chitto had brought him face-to-face with just how isolated this life he'd chosen really was. *Had* he chosen it? Honestly, it hadn't been much of a choice. He no longer had the money to make rent on his small apartment in San Francisco and afford the skyrocketing cost of living there. His childhood home was the only fallback he had. It was a free place to live, one that he technically already owned. More than that, it was a place to lick the wounds of his failed career. And he'd rather be lonely with his secret intact than walk through a friendly town with folks pitying him behind his back. *There goes Elijah Leith; remember, that cocky kid who thought he was too good for Point Orchards and moved to the big city to write the next great American novel? Guess he didn't make it after all.*

Elijah scraped his bowl with the spoon and licked it clean. Chitto was right; he couldn't hide out here forever. Sooner or later he'd run out of money and have to reenter the world. The whole town came out to watch the Fourth of July fireworks and half the reservation did, too. He'd be jumping in with both feet if he went. Elijah rose from his chair on the porch and stretched his sore legs. He had a few days to decide.

The far-off wail of a siren grew nearer, and Elijah paused in the doorway, watching the road until the red and blue lights zoomed past, headed toward the reservation. Elijah's imagination went with it, wondering if a certain woman who lived in a small house across the border would find her way down to the marina for the fireworks, too.

6

Sheriff Godbout cut the engine and squeezed the police skiff through the narrow inlet to the hidden lake beyond. He covered his head with his hands, wary of falling snow from the pines, but the lowest boughs, tucked protectively away from the elements, scratched dry needles against the metal boat as he passed through.

A trail of silver breaths followed him across the lake like the puffs of a tiny steam engine as he angled his boat toward the giant tree on the other side and rowed at the slow and steady pace his stiff bones allowed.

Perhaps it was the stark absence of the howling wind that had raged for days or the fact that every inch of the forest around him was covered in a sound-muffling layer of powder, but the crisp morning silence pressed in on all sides, demanding as much attention as the storm had. Jim rested his oars across his lap for a moment and drifted noiselessly across the opaline surface of the lake. The tall evergreens that leaned out over the water stood grand and bridal, their boughs so heavy with snow that many rested on the ground. Later in the day the temperature would rise. The sun would poke through the clouds and the woods would be full of the sound of wet, plopping piles of slush that fell from limbs springing free, but for now they remained heavily frosted, their trunks coated at an angle where the snow had blown hard against their western sides.

Jim allowed himself a moment to take it all in. It was like floating through a painting. The woods were stunning, dressed in their January finest, ensuring that it wouldn't be easy to poke around the crime scene for evidence.

He picked up the oars again and pulled with slow, even strokes toward the beach. When the bottom of the aluminum boat scraped pebbles, he climbed out and secured the skiff to a log.

The snow was just deep enough and wet enough to slide over the tops of his boots and instantly soak his socks.

"This is pointless," he said under his breath as he trudged through shin-deep powder. He stepped over the heart-shaped tracks of a deer and a couple of rabbit trails crisscrossing atop the snow, but there were no human footprints in sight. No surprise there; every sane soul in Point Orchards had been safely cooped up at home for the past few days, enjoying fireside laughter and the last of the holiday leftovers. He had to admit, he'd enjoyed being snowed in with his old German shepherd and the tin full of gourmet caramel-and-cheese popcorn that his niece had sent him from Chicago. It had given him ample excuse to procrastinate coming back out here to look for clues when, truth be told, he had no idea what he was looking for.

Jim circled the tree three times with shuffling feet, kicking at the snowdrifts. He knelt down to tunnel with his hands, quickly abandoning the idea when his gloves soaked clear through. He pulled them off and tucked his red, wet fingers into his pockets as he circled the tree a fourth time, this time peering up into the veiny branches.

"What happened out here, Doc?" he whispered.

As he turned to leave, his gaze snagged on the trunk, on a barely there indentation that gently shadowed the snow. Puzzled, he reached up to brush the powder away.

E.L. + N.M.

"Huh . . ."

The sound of a motor pulled his eyes back to the water. Jeremy was flying toward him in a jaunty little fishing boat, bouncing across the surface of the lake like a skipping stone.

"Slow down," Jim called, waving his arms.

The sound of the engine fell away and the little craft rode the momentum all the way to the shore, beaching itself noisily with several gurgling waves that lapped the icy bank in its wake. Jeremy released his grip on the wheel and leapt out, waving a letter above his head.

"Hey!" he called. "I heard back from the handwriting people. Just picked it up at the post office."

"Whose boat?" Jim asked.

"Mike Ginter's," Jeremy said, high-stepping through the snow with the paper outstretched in his hands.

"Well, you better tie it off, it's floating away."

Jeremy turned to lunge for the rope that was already dragging in the water and tied it to the felled log on shore.

"Can I read you what they said?" he asked.

"Go on."

"Dear Deputy Hart," Jeremy started, "greetings, yada, yada, yada, okay, here we go. The inconsistencies between the original note and the handwriting sample are suggestive of coercive handling from instruction to dictation. We suggest further investigation of syntax, punctuation, et cetera to ascertain alternate author."

The twenty-degree weather was not aiding Jim's patience, but he did his best to politely encourage his deputy to cut to the chase.

"Enough gobbledygook, Jeremy, plain English."

"It's her handwriting, but it's possible someone forced her to write the note."

"Kinda figured that," Jim said, turning back to the tree.

Jeremy shoved the piece of paper into his pocket. "What more do you want, Sheriff? I'm working my butt off here."

Jim turned to his deputy and offered a fatherly pat on the shoulder. Long years on the job would beat the enthusiasm out of him eventually. His get-up-and-go would have gotten up and left by the time he reached Jim's age. He couldn't fault the man for his youth.

"Take a look at this," Jim said, leading Jeremy to the tree.

"E.L. plus N.M.," Jeremy read aloud. He looked around quizzically before turning back to Jim.

"Erin Landry," the sheriff suggested.

"But she was married, right? What was her maiden name before Landry?"

The sheriff shook his head. "Kept her name."

Jeremy shrugged. "I guess I'd keep mine, too, if I was a lady doctor. That's kind of a weird coincidence though, don't you think? She happened to be hanging on the only tree for miles that had initials carved in it? And her initials at that." He brushed the carving with his fingers.

"Doesn't look fresh, does it?" Jim mused. "Couple years old at least."

Jeremy stood staring at the letters for a moment longer.

"It's not much to go on," the deputy admitted. "What do we do next?"

"I reckon it's time to start putting together a list of suspects," Jim said.

"Why not start with this N.M. guy?" Jeremy proposed, tapping the trunk. "Former boyfriend, you think? Who else would have sailed her out here to this spot where they'd been before, to the same tree where they carved their initials?"

"That's something else that's been bothering me," Jim said as he looked out at the water. "The coroner's time of death was around three in the morning on Sunday."

"So?" Jeremy shrugged.

Jim turned to meet his deputy's eyes. "Three in the morning was smack in the middle of low tide. You can barely get a boat through that inlet when the tide is up. You'd never make it in or out at low tide."

The two men stared at each other for a long moment before Jim spoke again.

"And if she didn't come by boat, that only leaves one alternative." He turned away from the lake to scour the dense white forest behind them, interrupted only by a single shadowy path through the trees.

"That one," he said slowly, turning the letters E.L. over in his head. "The trail that leads straight to Elijah Leith's cabin."

7

Elijah steered his motorcycle between tightly parked cars in the full lot of the Blue Goose Café, grateful that he'd bought the sleek and quiet bike instead of the rumbling Harley he'd considered that was designed to turn heads. He pulled his helmet free and left it hanging from the handlebars. The marina was swarming with families and Elijah slipped into the stream of people headed toward the water. So far, so good.

He was dressed to fit in: long-sleeved plaid shirt over dark jeans. The sun was just dipping beneath the horizon, and though he was sweating now, he'd be grateful for the warm outfit in an hour. Even in July, the nights were cool and often damp.

Elijah crossed the road behind the happy chatter of a young family toting a Radio Flyer full of toys and snacks. They veered right on the grass and Elijah ducked off to the left, taking cover under the shadow of a large fir tree. He didn't have to stay long, he reminded himself. They'd set off the fireworks in less than thirty minutes, and he could hightail it home the second the last spark went out.

He lifted his chin and risked a long look around at the townsfolk setting up chairs and blankets on the sloping lawn that led down to the docks. All around were the ghosts of his past, each a decade and a half further along life's timeline than when he'd last seen them. It was eerie, jarring almost, skipping forward a whole chapter in a small town's history to witness the effects of age on its citizens. Kids who had been running down the sidewalk with suckers in hand when Elijah left were now sipping beer in lawn chairs. Young men and women with vaguely familiar faces had grown up in the fifteen years he'd been gone and were now shouting after school-aged children.

Elijah scanned the crowd. There were at least half a dozen heads of long, dark Squalomah hair against straight, narrow shoulders. Elijah's gaze jumped from woman to woman before landing on the one who sat cross-legged, braiding her hair behind her. She was thin but curvy, and the breath left Elijah's chest as he watched her slim fingers weaving her hair with quick twists against the backdrop of the green horizon.

Turn around, he willed her.

A long minute passed and then a crying toddler ran on chubby legs toward the woman. She turned to wrap him in her arms, and Elijah let out the breath he had been holding. Her profile was unfamiliar, her nose longer and her mouth thinner than the woman he had thought she was. An emotion somewhere between relief and regret crashed over him.

"If I didn't know any better, I'd think you were hiding under there," a familiar voice said.

Elijah stepped sheepishly out from under the fir tree.

"Hey, Chitto."

"Come on, I brought a blanket."

Chitto spread out the patterned wool quilt on the grass, and Elijah sat beside him as the last of the light on the horizon fell under the curtain of a heavy indigo sky. Elijah relaxed. He'd made it to the cover of darkness, at least.

"Elijah Leith, is that you, Elijah?"

The voice was loud and female, and Elijah gritted his teeth as he stood to face her.

"Hey, Mrs. Bartlett." It was the mother of a close friend from high school. Another relationship he had abandoned to die when he left town.

"Oh goodness, honey, you just call me Elsie, you're plenty grown-up enough now. What brings you back? We were all so sad to hear about your dad's passing. He was so proud when you went to Sacramento to write plays."

San Francisco. Novels. Elijah didn't bother to correct her, and she went on without encouragement.

"My Nathan would sure love to see you, but he couldn't make it up for the Fourth. He's in Seattle now. Would you believe he's an art history professor at the University of Washington?"

"That's great," Elijah said unenthusiastically.

"They're talking tenure," she went on. "You'll have to swing by for dinner next time he's in town. Are you staying long? How's your play-writing coming, have you written anything we've heard of?"

"Actually, I'm not writing anymore."

"Oh," she nodded, "are you still playing soccer? I remember you were the best goalie the team ever had."

"Distance running." Elijah couldn't help himself. "No, ma'am, not anymore."

A balding man tapped Elsie on the shoulder and drew her away toward a hot popcorn cart.

"Survived it, did ya?" Chitto asked as Elijah sat back down on the blanket with a heavy sigh.

"Barely."

"Listen, son, I want to share the best piece of advice I ever got, you ready?"

Elijah nodded and Chitto lifted a hand into the air as though to spread out the words before him.

"Nobody cares."

Elijah waited for him to go on.

"That's it," Chitto said, dropping his hand. "Nobody cares."

Elijah laughed. "That's encouraging."

"Yes, it is," Chitto insisted. "It frees you up to fail. At the end of the day, no one gives a rip. It's okay that you didn't make it in California and had to come back. Nobody cares."

Elijah lay back on his elbows and smiled. There might be a little truth in that somewhere.

"Who's that?" Elijah asked, nodding to an unfamiliar figure a few blankets away, a tall woman who stood with her back to them, fine platinum-blond hair falling to her lower back.

"That would be the town's new doctor. She took over Doc Robertson's practice. Erin's her name. Smart lady. Heck of a doctor."

The woman turned, her belly protruding with the promise of new life as she reached for the snow cone her husband had returned with.

Oh.

The pregnant doctor caught Elijah staring and smiled brightly as she touched her belly. Elijah offered a small wave before she turned back around. She was probably used to people staring at her in this late stage of pregnancy.

Elijah received a few waves and nods of acknowledgment from nearby chairs and blankets, but was pleased to find that Chitto was absolutely right. His failure and return hadn't created the splash he'd feared. Hadn't even disturbed the surface, really. Nobody cared.

"Sheriff Godbout," Chitto called out, waving to a man in jeans and a dark jacket who was skirting around the edge of the blankets nearby.

"Blew my cover, Chitto," he said as Chitto and Elijah stood. "This is prime underage drinking territory. Remember last year? High school kid smuggled Jack Daniel's in a water balloon."

"Yeah, I remember," Chitto chuckled, "I remember because one of his friends didn't know what was in it and threw it at you. That's how you cracked the case."

"Took all of three washes to get the saloon smell off me."

The two men shared a hearty laugh. Chitto placed a hand on Elijah's shoulder.

"You remember Elijah Leith, don't you?"

"Sure do, it's been a while," the sheriff looked him over.

"How are you, Sheriff?" Elijah asked, reaching out to shake his hand.

"Cautiously optimistic," the sheriff replied, looking around. "It'd be great to finish out the night without any third-degree firework burns. It's been a long week."

"I bet." Elijah nodded. "Actually, I think I saw you driving by with the lights going the other night."

The sheriff's face fell. "You did. Bad hunting accident on the reservation. Couple of young guys tracking a bear in the woods on the south end. They should've called it a day while they still had some light left, but they didn't. One shot the other in the head accidently. Nothing I could do by the time I got out there."

"That's rough," Elijah commented.

"It is," Sheriff Godbout nodded. "Poor son of a gun. Not his fault, of course, but I always hate to see a young wife become a young widow. Such a pretty little woman, too."

Elijah opened his mouth to ask her name just as the sky behind the sheriff exploded in bright spirals of silver and red and green. The men turned to watch, and Elijah's question was left unasked in the crackling of fireworks.

8

AUGUST 6, 1988

Elijah crawled through the garden on his hands and knees, plucking weeds as he went. Beneath delicate, heart-shaped leaves, dozens of green beans hung ripe and ready. Next to the beans, four rows of electric-green snap-pea pods sat perfectly crisp, each the length of a finger. Elijah gathered the discarded weeds in the wicker basket and dumped them on top of the compost heap. He returned to the garden and filled the basket with ripe vegetables. A small zucchini and two bell peppers followed the green beans and peas, and Elijah topped off the pile with several handfuls of sweet cherry tomatoes. For a long moment, he stood staring into the basket at his feet, pride swelling in his chest. Had he really grown all of those beautiful vegetables himself? With plenty of hard work, sweat, and maybe one or two tears, he had coaxed food out of the land.

His body, too, was showing the fruits of his labor, sore muscles that had screamed with overuse at first were strong and lean now, adapted to the demands of this new, arduous lifestyle. He'd realized lately just how fortunate he had been to have those long summer days as a child, sitting in the garden among the growing plants and listening to his mother's fairy tales as she worked the dirt with her hands. He had apparently soaked up more knowledge than he'd realized. He knew by instinct or long forgotten instruction which plants loved sunlight and which needed a little shade, how to tell when a carrot was ripe just by looking at the top and when to clip back the leaves of the herbs to invite more growth. It seemed that all his mother's know-how was buried deep inside his head, just waiting for him to water it and let it bloom.

Elijah slung the basket over his arm. It was just after seven in the morning, and gentle rays of watery sunlight fell at pretty angles over the cabin and into the backyard. Summer was already starting to lose some of its punch. There was an undeniable bite in the air, one that lifted the hairs on Elijah's arms as he stepped outside with his coffee each morning. Now his mug sat forgotten on the dewy grass as he stood combing his eyes over the garden for anything else he could sell. It was a little sad, stripping the plants of their harvest, but it was good for them. It would encourage more produce over the final two months of the growing season, and there were still plenty of half-ripe vegetables that needed just a little more time. Acorn and butternut squash now the size of his fist would be ready in a month or so, and the pumpkins at the far end would follow just in time for October.

He ran the math in his head as he carried the basket to the kitchen. All in all, he could bring in maybe twenty or thirty dollars at the farmer's market. Any leftover vegetables could be brought home and canned afterward. Elijah popped a cherry tomato into his mouth and grabbed a backpack from his room. He carried it outside and walked slowly along the front fence, reaching up to pinch the low-hanging fruit for ripeness. The red plums weren't quite ready and the apples were nowhere close, but at the end of the row Elijah found a few yellow plums already on the ground, a sure sign that the tree was peaking.

He climbed the fence, keeping his balance with the top board pinched between his shins. Before filling his backpack with dozens of the small yellow plums, he ate six for breakfast. They were perfectly sweet, with flesh that was both soft and meaty. They would sell well to housewives wanting to put up preserves in mason jars before the first frost claimed the best of the year's fruit. He smiled at the thought of his mother stirring a steaming pot of plum preserves, the rich, Christmassy smell filling the cabin.

Now, get me that plate out of the refrigerator and let's see if it's ready, she'd say. Elijah always hurried to the refrigerator and lifted the cold plate with both hands, passing it to her carefully. That was his job to do. Then, he'd watch as his mother let a drop of the hot preserves run down the plate. *See that? Slow as a snail's trail. It's good and ready.* The preserves were devoured faster than anything else on the pantry shelves, but his mother always stashed a jar away for the winter and surprised him on snowy mornings by layering homemade sourdough toast with a generous helping of what tasted like summer sunshine in a jar.

Maybe he'd whip up a batch of preserves this week. There was nothing better on pancakes than butter and plum preserves. Elijah made a mental note. *Learn how to make pancakes.*

He dressed quickly and started for town, the backpack full of plums safely strapped to his shoulders and the basket of vegetables wrapped in a tea towel and slung over the handlebars. He rode slowly. The last thing he wanted was to take a corner too hard and leave a pile of bruised vegetables behind him on the road. The air was fresh, sweet, and still beneath the pines, and the sky above was mercifully cloudless as he cruised the three miles to the marina. Couldn't ask for a better day to sell at the market; it was sure to be packed.

Elijah pulled in just after eight o'clock to find most of the booths already set up and doing business. Chitto sat in the shade of a white tent, his boots resting atop a table laid with ornately carved wooden flutes. Elijah waved as he carried the vegetables over.

"Morning," Chitto called, reaching behind him for a small folding table. "Brought you your own table this week. Figured you'd have a big haul."

"You figured right." Elijah uncovered the basket and opened the backpack for Chitto to inspect.

Chitto whistled.

Elijah laid out the produce on the folding table and busied his hands arranging it attractively as the market began to fill with Saturday shoppers.

"Morning, Elijah." A stooped woman with fine puffs of white hair shuffled over to inspect the vegetables.

"Hey, Mrs. Macbeth, nice day out."

"I'll take those cherry tomatoes off your hands for the right price," she said, her voice scratchy with smoke. "Mr. Macbeth loves tomatoes in his pasta salad, but he won't let me grow them. It upsets him to have a plant as tall as a person in the yard."

"I could let you have all of them for three or four bucks, I think."

"Two and a quarter?" she asked, and Elijah didn't have the heart to hold firm on the price.

"Sure."

Mrs. Macbeth loaded the tomatoes into her basket and walked on.

"Flute?" Chitto called after her.

"Maybe if you played one you could draw a crowd," Elijah suggested. "I've seen you sell maybe five flutes this summer."

"It's not about the money. Someday you'll learn that every man must fill the need to create something with his own two hands. Even the richest man in the world probably hides out in his garage to put together an old Chevy or paint terrible pictures."

"Or write terrible books," Elijah said under his breath.

"Or pull good food from his land," Chitto said with a nudge. "That's not nothing, kid. Ah, look at that." He nodded to a couple walking toward them. It was the pretty doctor Elijah had seen at the fireworks, walking arm in arm with her husband. A gray shawl was wrapped tightly around her chest, snuggling her newborn inside.

"Good morning," she said, stepping up to the booth, a glimmer of recognition sparking in her eyes as she met Elijah's gaze.

"You had your baby," Elijah said with a smile. Chitto side-eyed him for stating the obvious, but Elijah ignored it.

"I did," she nodded. "It's our first time venturing outside the house with her, but we're surviving."

The dark-skinned husband wandered off to another booth while Erin looked over the vegetables. The baby in the wrap stirred with a soft coo, and Chitto stood, leaning over the table.

"Let's have a peek," he said. The doctor pulled back the wrap to reveal a perfectly pink little face with round cheeks and puckered lips.

"She's an angel. Congrats, Doc."

"Well, she'll definitely grow up to be a beauty if she looks anything like her mom," Elijah said, then immediately cast his eyes down at the table, his face reddening. He wished he could just learn to keep his mouth shut. She really was stunning though, with eyes the color of sea-foam and a million-watt smile. Not to mention that hair.

"Thank you," she said with a little laugh.

"Are you back to work yet?" Chitto asked.

"Next week," she said, and nodded. "Actually, you're due for a physical, Chitto. I want to see you before the end of the month." She turned to Elijah. "And what about you?"

"Elijah," he offered.

"Elijah," she repeated.

"It's been a few years since I've had a checkup," he said. "I probably should."

"Any time, just give the office a call."

"I'll do that," he promised. "So"—he gestured to the spread of produce—"are you interested in anything today?"

"Those plums look tempting." She reached out to touch one. Her husband returned and she placed a hand on his arm.

"Manny was hoping to make some plum preserves this week."

Elijah hid his smile.

"Can't make plum preserves without plums," he said jovially.

The doctor's husband picked up a few plums and squeezed them lightly.

"How much?"

Elijah's eyes lingered on the man's expensive watch. "Four-fifty."

"We'll take them," he said, reaching for his wallet and handing Elijah a five-dollar bill. "Keep the change."

Elijah watched the couple leave, then rearranged the vegetables on the table to cover where the plums had been. On the opposite side of the market there was a commotion. Elijah heard loud shouts and the unmistakable squawking of chickens. He leaned forward to stare down the row of booths. A cloud of feathers was settling beside several small metal cages.

Elijah sat back in his chair, the wheels spinning in his mind.

"I'll be right back," he told Chitto, springing to his feet and sweeping all of the vegetables into the wicker basket.

In the booth with the metal cages he found a man from the reservation selling eggs and chickens.

"Do you have a rooster?" he asked.

"One, but he's not for sale," the man said as he thumbed through dollar bills.

Elijah looked through the cages and found the rooster. He was strutting proudly back and forth in his metal box, feathered chest puffed to full capacity.

"If he's not for sale then why is he here?"

The man looked annoyed. "He's already spoken for. Someone asked about a rooster last week so I brought him with me today."

"How much did the guy say he'd pay?" Elijah pressed. This wasn't his first rodeo. He had spent many Saturdays dickering prices over good bread in San Francisco's outdoor markets.

The man placed the bills down on the table and looked at him appraisingly. "Twenty."

Elijah waited a beat. "How much did he really say he'd pay?"

The two men stared at each other without speaking for a long minute. Then, the faintest hint of a smile lifted the corner of the man's mouth.

"Fifteen."

Elijah fished in his back pocket. "I don't have quite that. Here's seven and a quarter. Plus, I've got all these vegetables. Worth another ten at least. Probably more."

The man stood and peered into the basket. He held out his hand. "Done."

Elijah grinned and pumped his hand up and down. "Done!"

The man opened the cage and wrapped large hands around the rooster's wings, pinning him tightly.

"Here you go."

He handed the bird to Elijah, who instantly realized he hadn't thought this fully through.

"Thanks."

Chitto was standing in front of the flutes with his arms crossed, laughing as Elijah approached holding the kicking rooster at arm's length.

"Why don't I give you a ride?" he suggested.

The rooster, promptly named Houdini, managed to escape Elijah's tight grasp three times on the way home. The cab of the small pickup had become a flurry of feathers and squawking and two very loud cock-a-doodle-doos by the time they pulled into the driveway. Elijah considered it a small miracle that Chitto hadn't crashed into anything along the way.

"Good riddance, Houdini!" Chitto yelled out the window as he pulled away. Elijah heard him laughing all the way down the road. Houdini was dumped inside the chicken coop with mercifully little fanfare, and Elijah fiddled with the fence, constructing a clever little door through which chickens could enter but not exit.

"Build it and they will come," he said with satisfaction as he stepped back to look over his work. With just a little luck, he'd have a brand-new generation of chicks running around before long and, soon after that, an endless supply of eggs at his fingertips. Elijah left Houdini squawking at the top of his lungs and ducked into the shed in search of feed.

Beneath a pile of tools, Elijah saw the canvas corner of a bag poking out. Moving wrenches and clippers to get to it, his hand closed around a familiar handle. He lifted the machete and blew the dust away. The blade was still sharp; no rust. If he wanted to use it to clear the trail to the lake, he could.

Elijah propped the machete against a wheelbarrow and carried the bag of feed over his shoulder to the coop. He flung handfuls of corn toward Houdini, but his eyes were on the woods. It would be nice to have a trail again. Easier access to wild berries that he could can and sell, and it would make it easy to hunt in the woods if he wanted to. That would be a game changer, definitely worth the hard work of clearing the trail.

Elijah grabbed the machete and headed for the woods. For the better part of an hour, he hacked at the brambles and bushes just feet past the fence. He was pretty much starting a trail from scratch, a task that his shoulder would certainly pay for tomorrow. Twice he startled wild chickens from their nests and sent them running, but at least they ran back toward the cabin and not deeper into the woods. Perhaps they'd be curious enough to poke around the coop.

The afternoon wore on, growing hot and sticky, but Elijah didn't rest. He kept clearing until he reached the first fallen tree. Then he jogged back to the shed and traded the machete for his dad's handsaw.

The rigorous back-and-forth motion of the saw brought beads of sweat to his forehead that ran down into his eyes and stung like seawater, but he refused to quit. He was only halfway through the log before the shadows grew long enough to choke out the last of the sunlight in the woods. Elijah looked up, surprised by the falling dusk. The sky above the treetops was lavender and clear. It would be a dry night. He leaned the saw against the log and walked slowly back to the house.

He was so hungry and so tired that he couldn't decide whether to eat or sleep. In the end, he opened a tin of baked beans and ate them cold over the sink before staggering to his bedroom and falling onto the bed, out like a light in seconds.

He woke to bright morning sunlight streaming in through the blinds and blinked at it, confused. It felt like he had closed his eyes just minutes before, but eight full hours had passed. It made no sense to start the day with a shower when he was planning on spending the rest of it in the woods in dirty, sweaty work, but he did anyway, letting the hot water pour over his aching muscles and stiff joints. His right hand was raw in places from tightly gripping the machete for hours, and it burned beneath the water. He'd have to wear gloves today.

The saw was right where Elijah had left it against the log, and he startled a small russet finch nosing around behind it for bugs. It was a beautiful morning. Cool and fresh and full of birdsong. Elijah cracked his knuckles and got to work.

Dew and moist earth had made the bottom of the log soft and he worked through it quickly, rolling the round center piece back to the woodshed for later chopping. After that, the going was easier for a while, wide swings of the machete making quick work of the trail. He kicked away puffy fungi and moss, leaving a clean brown path behind him as he went.

When his stomach grumbled loudly, he set down his tools, stripped off his gloves, and jogged back to the cabin. He slathered two slices of bread with mayonnaise, layered them with sliced tomatoes from the garden, and topped them off with salt and a few flecks of pepper. After lunch he returned to the trail, hacking away, his mind elsewhere as his body worked one step at a time deeper into the forest.

"What the—"

Elijah dropped the machete and inspected his forearm, convinced he'd been stung by a bee. Tiny blisters bloomed on his skin and he knelt to inspect the knee-high plant. Stinging nettle. Elijah stood and rubbed his forearm as he stared at the tangled masses of waist-deep plants crowding the forgotten animal path. He was at the fork in the trail, the one that led to the secret lake.

Unchecked, the nettles had completely swallowed the path. There were thousands of them, each gently tilted green head promising blisters and pain. Elijah's eyes assessed the many plants as he pulled off his gloves and let them fall to the ground. Something wild was coming over him, something wild and reckless and fierce. He took a deep breath and charged right into the middle of the nettles, hollering at the top of his lungs as he broke through them with his bare torso, knees, and hands. Within thirty seconds, his entire body was on fire, but he kept pushing, breaking into a run as the nettles thinned, amazed to hear his own shouts turn into laughter as he kicked forward, swinging his arms with all his might. Sprinting now, he burst through the last of the nettles to the other side, open forest with the promise of water beyond.

Elijah ran for a long, lung-busting minute toward the lake and came upon it at full speed. Limbs burning, he threw himself into the cool water and let it swallow him whole. How good it felt, to be totally submerged. To be weightless and free.

He stayed beneath the water as long as his lungs would allow before popping up to swallow air in hungry gasps. The water around him stilled and all was quiet, his unexpected splash having frightened away all birds and rustling critters.

Behind his legs there was a flicker of movement as a startled trout dove past his knees and something clicked into place in Elijah's mind. How had he not realized it before? There was more to eat than berries back here. There was a whole lake full of fish just waiting to be caught.

After his mom died and before his dad's drinking spiraled out of control, they would spend warm afternoons sitting on the bank with a tackle box and a bag of ham sandwiches between them, swapping bad jokes or just sitting comfortably in the silence that settled after the frenzied commotion of a bite on the line. Elijah was the one who fried up the fish in his mom's old cast-iron pan, always careful to clean it the way she had taught him to, gently and without soap. Those dinners with his dad, though painful with the empty third chair at the table, were good days.

Elijah shook his head again, more to clear it than dry it. Somehow, the happy recollections of his dad on sober days were more painful than the unhappy, drunken memories.

Elijah wiped the lake water from his eyes and looked around with the dawning realization that this was the first time he had ever come here alone. That dreamlike summer before he left, he had come to the lake nearly every day, but always with Nakita by his side. Even now, fifteen years later, his arms felt empty as he stood in the water by himself, no one to carry to shore.

Elijah shook his head back and forth to dry his hair, suddenly full of an awareness that had been growing in him since he returned home. The lake had washed away the foggy denial he'd been living in. Hadn't he been waiting with equal parts hope and dread these past few months to accidently run into her somewhere in town? Hadn't he been hoping deep down every time he rode his motorcycle into Point Orchards that they would stumble into each other and find themselves face-to-face with nothing between them? Nothing but the past. For years, Nakita had been hundreds of miles away, but now, with the reservation just minutes up the road, she was so close. There was nothing standing in his way of going to see her. There was nothing but his pride keeping him from going to her to say the words he ached to say, even just to apologize and tell her that he was a fool, a sorry fool for putting his stupid dream ahead of her and everything else.

Elijah waded purposefully out of the lake, drops of fresh water running quick paths down his arms and legs.

Enough. It had been long enough. He just needed to see her.

9

The police skiff slid into its tight dock with ease and Sheriff Godbout climbed out. On the other side of the marina, Jeremy was mooring Mike's boat and had angled himself too far to the left. He skidded into the dock with a metal screech so loud it made Jim flinch from fifty yards away. The kid would have some explaining to do when Mike saw the scratches on his neat little boat.

"Come on," Jim shouted, waving Jeremy over to where he'd parked the cruiser. The sheriff climbed in and cranked the heat, turning the vents away when frigid air blasted into the car. It was still well below freezing, and he felt the damp cold in his bones.

Jim had heard the snowplows going in the early-morning hours, but the road was still slick. The slush left behind by tires had a bad habit of turning into black ice when it refroze at night, and he'd bet his next month's salary he'd be called out to at least one accident today. He eased the cruiser onto the road and turned right toward the Leith place.

"Keep an eye on the road for ice, it's cold out," Jeremy said, and Jim was proud of his restraint in not sarcastically responding, *Ice? Swell idea, I was keeping an eye out for crossing flamingos.*

At the sound of a pencil scratching paper Jim turned to find Jeremy scribbling in a small notebook.

"What's that?"

"Suspect list. I've divided them into rows and here at the top, the columns are: Name, Evidence, Alibi, and Motive."

"Snappy," Jim said without inflection. "So far, how many suspects do you have?"

"Well, so far just two."

Sheriff Godbout lifted an eyebrow and Jeremy elaborated.

"Elijah Leith for one, and in the evidence column we've got that she was found on his property and couldn't have been brought in by boat, so at the very least she had to pass his cabin that night. Don't have an alibi or a motive yet."

"And who's the second suspect?"

"Ah, you'll like this, that is our Unknown Suspect with Unknown Motive. Little trick we learned at the police academy. Always keep that one on your list so you don't get blinders with the names that you have and rule out someone you haven't thought of yet. Might not have been a strategy in your day."

Jim rolled his eyes but couldn't hide the smile that tugged at the corner of his mouth. It was in moments like these that he truly felt his age. He used to wonder how he'd know when it was time to retire, time to hand the reins over to some eager young buck and plant himself on his porch rocker with his German shepherd snoozing at his feet, ready to offer the wisdom of experience to anyone who trotted up the steps. Turns out, the younger generation lets you know when it's time.

A wet pile of snow dropped from a bough that overhung the street and fell thirty feet down, exploding in a feathery mass on the windshield and making both men jump.

"I hate winter," Jim grumbled, switching on the wipers to brush the snow away. The air circulating through the vents finally warmed, and the sheriff flicked them open, gratefully stretching his stiff fingers.

Around a bend in the road, the log cabin appeared, tucked back behind frosted fruit trees, as inviting as a gingerbread house in the snow, though no smoke puffed from the stone chimney and the windows were dark.

"Nice place," Jeremy commented. "You ever been out here before?"

"Not since Jake died. It wasn't much to look at then. Hard for him to take care of the place at the end. Terrible way to go, liver failure."

"I heard he pretty much drank himself to death."

Jim didn't respond as he pulled into the driveway and parked, noting the bald patch in the snow where a car had sat through the storm, tire tracks leading out to the road. He doubted Elijah was home, but they were here now and might as well check.

"Let's go," he said, unbuckling his seatbelt.

Jim climbed the porch steps, boots crunching in the snow, and covered his eyes with his hands as he peered into the dark window. He rapped on the glass with his knuckles and called Elijah's name. Jeremy tried the same at the window on the other side of the door, with no luck.

"Elijah?" the sheriff called again, leaning around the porch to scan the backyard. "You there, son?"

"Hey," Jeremy called, his hand on the doorknob. "It's unlocked."

"Quit," Jim scolded. "You know good and well we don't just barge right in."

"We could if we had a search warrant."

The sheriff turned tired eyes on his deputy.

"And what exactly would we be searching for? We've already got the murder weapon. I just wanna talk to him. Find out if he was home Saturday night and if he's got anything to say about it."

The deputy's hand stayed on the knob. "He could have drafts of the note in there, couldn't he? Or a notepad with an impression we could trace."

Jim stared at Jeremy as if truly seeing him for the first time that day. "Yeah, I reckon he could. We'll see if we can catch him here tomorrow, but in the meantime I'm putting you in charge of getting that warrant." Sheriff Godbout retreated down the porch steps, his deputy on his heels. "Let's get to the station."

"Can we eat first?" Jeremy asked. "Blue Goose is on the way and I've only had coffee."

"Best idea you've had today."

Della set two plates of eggs over medium and hash browns before the grateful eyes of the sheriff and his deputy. For the next few minutes, the sound of chewing was only punctuated by sips of coffee and appreciative grunts. Della shuffled over to refill their cups just as Sheriff Godbout finished wiping his mouth with his napkin.

"Eggs were perfect," he said, sliding his plate to the end of the table.

"How's the case coming?" she asked.

"We're making progress," Jeremy piped up sunnily before the sheriff silenced him with a warning look.

"Any suspects yet?" she asked loudly.

"Cheese and rice, Della, will you keep your voice down?" Jim hissed.

"Sorry," she whispered loudly. "I just thought you should know I've been hearing Elijah Leith's name thrown around, but if you ask me, and I'm not one to spread rumors mind you, but I think it's way more likely her husband did it."

"You're losing your edge, Della," Jim said dryly. "He's been gone over a year now."

Della pressed her already thin lips together and shook her head.

"What do you mean?" Jeremy asked, sitting up straighter.

Della pulled a rag from her apron and rubbed at a spot on the table, stooping to speak between them. "They were in here together not two weeks ago, sat over there in the corner booth."

"Are you sure it was Manny?" Jim asked.

"Unless he has a twin brother."

Jeremy nearly upset his coffee mug in his rush to pull out his notebook and add Manny's name to the suspect list. Jim was sure he knew the answer, but he asked Della the question anyway.

"Did you happen to catch any of their conversation?"

"Some," she nodded. "There was a lot of awkward silence every time I came over to refill their drinks, though. They sure as heck weren't getting back together if that's what you're asking."

"Did he seem agitated at all?" Jeremy asked eagerly, his pencil poised. "Angry?"

Della stopped scrubbing as she thought. "No . . . No, maybe tense, but mostly sad, I'd say."

Jeremy turned to Jim with eyebrows lifted and Jim gave a subtle nod that said, *We'll look into it.*

Over their heads, Della was still talking.

"The Nelsons think it's Elijah, but I told them it's pretty hard to believe anything like that about Jake and Laurie's sweet little boy. He used to run around in here, giggling and making paper airplanes out of napkins, but they think he did it, being that she was found in back of his property and all."

Sheriff Jim kept his face wiped clean of emotion.

"Is that so?" He sat back in the booth and rubbed his chin like the idea had just occurred to him. "You ever seen Elijah and Doc Landry in here together?"

"No," she said slowly, thinking, "no, I don't know that I ever saw the two of them together, here or anywhere else for that matter. But I did hear about that big row down at the docks."

The skin along Jim's forearms prickled unpleasantly.

"How's that?" he asked, leaning forward.

"I guess it ain't gossip if police are asking straight out, but I heard about it last summer. I remember because Kim and Kevin Walsh came in here for their anniversary and brought their kids with them. You wouldn't believe how many people celebrate anniversaries in here with their kids. Seems to me if I wanted to celebrate a romantic occasion, I'd hire a sitter and get as far away from my kids as possible."

"The fight, Della," the sheriff steered her back, "what about the fight?"

"I was serving up pork medallions to Kim and Kevin and their little ones, and they were talking about the scene at the marina that morning. I guess Doc Landry took Elijah out in her boat, and when they got back, they exchanged words and I think he grabbed her arm or wrist or something. Anyway, bein' that it was summertime and a nice day and all, the docks were pretty full, so everyone saw her telling him to get off her boat and speeding back out to the sound by herself."

"Is that right? Well, thanks, Della"—he lifted his mug—"for break-fast, I mean."

Della vanished through the kitchen doors, and Jeremy held his finger in the air to tick an imaginary box.

"Motive."

10

Elijah held his breath as he crouched beside the tree, his fingers holding the taut bowstring against his cheek, his eyes locked on the rustling ferns across the trail. The rabbit was teasing him, popping its head up and ducking down again, then emerging to peer at him for a quick second before darting back under cover. It knew he was here. Elijah wasn't trying to hide; his long minutes of stillness would eventually gain the rabbit's trust and it would show itself, accepting that Elijah was merely a stationary part of its environment.

He'd gone hunting with his dad a handful of times out in the woods, but he had never shot anything that drew breath. His time with the bow as a teenager was spent aiming for the bull's-eye he'd drawn on a cardboard box and hung from the fence.

It's not that he was afraid to kill, exactly; he just hadn't wanted to face the moment right afterward, standing over an animal as it stared up at him with dead eyes, his gut twisting with the knowledge that he'd been the one to kill it. This was different, though. He wasn't killing for sport. He had been home for months and was staring down winter with an empty freezer. Unable to afford meat any better than bologna, he had shouldered his dad's bow and headed for the woods.

The rabbit stuck out its nose, whiskers twitching as it considered his scent. One inch at a time, it emerged from behind the ferns. The moment its tail was clear, Elijah released the bowstring and the arrow launched straight and true, a hundred and ten miles an hour, right into the rabbit's side. Death was nearly instant, just a few skittering twitches and a shrill squeak, then the rabbit flopped to the side and lay still. Elijah stood and shook out his legs. His right one had fallen asleep, and painful pins and needles were running from his knee to his ankle.

He stood over the rabbit, who was indeed staring up at him with one round, lifeless eye. Elijah waited for the wave of remorse to come crashing over him, but he felt nothing deeper than hunger. He yanked the arrow out and wiped it on the ferns before tucking it into the quiver, then he slung the rabbit over his shoulder and walked back to the cabin.

Skinning the rabbit was another matter. He didn't like blood, but he knew how to do it. His dad had always spared him the guilt of actually killing their prey, but insisted that Elijah learn how to skin and prepare it if he wanted to partake in eating it. He had agreed begrudgingly as a kid, but now, as a man, he could appreciate the wisdom in the lesson. He'd probably have done the same if he had a son.

Elijah left the bow on the back porch. Given the choice, he would have killed the rabbit in some cleaner way, like snapping its neck, but catching a rabbit with his bare hands didn't exactly fall under his skill set. Maybe he'd figure out a way to set up some snares in the woods and kill the next one that way. A quick break of the neck seemed a more humane way to die than a sharp arrow through the middle.

Elijah seared half of the rabbit in his mother's cast-iron skillet, his stomach responding to the mouthwatering scent with loud gurgles. He made sure to cook it completely through, then carried it to the front porch and devoured it in minutes. He leaned back in his chair and wiped his mouth, realizing that this was the first time in weeks he'd been completely full. It was good timing, too. He needed fuel for what lay ahead today. Today, he was running to the reservation.

Elijah wrapped the rest of the raw meat and stored it in the freezer before stepping outside for his morning chores. He carried the bucket of feed to the chicken coop, where Houdini and two golden hens were still sleeping. He gave the chicken wire a little rattle and their heads popped up, beady eyes angled toward the bucket.

"Breakfast," he called, tossing in handfuls of feed. The birds hopped from their roosts and ran toward the kernels. Elijah laughed. They always sprinted for the feed like they hadn't eaten in weeks, fighting each other over individual kernels when hundreds more lay at their feet. He circled around to the back of the coop and lifted the wooden flaps where the hens had slept. One brown egg lay in the center of a nest, still warm.

"Yes!" he whispered, grabbing it. It was still every bit as exciting as an Easter egg hunt when he discovered that one of the hens had laid.

Chickens fed, Elijah dragged the hose over to the garden and watered it generously. It was a rare dry spell in Point Orchards, three full weeks without so much as a drop of rain and none in the forecast ahead.

Elijah pulled the hose back to the well, passing the woodshed where two and a half rows of firewood sat to age and dry. The dirt floor around the chopping stump was raked clean and the axe was stored safely in the shed for winter. As he passed the tall rows of firewood, his gaze lingered appreciatively on his work.

Back inside, Elijah found an old pair of running shoes in his closet and inspected them for wear and tear. There was a small hole in the upper mesh on each shoe, but the tread on the bottoms was still in good shape. They'd do. He pulled on shorts and a T-shirt and laced up, his belly full of the same fluttering nerves he always felt before a cross-country race. He'd run the two miles out to the lake and back several times in the weeks prior, but today he was asking his body for four times that distance, writing a check he wasn't completely sure his legs could cash.

He started jogging slowly down the road at a pace just faster than a walk. It was closing in on eighty degrees, and sweat beaded quickly at his temples, running down his neck to soak the front of his T-shirt. Now and then, a car would come rolling around a curve ahead and he'd edge toward the shoulder of the road, lifting his hand in greeting at whoever passed.

He jogged along the curving white line that hugged the road, through dappled sunlight and past the quaint summer homes that were tucked here and there in deep green pockets of forest, pretty as doll-houses behind their picket fences. Around a wide curve, Elijah came upon the brown sign that read SACRED MOUNTAIN RESERVATION I MILE, and he reached up to tap it with his fingers as he passed. The evergreens that edged the road thinned as he climbed a gentle hill out of the woods. The reservation was dotted with trees, but it was mostly farmland; flat and fertile at the base of the eastern mountains. Many of the Squalomah grew crops: corn, hay, even tulips, in quilt-like patches soaked in both rain and sun.

Elijah ran for another few minutes, until he looked up to see the border of the reservation looming ahead, marked by a large wooden sign that announced: ENTERING SACRED MOUNTAIN RESERVATION. Elijah slowed to a walk as the pavement dropped abruptly away into dirt. Up ahead, almost half a mile away, he could see the first house across the border, Nakita's house.

Elijah hadn't spent much time on the reservation. Nakita always came to him when they trained together, but he'd picked her up from her family home in his dad's car a few times and he remembered it well, though he had never been inside. It was small but kept-up, and in some pocket of his memory was a vague recollection of Nakita's father kneel-ing over the porch steps with a hammer in his hands. Nakita had always waited for Elijah at the end of the driveway when he pulled up, jumping in and waving goodbye to her grandmother sitting on the porch.

Elijah walked along the road, leaving indented footprints on the soft dirt and feeling completely unprepared. He should have at least spent some time figuring out what to say to her. What if she was still furious that he had left? What if she didn't even recognize him after all these years? What if she did recognize him and slammed the door in his face?

Elijah started running again, keeping time with the river that met the road from the east. As he neared Nakita's house, he realized he didn't have to worry about her slamming the door in his face or any other scenario for that matter. For one thing, the house no longer had a door. The once-cared-for home was clearly abandoned now, with broken windows and hot-pink spray-painted graffiti on the side. Elijah climbed slowly up the porch steps. The chairs he remembered were gone, and the ragged, filthy remains of a white curtain flapped gently in the wind behind a shattered pane. Through the gaping front entrance was a vandalized kitchen with broken cupboards and a bathtub-sized hole in the middle of its peeling linoleum floor. No one had lived here for years.

Nakita and her family were long gone. Probably someplace else on the reservation. He could search for days for the right house. There were easily twice as many people on the reservation as there were in Point Orchards, and he had no idea how far these roads stretched toward the mountains and beyond. Elijah jumped off the porch and ran north. There was one obvious place he could start.

For twenty minutes, he jogged past houses that ran the gamut from ramshackle mobile homes patched together with plywood and tin to well-maintained single-family dwellings. There were children and dogs running and playing in some yards, and most had wooden canoes propped on the riverside bank of the road.

The river bent sharply back toward the eastern mountains and the road went with it. Around the bend, a tiny wooden church came into view up ahead. It was as old and beaten down as some of the houses, warped boards lending it a permanent forward lean over the dirt road. The roof was sharply peaked, rusted by the rain until it was nearly the same color as the wooden sides. At the very top, a humble wooden cross announced sanctuary for the Squalomah who had converted to Christianity.

There was a rusty red two-door sedan in the gravel lot. Yes, he would be here.

Elijah slowed to a walk and took a deep breath as he stepped under the awning. He knocked lightly on the front door as he pushed it halfway open to peer inside. Twelve rows of backless wooden pews rested between him and the pulpit, and the man who stood with his head bowed over the text, long hair spilling onto his Bible and a pencil pinched between his teeth.

Elijah cleared his throat as he stepped inside. "Reverend Mills?"

The man looked up, the sharp bone structure and deep black eyes he shared with his daughter as striking as ever. He stared down the aisle at Elijah, who took a cautious step forward.

"Elijah," he said slowly, pulling the pencil from his teeth. "Would you believe I'm halfway through writing a sermon on the prodigal son?"

Elijah gave a nervous laugh and risked a few more steps forward.

"Yeah, I'm . . . I'm back. I mean I'm here for a while, I'm not sure if I'll be staying or not." He was rambling. Scrambling.

Reverend Mills kept his eyes on Elijah as he closed his Bible. The silence between them swelled until it was unbearable.

"And you'd like to know where Nakita is."

Elijah swallowed hard, his mouth as dry as the dusty road outside. "Yes, yes, sir."

The reverend sighed as he stepped out from behind the pulpit.

"Sit down, Elijah."

Elijah sat in the very last pew as Reverend Mills came toward him with the Bible tucked under his arm, boots clicking on the wooden floorboards. He sat on the pew beside Elijah with a straight back, turning to face him gravely.

"I'll spare the small talk and tell you right now that I'd like you to turn around and head back where you came from."

Elijah's face fell as Nakita's father went on.

"Whether or not you know that Nakita is mourning her husband's death doesn't matter. I would say that this isn't the right time for you to show up at her door, but I don't believe there is a right time for you to come back into her life."

Elijah couldn't have spoken if he wanted to. All the blood from his brain seemed to be pooling in his feet. Nakita's husband was dead. He had wondered. Considered the possibility. Even, though the thought made him sick to his stomach now, lain in his bed late at night hoping that the young widow the sheriff had mentioned at the fireworks was Nakita, but he had never truly believed it was her.

He opened his mouth to say something, to offer his condolences, but was silenced by the stony look on Reverend Mills's face. Nakita's dad had always been friendly while they were dating. Actually, Elijah couldn't recall if he'd been friendly toward him *because* they were dating or merely because he had known Elijah's parents long before Elijah was born.

"But," the reverend went on after the long pause, "you're an adult and so is Nakita, and if you're here, it must be because you feel at least a little regret for leaving her high and dry all those years ago. You're not the eighteen-year-old kid that broke my daughter's heart anymore, are you?"

Elijah didn't know how to answer that. How much had Nakita told him? Did he know that Elijah had promised to come back and broken his word? It didn't matter. Even without kids of his own, Elijah could guess that a father didn't have to be told when his daughter's heart was broken.

"Unfortunately," Elijah said, finding his voice, "I am. I'm the same guy that left without coming back. It was me who left her, not anyone else. I've felt guilty about it for a long time, but I can't go back and change it now. All I want to do is apologize. That's it." Elijah paused. "And I had no idea her husband died. Actually, I didn't even know she was married."

Reverend Mills leaned back slightly, assessing Elijah with sharp eyes. It was a long moment before he spoke, and when he did, his question was unexpected.

"Do you know why your mother named you Elijah?"

Elijah blinked, surprised. "No. They never told me. I mean, it's biblical, right?"

"Yes," Reverend Mills said, laying a hand on the worn leather Bible in his lap. "Elijah is thought to be the greatest prophet before Christ by most who study the Word."

Elijah smiled weakly. "So that's it, then? She wanted me to live up to some sort of moral greatness."

"No," Reverend Mills said, gently shaking his head. "It wasn't his faithfulness that she admired, it was because he was deeply flawed."

"How so?"

"That same Elijah who slaughtered hundreds of false prophets and called down fire from heaven had one death threat from an evil queen and abandoned his faith. He ran for his life. He hid in a cave and cursed God for the day he was born. He became depressed and suicidal, a pitiful excuse of a man."

Elijah tried to laugh, but the sound that came out was hollow and flat, echoing in the empty church. "I guess I lived up to him after all, then."

The reverend shook his head. "That wasn't the end of his story."

Elijah's eyes fell on the Bible. "I guess I don't remember that one from Sunday school."

"Redemption," Reverend Mills said softly. "Elijah's story is one of great redemption. But first, he had to be willing to come out of the cave."

Elijah cleared his throat, unable to meet the reverend's eyes.

"I'm trying," he whispered.

Reverend Mills's wide hand landed on Elijah's shoulder and gave it a reassuring squeeze. "This is a good place to start."

Elijah looked up and was surprised to find Nakita's father smiling at him sadly.

"She's not here, is she?"

"No. She's in Bellingham. She left after Kailen died. His parents own land on one of the islands off Bellingham Bay. She wants to be alone with her grief."

"Will she . . . come back?"

"She will," her father said with certainty, rising to his feet. "In time. We mourn our dead for a year, sometimes longer, but she will return. This is her home. I can tell her you came looking for her next time she calls."

Elijah stood. "No. No, don't tell her."

Reverend Mills walked him to the door, and Elijah held out a tentative hand. Nakita's father shook it and Elijah turned, breaking into a run as he headed west, back toward Point Orchards. When he glanced over his shoulder, Nakita's father was still standing tall in the doorway of the old church.

As he ran slowly home, Elijah's mind traveled back to that day, the twenty-second of August in the year he graduated college. Nakita probably assumed he had simply forgotten his promise, but he hadn't. The truth was, he'd had every intention of coming home. He had the money set aside for a plane ticket and he'd even packed a bag. But life had given him a choice, and he'd made the wrong one.

He had finished writing *Middletide* in May of his senior year, and in June he sent out letters to literary agents all over the country, asking for representation by someone who knew the publishing world and could land a book deal for him with a traditional publishing house. On Friday, August 19, his phone rang. It was an agent, one who lived just a few miles away in San Francisco. She had read his manuscript and was eager to represent it. He had bounced from foot to foot with the telephone gripped in his fingers, wanting to leap right out of his skin and through the ceiling, but he was tethered to reality and the table by the tightly spiraled phone cord as the agent poured out compliments about the intricacies of his plot and how well he'd fleshed out his characters. When she asked if they could meet for lunch on Monday to sign the papers officially making him part of the agency, he'd said yes without a second thought. After all, this was his dream, the opportunity of a lifetime, and it was being handed to him on a silver platter.

He'd barely slept through the weekend, floating through Saturday and Sunday on happy daydreams about cover meetings and book tours and signings, and when Monday finally arrived, he'd tucked the money for the plane ticket home into his wallet, intent on making a good first impression with the agent by offering to pay for lunch at the astronomically expensive restaurant in ritzy Pacific Heights.

On Tuesday the twenty-third, he'd unpacked his suitcase, still floating on the elation of signing the contract. As he tucked his clothes back into his dresser, he convinced himself that Nakita had probably forgotten all about their plan to meet, anyway. They hadn't written to each other since the handful of letters that tapered off after his freshman year, and her family's home didn't have a telephone, so it wasn't his fault that they'd lost touch. And, even on the off chance that she had gone out to the lake to wait for him, if she knew that he had been signing with an agent that very day, she'd forgive him for it. It was his dream; she would understand.

Elijah ran across the border of the reservation, where the dirt road turned to pavement, without looking back. He was headed home to a cabin hidden deep in the woods, no one waiting for him with a smile in the doorway, no one to talk to, and no one to blame for it but himself.

11

Elijah found a tapered wax candle hiding in the back of one of the kitchen drawers and placed it in a mason jar. He flicked the lighter and lit the wick. He didn't need the extra light, but he wanted something symbolic to mark the occasion as he sat down to this special meal.

He lifted the knife, the sharpest one he could find in the kitchen, and carved the chicken. He had killed and plucked it himself, then roasted it in a shallow pan and basted it every twenty minutes with its own juices. It was dressed with bounty from the garden, carrots and onions stuffed inside and herbs sprinkled on the crispy skin when it came out of the oven. He placed a leg and two slices of the breast on his plate and turned to the glass bowl that held green beans, cooked to perfection and well seasoned. He lifted a few out with his fork and placed them beside the chicken, then gave up the attempt at pretty plating and overturned the bowl, sliding them all onto his plate in a pile.

At first, he tried to eat slowly, intending to savor the meal, but he was hungry, and before long the food was going down in heaping forkfuls. He was eager to get to dessert, the smell of it filling his nose as he ate dinner. Apples had been stewing in cinnamon and sugar on the stove all day until they were tender and gooey. He pushed his empty plate back and filled a bowl with the sweet cooked fruit, carrying it to the recliner that had always been reserved for his father after dinner. He took a bite and frowned. Something was missing. He returned to the kitchen and hunted the spice cupboard, still full of tin containers labeled in his mother's handwriting. He opened them one at a time and held them to his nose. Allspice. That was the one. He sprinkled a little on top of his dessert and took a bite. Perfection. Like an apple pie without the crust.

Elijah placed the needle on his father's record player and let the voice of Etta James, smooth and slow as plum preserves on a cold plate, fill the living room. As she sang about her lonely days being over, Elijah enjoyed his stewed apples bite by bite, gazing absently across the room at the carved bones of the chicken.

The hen was one that had found its way into the coop last week. He had guessed it was past its egg-laying years, but he had waited a week to be sure, checking its nest every morning and finding it empty. So, tonight, it was dinner. And that was the special occasion; everything he had eaten for dinner had come from the land within his fence. He had provided a fully sustained meal all by himself, and he was pretty sure that, unlike a can of beans, it would tick the boxes of that food pyramid he learned about in middle school.

The record scratched to a stop and he rose to place the needle again. When his apples were finished, he set the bowl in the sink and fell back into the recliner with a sigh that was half satisfaction, half longing. The dinner had been perfect, other than the lack of someone to share it with.

He closed his eyes and let the music bathe him in "the ache." That was what he had come to call this feeling, the nostalgia so sharp that it was physically painful. Through his closed lids he could see his mother and father dancing to this song when he was little, slow and graceful, embracing as the violins swelled between choruses. He would hear the music from his bedroom at night and creep down the hall to peer at them, at the hem of his mother's skirt that swayed like tall grass, and the love in his father's eyes as he looked down at her, lifting her chin with his finger to keep her gaze locked on his.

"The ache" was both pleasant and painful, and he had been indulging in it more and more lately. Even though it carried him to a time and place that was tinted with loss, at least it carried him away. For a few minutes at a time, he was no longer living alone in the cabin, desperately lonely.

The farmer's market had closed for the season, and with it had gone the thing Elijah had looked forward to most during the week, regular human interaction.

Perhaps it was time.

Elijah pushed out of the recliner and went to his room. The envelope on the nightstand that held his money was quite thin now, and he dumped it onto the bed to count the contents.

There was one ten-dollar bill, two fives, six ones, and a handful of change. Yes, a job would kill two birds with one stone, he could work all day in friendly conversation with Chitto *and* begin stashing away savings, especially now that the first freeze of the year had been forecasted for the coming week and living off the land would be harder and harder to do.

Elijah headed for the kitchen. The new phone he'd splurged on was one of the reasons the envelope on his nightstand was so thin, but it was worth the dent in his savings. The old pea-green phone with an actual rotary dial had been around since he was a child. He had to keep up with the times. Chitto picked up on the first ring.

"Hello?"

"Did I wake you?" Elijah asked.

"Did you wake me? It's eight-thirty."

"Oh," Elijah glanced at the clock, "I guess it is. Listen, I was wondering if you were still looking for help at the garage? I still remember plenty from when I used to help you and dad out back in high school, and you can catch me up on what's changed since then. I learn quick."

There was the hint of a laugh in Chitto's reply.

"Kid, I thought you'd never ask. Can you be in tomorrow at nine?"

"I'll be there," Elijah promised. Chitto hung up and Elijah replaced the receiver, wondering now what had taken him so long to reach out for work.

Truth be told, he wasn't keen on that particular brand of labor, working beneath greasy cars, staining his hands and clothes with oil and tinkering around with tools. It's not that there was anything so difficult about it, but the plain fact of the matter was that that kind of work was beneath him. Or at least, that's what he had told himself since he left for San Francisco. He had always wanted to work with his brain. That's what had drawn him to writing in the first place. Instead of building and fixing machines with his hands, he wanted to build worlds and fix characters with his mind. He wanted to be known and admired for masterful works of literature, and now, within the span of three minutes, he had hoisted a white flag of surrender up the pole. He had officially resigned himself to the manual labor that his father had done, and it stung like a big, fat nail in the coffin of his future. But his writing career was dead anyway, and winter was coming. He had to survive somehow. Anyway, he'd made the call and what was done was done.

Elijah retreated to his room and laid out clothes for the morning, old jeans and a T-shirt that he had stained varnishing the deck. There would be no one to impress at the garage.

He slept poorly, his nighttime hours punctuated by dreams that woke him, dreams about dripping oil pans and engines that dropped parts like loose teeth. He stepped out of bed before the sun was up and ate a bleary-eyed breakfast of plain oatmeal and coffee. When it was light enough outside, he completed his morning round of outdoor chores. There were now five hens in the coop with Houdini, and three warm eggs sat waiting for him behind the wooden nest flaps. He carried them carefully inside and wrapped them in a shirt before tucking them into his backpack. It wasn't much of a gift, but it was all he had and he owed at least something to Chitto for offering him the job. At a quarter to nine he kicked the bike engine to life and rode to the garage.

There was only one street that defined the "downtown" of Point Orchards. It sliced through the quaint residential neighborhoods and was lined with small businesses that kept the townsfolk who didn't commute to Seattle employed.

The garage was smack in the middle of Main Street, sandwiched between the post office and the bakery. Its front door stayed pulled up to the ceiling during business hours, inviting passersby to gawk at the elusive underbellies of cars as Chitto worked beneath them, the sounds of whirring drills and cranking wrenches spilling out to the sidewalk beyond.

Main Street looked pretty much the same as it had fifteen years before. The mural of a cow chewing hay in a pasture on the side of the Point Orchards Market was peeling a bit more, and the small storefront that had been Terry's Hair for All was now a bait-and-tackle shop, but other than that, nothing notable.

The garage door was already open when Elijah rode his bike up onto the sidewalk and pulled straight in. Chitto was sitting in the small office off the main floor, squinting at receipts and carefully punching numbers into a calculator.

"Come on in," he called through the open door.

Elijah stepped into the office and took a seat, looking around. There wasn't an inch of wall that wasn't covered with photographs, various pieces of paper, certificates, and even a few drawings clearly done by children. Elijah blinked at those, confused.

"You don't have kids, right?"

Chitto didn't look up from the calculator as he answered.

"I keep blank paper and crayons in my desk. You wouldn't believe how many people drop off a car and ask if their kid can stay to watch. I oughta run a daycare service. The kiddos love watching me work."

Elijah chuckled. His eyes followed the photographs around the room. There was picture after picture of Chitto and his father through the years. In fact, Elijah could pinpoint exactly where in the room Chitto had started decorating. Near the door were photos of his dad and Chitto as young men, both smiling, both in good shape as they held up fish and deer for the camera. Most of the early photographs were black-and-white, but as he followed the pictures across the wall and around the back of Chitto's desk, they became colorful, his dad and Chitto a little older, a little less fit. On the far wall, the photos with his father tapered off and many were just pictures of cars, some scenic shots of mountains or waterfalls, one or two Christmas cards, and a few faces from the reservation that were unfamiliar to Elijah.

"Oh, here, I brought you some eggs."

Chitto put down the last receipt and stood, his back popping loudly.

"Thanks, kid. Must've got the coop sorted out, then," he chuckled, taking them from Elijah's outstretched hand. "Come here"—Chitto stepped around Elijah into the garage—"I've got something to show you."

Elijah followed him to where a car was hidden by a beige cover. Chitto loosed the straps and pulled the cover off, revealing the car underneath.

Elijah ran his eyes over the silky curves of the pool-blue Camaro. It gleamed under the fluorescent lights like water, its profile low and furtive.

"Wow," he breathed. He'd always been partial to the sleek Chevy model. "Where'd you get it?"

"It's not mine," Chitto said. "It's yours."

Elijah turned, confused. "I don't understand."

"After you left, your dad spent his free time in here pouring his heart and soul into restoring this baby. Then he got sick and couldn't work anymore so it just sorta sat here. Before he passed, he made sure to tell me that you would get it when you moved back. He never stopped believing you would come home."

Elijah didn't know what to say, but that familiar tug of guilt in his chest pulled at him.

"Does it run?"

Chitto snorted. "Not by a long shot. The engine still needs to be rebuilt. Unfortunately, your pops spent most of his time on her looks, but inside she's a dud. I don't know, maybe he did it on purpose to make you earn her. We've got plenty of work coming in this month, but between clients it'll give you something to do."

Chitto pressed the cover into Elijah's chest and walked back to his office, leaving Elijah alone in the garage, deep in thought. For the first time, he was wondering how well he had even known his father. His dad had changed, withdrawn, after his mother died. She was the glue that held the family together. She had made them whole and given them purpose, but Elijah hadn't known that she provided their guiding light until it was snuffed out and his dad spiraled down into the darkness of drink. The more his father drank, the more desperate Elijah became to leave town, counting down the days until he turned eighteen and running more miles than anyone else on the team to earn the scholarship that would get him out. He hadn't lied to Nakita; there was a new life that he craved in San Francisco, a chance to make it as a writer, but she hadn't known how badly he needed to escape that suffocating cabin and the man inside it. The man who drowned himself in booze until he couldn't remember his own name.

The longer he spent in Point Orchards as an adult, the more he had to face the fact that he might not have fully understood his dad. Perhaps the guy had changed in the last fifteen years. If he had come back to town sooner, maybe they could have spent a little time together as men. Maybe Elijah could have come to know him as a person rather than a parent, perhaps even as a friend.

Elijah gazed at the Camaro, lost in thought. For a moment, he could almost picture his dad behind the wheel. Turning away, he headed for the wall of tools. It was time to pop the hood and figure out what was going on inside.

12

A light knock sounded on the door frame of Sheriff Godbout's office, and he looked up to see the Point Orchards postwoman holding a box.

"Oh, hey, Trudy."

"Package for you," she said, crossing the room and setting it on his desk.

Jim signed her clipboard and she bustled out.

"Stay warm out there," he called after her.

"Rain, sleet, or snow, Jim," she quipped from the hall.

Jim picked up the package and gave it a light shake. It was a small box, not heavy, and gave a gentle rattle when he shook it. He hadn't ordered anything. And if he had, he would have had it sent to his house, not the station. But, sure enough, it was made out to Jim Godbout at the station's address, and where the return address should have been was only blank cardboard.

Jim reached into his desk for scissors and slid a blade through the tape. Lying faceup inside the box was a paperback book.

"The heck is this?" he said under his breath as he ran his eyes over the cover. It was a forest scene. The dark green trees, raised to give the paperback texture, covered the whole page, except an inch or so of dark blue at the top and bottom for dramatic effect. Perplexed, Jim looked

79

closer. From one of the trees in the center hung a tiny noose. The title was written in bold white letters across the front: *Middletide*.

Jim opened the cover and a printed note slipped out, fluttering to the floor beneath his chair. He retrieved it and flipped it over, and his blood ran cold at the nine words addressed to him.

Sheriff Godbout,
Erin Landry's death was not a suicide.
Please read.

Jim closed the book and looked at the cover again, this time finding the author's name along the spine in small red letters: E. M. Leith.

Jim set the book aside and picked up the box again. He turned it upside down and checked the bottom and all the sides, but there was no clue as to the sender. He turned the note over as well, but it was typed on plain white paper and gave nothing away. Mystified, he opened the book and started reading.

The clock on his desk rounded three full hours while Jim sat hunched over the book, turning pages every few minutes. He didn't hear Jeremy enter the station and greet him as he walked past. He didn't hear the phone ring out in the main room, answered by the station secretary. He didn't even hear the snowplow that roared past his window twice.

He ran his index finger down page after page, chapter after chapter, reading the story as quickly as he could comprehend it. It was absurd, an absolute impossibility, and yet there it was on the pages before him. The lunch hour came and went and Jim stayed where he was, nearly halfway through the book. Only once did he pause, and that was to flip back to the cover page and read the date of publication. May 20, 1981. Almost thirteen years ago.

With only three chapters remaining, Sheriff Godbout closed the book and placed it on his desk. He didn't need to read the end. He didn't need to know how the remaining loose ends tied up.

"Hey."

Jim looked up to find Jeremy leaning into the door frame.

"When did you want to get out to the Leith place?" the deputy asked.

Jim hadn't realized his heart was racing until he tried to speak and found himself short of breath.

"Sit down." He gestured to the chair across from him and slid the book to Jeremy.

"What's this?"

"Buckle up, kid. You're not going to believe what I just read."

"*Middletide*." Jeremy frowned at the cover. "Why are you reading a book?"

"Because Elijah Leith wrote it," Jim said.

"Huh," Jeremy looked impressed as he picked it up and fanned his thumb across the pages. "He actually wrote something?"

"Oh, it's something. It was published in eighty-one, before he moved back to town. He left Point Orchards after he graduated high school and tried to make it as a writer. His dad used to brag on him all the time about it. But, you ready for this? It's a mystery novel about a murder that was made to look like a suicide."

"Wait . . . what?" Jeremy dropped the book onto the desk like it was white-hot.

"It's the same, and I mean the exact same, down to the details of the crime scene. In this version, there's a town off the Louisiana Gulf Coast that's only accessible at low tide. When the water rises, the only road to the town is cut off from the mainland. A woman is found hanging from a tree in what looks like a suicide, only there's discrepancies, just like with Doc Landry. There's blood under her fingernails and missing shoes. And get this, she was killed in the middle of the night, at high tide, which limits the suspects to the folks in the town."

Jeremy's jaw had fallen open and stayed there as Jim finished summarizing the plot of the novel.

"Okay, so it means he'd know exactly how to commit this sort of crime, but why?" The deputy shook his head, incredulous. "Why would he incriminate himself like this knowing it was possible for us to get ahold of the book and read it? It makes no sense."

"You're looking at it wrong," Jim said, leaning forward. "It's the perfect alibi. He'll say the same thing you just said. He'll ask who in their right mind would commit a crime exactly like the one they wrote about in their novel. He'll say he was framed, that someone read his book and made it look like he'd done it. He knows how crazy it'll sound and that it would make much more sense for someone else who wanted her dead to use him as a scapegoat."

"This is nuts . . ." The deputy trailed off in a whisper.

"I know," Sheriff Godbout nodded. "I know. But there's something else here. In his story, the woman's high heels were found near the murder scene, shoved into the hole of a tree."

"How come?" Jeremy asked.

"They had traces of the killer's blood on them from the struggle."

Jeremy's brows cinched together. "But DNA evidence wasn't a thing back in the early eighties. It's barely a thing now. He wouldn't have known you could identify someone based on DNA yet."

"Not DNA," Jim said, "but blood type. In the book, the victim opened a pretty good gash on the killer's leg and that's where the blood came from. He hid the shoes because if she committed suicide by hanging and they found her wearing high heels covered in blood, they'd wonder where it all came from, and later his blood type was used as evidence in court."

Jeremy stood suddenly, upsetting his chair. "Wait, do you think—"

"Let's find out." Jim finished his deputy's thought as he stood to grab his coat and hat. He snatched the book off the desk as he left, tucking it into the inner pocket of his jacket.

It was a short walk from the station to the marina and the roads were mostly clear. The snow was melting in the sun with temperatures in the high forties. Sheriff and deputy climbed into the silver police skiff and kicked the motor to life. It carried them out of the marina and into the sound.

Within ten minutes, they were sliding through the inlet to the lake, engine silenced. Jeremy rowed across the water as the sheriff scanned the trees on the far shore.

"Nice and easy," he instructed in a low voice as Jeremy pulled the boat onto the shore. For the first time, he was unnerved by the thought of the man who lived on the other side of these woods, the one who had access to the lake by way of a trail and could, at any moment, be watching him and Jeremy nosing around the scene of the murder. He glanced at his deputy and found the same look of unease written across his features as his gaze jumped from shadow to shadow along the shore.

There were still thin patches of snow scattered along the bank. Much of it had melted and run into the lake, leaving the bare ground slick with mud that slid beneath their boots.

"We're leaving a pretty noticeable trail," Jeremy said, looking back at their tracks.

"No way around that," Jim replied, sliding forward, arms out for balance.

Beneath the trees, the footing was firmer, and Jim came to a stop beside the hemlock. He reached into his jacket for the book and flipped through the pages, searching.

"Here it is," he said, then proceeded to silently read the passage about the victim's shoes.

Night was falling. Night always started in the middle of the forest here and worked its way out. Daylight started at the edges and worked its way in. James had mere minutes to search for the piece of evidence that would condemn Hannah's killer, and he moved in a feverish spiral out from the tree where her body had been. Foot by foot, he searched. Had any earth been recently overturned? Had the shoes been thrown into the gulf and washed up onto the shore?

The darkness did not wait for him. It descended with the swiftness of a gavel and James relented, ceasing his search beneath the umbrella of a dense oak. Sweeping tendrils of Spanish moss swayed around him, one kissing the side of his face, and as he turned to brush it away, he saw it. There, in the hollow between two of the oak's great arms, glinting in the first ray of moonlight, was the satin heel of a woman's shoe.

"Well?" Jeremy asked.

"It doesn't say where exactly, just that they were in the hollow of a tree."

Jim handed the book to Jeremy, who scanned the passage quickly.

"The heck is Spanish moss?" he asked.

"It doesn't grow here," Jim said. "Oaks don't either, for that matter. Come on, let's start looking."

They started at the hemlock, Jeremy walking one way, Jim another. There were no hollows in the evergreens along the lake. The trunks of the Douglas firs were made of solid, impenetrable stuff. It was one of the reasons they lived so long. There were no cavities through which rot could enter and grow, eating the tree from the inside. They were built to withstand centuries of Pacific Northwest weather. Here and there were the minutest of woodpecker holes, but nothing larger than a golf ball. Jim moved deeper into the forest and worked his way back toward the hemlock through the second layer of trees, finding nothing. He met Jeremy on the way and found his own frustration mirrored on the deputy's face.

They moved another length deeper into the woods and searched outward again. Jim glanced at his watch. They'd been hunting for nearly an hour and his high hopes of finding Erin's shoes had dwindled to empty. After a final fifteen minutes of poking around trunks, he gave up and returned to the hemlock, finding Jeremy already there, dejected.

"There's no point," the deputy said. "We could spend days looking at every tree between here and Elijah's cabin and still not find anything."

Jim stood silently for a moment, watching the police skiff bobbing up and down lazily in the lake. In Elijah's novel, the main character had found the shoes at the very moment he gave up searching. Giving up the search right now meant he and Jeremy would untie their boat and leave. Jim's eyes left the boat and followed the rope that anchored it to shore. It slithered in the frigid water like a snake and stilled where it hit the dirt, running in a straight line to the felled log he and Jeremy always tied it to. The log anyone would tie their boat to when they came ashore.

The log was hollow, rotting from the inside out. Eventually the trunk would collapse and there would be nothing but a line of bark dust on the shore that would hint that a tree had been there, but for now, the inside was open and dark.

Jim walked to it, knowing before he knelt down to peer inside what he would find there.

Wedged an arm's length into the log were a pair of beige suede boots. Jim reached in and pulled them out, staring at the dappled trail of blood that crossed the right toe.

Behind him, Jeremy made a sound that was half gasp, half triumphant whoop and he dashed forward, nearly slipping on the wet ground.

"No way," he said, gazing at the boots, his eyes alight with the excitement of a child who had just discovered a pirate's treasure. "Look at that, blood and all, just like in the book. I mean not exactly like the book, just a few drops, but this is nuts, I don't believe it!"

"I don't, either," the sheriff said slowly, evenly, as he looked down at the boots in his hand. It was too easy. Too convenient. Jim turned to his deputy.

"Makes just a little too much sense, doesn't it?"

13

Elijah turned the key and the Camaro roared to life. He let it idle for a moment as the engine warmed, enjoying the vibration in the soles of his feet. It had taken two years of hard work to rebuild the engine, but he'd done a thorough job and now it purred like a sleeping cat. He lifted his thermos to his mouth and took a sip of hot, black coffee, warming his insides and stiff fingers.

So far, this September had been an unseasonably cold one. Point Orchards had hit its first frost during the second week of the month and half of the vegetables in his garden had spoiled. It had pained him to toss them onto the compost pile, but not as much as it would have back when his survival had depended on whatever the garden produced.

Every morning since that initial frost, the backyard had been iced with glittering frozen dew when he stepped outside. Spiderwebs on the fence hung like intricate diamond necklaces and his boots left dark tracks in the grass wherever he went. The fruit trees up front that usually began to turn around this time and graced October with vibrant colors had faded prematurely brown, their sap slowed to a crawl by the cold weather. Half of the leaves had already dropped, and as Elijah pulled the Camaro onto the road, his tires scattered a cloud of the crunchy, brown shavings.

Elijah beat Chitto to the garage and rolled the door up. They didn't have anyone scheduled until ten, and he wanted the morning hours to work on blowing out the Camaro's fuel line.

At half past nine, Elijah's head turned at the familiar rumble of Chitto's pickup as it slid into his parking spot along the sidewalk.

"Hey!" Elijah called, wiping his greasy hands on a rag as he stepped into the morning sun. The door of the pickup opened, and from inside came the sound of a hacking cough. When Chitto finally emerged, he was hunched over a handkerchief.

"You all right?" Elijah asked. "That cough sounds bad."

Chitto waved the handkerchief dismissively. "Just a cold. My lungs don't like this weather."

He broke into another round of coughing, and Elijah fought back the urge to help him inside. Chitto didn't have many dislikes, but being patronized fell right at the top of the list.

"You oughta at least take a break from the pipe while your lungs are aggravated," Elijah said, turning back to the Camaro.

"Yeah, yeah," Chitto ducked into his office, "both you and Doc Landry need to lay off about the pipe. If I have my way, I'll be buried with it so I can blow smoke rings from the Great Beyond."

"You'll live longer without it," Elijah shouted after him.

"Nope," Chitto called back, "it'll just *feel* longer."

Elijah laughed and went back to work on the fuel line. The days he spent working with Chitto were easy and comfortable. They had become true partners at work and good friends outside the garage. Chitto came to the cabin for dinner most Friday nights and never left before midnight. They stayed up playing cards, swapping stories, and reminiscing about the past, when as a boy Elijah used to tag along with Chitto and Jake in the garage or out to the lake. The thing he appreciated most about Chitto was that he didn't try to be a father figure, and it was for that reason he became one. When Chitto's smile faded in moments of seriousness at the table, telling Elijah he shouldn't live in isolation forever, shouldn't tuck himself away from the world, should find himself a good woman and raise a family, Elijah listened. The man was right—the empty cabin got to him at times, and having Chitto's company in the kitchen every week meant more to him than he cared to admit. Elijah felt his absolute happiest when he was serving up food grown on his land to his closest friend. *His* friend. He sometimes forgot that his dad was the reason Chitto was in his life at all, but there were other times he couldn't miss it, like when he would glance out from under the Camaro and see Chitto leaning in the doorway of his office with a wistful expression on his face, almost as though it was Jake he was watching under the old Chevy instead of his son.

The workday picked up with oil changes, tire rotations, and a transmission replacement. Elijah offered to shoulder the day's appointments so Chitto could rest, and Chitto took him up on it, leaving for home just an hour after he'd arrived. At one o'clock, Elijah pulled down the door of the garage for his lunch break. He fished in the glove compartment of the Camaro and pulled out a worn leather notebook and pen. Normally, he brought lunch with him to work, but every now and then he treated himself to a real meal at the bakery next door. The chicken salad sandwiches on fresh croissants were always worth a few extra bucks. Notebook in hand, he stepped into the bakery and took a seat at his favorite square table next to the window.

"Chicken Salad, hun?" the woman behind the counter called.

"Yep, thanks, Janelle," he said and waved.

Elijah opened the notebook and flipped to a clean page to begin writing. He'd started a habit he called his "daily pages," committing to writing three pages' worth of whatever came out of his head with no expectations at all each day. It didn't have to be a story, didn't have to be brilliant, didn't even have to make sense, but the process of spewing whatever was in his mind onto a few blank pages had become an addiction. It felt good to write again, even on the days when what poured out was complete nonsense. One day he wrote about a patch of forest he'd driven by that was in the process of being logged for timber and how it hurt to see the land stripped of what it had grown. Another day he wrote about the work he'd done in the garage. Sometimes he wrote about Chitto or about his dad. It didn't matter; he never went back to read it.

The chicken salad sandwich arrived on his table and Elijah took a bite, chewing slowly as he scribbled.

*Running the math today I realized that I'm half the age Dad was
when he died. I'm halfway to seventy. I don't feel it. If I woke up
from a coma today and had no way of knowing how old I was,
I guess I'd feel about twenty. Maybe I'll always feel twenty, and
looking in the mirror to find gray hair and sagging skin will come
as a surprise when I'm old. The only difference is, at twenty, the
entire world seemed spread out into eternity before me, endless paths
to take, endless time to explore each one. Twenty was old enough to
know that someday I would die, but young enough to forget about
it, too. It's harder to forget now. It's harder to ignore the sense of
urgency I feel about the time I'm wasting. For two years now, I've
been working a job I don't have any passion for. I'm grateful for the
steady income, but do I really want to end up like Dad? Headed
to my grave with nothing to show for it? "Here lies Elijah Leith,
he changed five hundred brake pads." The only thing I've ever felt
truly passionate about was writing, but I tried. I tried and I failed.
I don't want to waste another decade on a new book that's just
going to bring me more heartbreak. I still love it though. I still love
opening the tap and letting all the words run out.*

Elijah took another bite of his sandwich. The chicken salad was
perfect, bursting with fresh red grapes and the crunch of celery, but
Elijah found himself thinking about the chicken itself. Where had it
come from? How long had it lived before being slaughtered for its meat?
Had it ever enjoyed the freedom of running where it pleased or had it
lived out its days in one of those massive airplane-hangar-sized sheds
full of thousands of chickens, never enjoying the sun on its feathers?
He couldn't help thinking like that after living mostly off the food from
his property for these last few years. He was making enough money to
afford groceries, but homesteading was in his blood now, an addiction
just like writing. Perhaps pride was the thing he was really addicted to.
The pride of seeing his own work on the page or on the plate.

*Ran out to the lake last Saturday. There were a couple of guys
fishing. Too far away to see who they were, but I sat and watched*

them for a while from the woods. I've pulled some pretty big trout out of that lake, but I saw one of them reel in a whopper, at least twenty-five pounds. At first, I had no idea how they got in, but I watched them leave through a tiny inlet on the far side that I didn't know was there. After they left, I walked a loop around the lake to check it out. Barely big enough for a boat—if the tide had gone out, they would have been stuck there for hours. Thought about putting up a no trespassing sign, but at the end of the day, they're not hurting anyone. It was weird seeing people back there though. I haven't been back there with anyone since that summer. Yes, that summer. I know it's long past time to move on, to start thinking about someone else, but pride's probably keeping me from dealing with that, too.

Elijah's pen stopped abruptly in its looping path across the page, and he closed the notebook. That was enough for today.

He finished his sandwich and laid a few bills on the table. He had fifteen minutes left until he opened the garage again, and he sat idly staring out the window at the storefronts across the street. On the bench outside the grocery store sat two men, one stooped and white-haired, hand resting on a cane, the other perhaps twenty years younger, salt-and-pepper hair and just starting to sag in the middle. Perhaps father and son. Elijah watched them as they watched the street, eyes roving back and forth with the cars that passed by. A sleek silver sedan parallel parked in front of the store and a woman climbed out, long black hair woven in a thick braid down her back. Elijah stopped breathing.

Time seemed to slow, dreamlike, as she turned around.

It was Nakita, tall and slender and more breathtakingly beautiful than he remembered. Her eyes were still the deep black of a moonless night, but they possessed a womanly intelligence that they had lacked when he saw her last. Her lips were full and deep red over a jawline that had become sharper and more defined. Her shoulders were still straight and her posture proud, but she looked thinner, her appetite undoubtedly stolen by grief.

She reached into the sedan for her purse, closed the door behind her, and disappeared into the grocery store. Elijah's heart was thudding madly in his chest, his vision tunneled on the sliding glass doors that had swallowed her.

He stood too quickly, bumping into the table and upsetting the half-full glass of water that spilled all over his notebook and pants.

Janelle rushed over with a towel and he wiped himself down, apologizing to her even as he kept his eyes locked on the grocery store doors.

"Here, let me," she said, taking the towel and mopping the table.

"I'm so sorry," he said as he snatched up his wet notebook and ran out of the bakery, ignoring the bewildered stares of the couple who had stopped mid-bite to watch him leave. He made it halfway across the street before abruptly changing directions and running back toward the garage. A jeep honked as it swerved around him in the middle of the road and he pulled up short, shouting another apology as the driver flipped him off. He sprinted to the garage and ducked in through the side door. From Chitto's empty office he had a perfect view of Nakita's car as he peered through the blinds. Ten minutes passed and Elijah stayed frozen behind the window, waiting, deliberating, trying to catch his breath. Twice the doors opened to let customers out, and each time Elijah felt as though his heart would leap right through his ribs. He could do it, right now, run back across the street and stand next to her car to confront her when she walked out.

Hey there, long time no see!

No.

Nakita? Is that you? Remember me? It's Elijah, the guy who promised to come back that one summer and didn't.

Definitely not.

Hello, I saw you go into the store, thought I'd pop over for a chat.

There was no right way to break the ice of seventeen years.

Nakita emerged from the store with a plastic bag in each hand and loaded them into the trunk of the sedan. Elijah watched her with a new kind of ache, a desperate desire to run back across the street and just stand there, just to feel her eyes land on him, to feel her acknowledge his presence, even if it was with hatred. That would be better than this, better than her not knowing that he was just feet away behind a brick wall, watching her. He wanted to make himself known, but his nerves kept him glued where he was. That, and the fact that the water he'd spilled made it look exactly like he'd wet his pants.

She climbed into the driver's side and the sedan pulled away. Elijah released the blinds and they sprang shut, hiding the world outside. He turned and sank into Chitto's chair, numb. With a groan of resignation, he let his head fall onto the desk with a thud.

At last.

At last, he had seen her. And it hadn't been the casual, adult conversation he'd envisioned, the show of maturity that he had hoped to display. No. Just one glimpse of her and he had been a boy again, out of control and scared, making a complete fool of himself. The moment he'd been imagining had arrived unexpectedly and he'd hid like a coward. He had been eighteen again, knocked flat on his face by a wave of the exact same reckless, stupid, overwhelming infatuation.

14

A slick, black drop of oil landed on Elijah's face, and he brushed it away with the back of his hand, smearing it across his cheek. He was on his back, sorting his way through a tangle of pipes and wires to get at the head gasket that needed replacing. This was his least favorite kind of mechanical work, the kind that meant he had to take an entire engine apart piece by piece just to get at a leaky gasket the size of a quarter. It wasn't taking the engine apart that bothered him so much, it was piecing it back together. In truth, actually replacing the gasket took all of three minutes to accomplish, but the hours of labor before and after were tedious, and more than once he'd had to explain the high bill to an angry customer, confused about the triple-digit number at the bottom of the page. It was half a day's work; that's why it cost so much.

He cranked the wrench, muscles straining as he loosened a large bolt. A welcome gust of chilly air blew in through the open door and met him under the car, wicking away the beads of sweat on his forehead. The temperature outside was hovering just above freezing, but Elijah had left the door rolled up, grateful for the draft.

Another drop of oil landed on his face, this one right at his temple, and Elijah swiped at it, smearing the black stain into his hair. This wasn't what he'd pictured himself doing for a living at thirty-six years old. For some reason, thirty-six felt like a benchmark number, like he had lounged through his early thirties until this past birthday, when he found himself suddenly strapped to the front of a train hurtling toward forty with no way to pull the brake. Forty was serious. Forty was the age at which most people were settled in a well-established career.

There was a bold line between a job and a career, and this work fell decidedly into the job column. It was an occupation that brought in regular income, steady and predictable week after week, but it was no career. A career was what happened at the intersection of passion and paycheck. For Chitto, this work *was* his career. The man loved taking apart cars more than anything else on earth. He talked about it even when he wasn't at the garage. He probably dreamed about it. This was all he had ever wanted to do. For Elijah, it was a job that he left at five o'clock and didn't think about again until he arrived back at the garage the next morning. And, even at work, even now with oil dripping onto his face and his shoulder aching with every torque of the wrench, his mind was thousands of miles away, daydreaming about the writing bungalow on the coast of Maine he'd been constructing in his mind.

He could see it now, whitewashed and weathered by the salt air, the outside decorated with wind chimes made of shells and wooden carvings of seagulls. Surrounding it, an old ship's rope strung through wooden posts for a fence. Inside, there was a small galley kitchen against one wall, a plain canvas cot for a bed on the other, and an old desk beneath a round window that looked out on the ocean. The desk was simple and inviting, with a half-finished manuscript spread across it. Beside the manuscript, a steaming mug of coffee that never grew cold. He found himself daydreaming about this fictional retreat more and more of late, and he could see with vivid clarity every single detail of the place—the chair, the pen in his hand, and the paper waiting for words. He could picture every detail, except the story that would be on those pages.

Above the sound of Kurt Cobain's voice in his headphones, Elijah heard the phone ringing in Chitto's office. He rolled out from underneath the Volkswagen and pulled his headphones down around his neck. The phone rang again.

"You gonna get that?" he called.

There was no answer from Chitto, and the phone rang a third time. Elijah ran to answer it.

"Begay's Service and Oil," he said into the receiver. The office was empty; Chitto must have stepped out while Elijah was working.

"You don't sound like Chitto," the female voice on the other end said.

"No, ma'am, Chitto's not available, this is Elijah Leith, how can I help you?"

"Oh, hi, Elijah, this is Dr. Landry, I'm not sure if you remember me."

Elijah stood a little straighter behind the desk.

"Sure, how are you, Doctor? How's the little one?"

Dr. Landry laughed. "You can call me Erin, and thanks for asking, she's doing great, talking up a storm, which is amazing, but we're also in the throes of the terrible twos."

Elijah smiled.

"Anyway," she said, "I'm calling about my Mercedes, it's starting to stutter between first and second and it's having trouble reversing as well. I'm worried the transmission might be going out."

Elijah jotted down a few notes on Chitto's desk as she talked.

Landry, Mercedes, Transmission check. He knew which car Erin drove; he'd eyed it lustfully every time it rolled past on Main Street, a black Mercedes SUV that was basically a Jeep Wrangler on steroids. It was more suitable to Indiana Jones rolling through the Amazon or bumping along the African plains than a slender female doctor in the small town of Point Orchards, but that was one of the reasons it worked for her: it was such a stark contrast to its driver's looks.

"Do you feel safe enough to drive it or do you want us to tow it in?"

"I can get it there," she assured him. "Do you have anything available today? I'm not off work again for another nine days."

Elijah glanced at the Volkswagen in the garage.

"Actually, if you want to bring it in around one, I can get to it over my lunch hour, as soon as I'm done with the car I'm working on."

"I can't ask you to give up your lunch hour," she said.

"It's no problem, I'll just run over to the bakery for a quick bite when I'm done."

"Thanks so much. I'll go ahead and drop it off at one, then."

Elijah hung up and went looking for Chitto. He found him sitting behind the garage, facing the alley with his back against the wall, pipe in hand, mumbling something to himself as he stared absently into space.

"Having a nice chat with the dumpster?" Elijah asked.

Chitto laughed, and beneath it, Elijah heard the rattle in his chest that had never fully faded since his fall cold.

"Doc Landry's bringing her rig in. I promised her I'd take a look at the transmission over lunch."

Chitto nodded. "That's my cue to head home early then. She'll smell the smoke on me and rag about the pipe. I'll be back later this afternoon after I grab a nap."

Elijah held out a hand and pulled Chitto to his feet.

"Stay home, I've got it covered today."

Chitto nodded again, and Elijah walked him to his truck.

No sooner had Elijah backed the Volkswagen out onto the street and parked it than Erin drove up in her black SUV with a friendly honk.

Elijah waved her forward into place and she parked. She stepped out of the driver's side wearing a white linen blouse tucked into dark jeans and knee-high, heeled boots. Her long blond hair was pulled into a loose ponytail, and she wore just enough makeup to highlight her fine bone structure and wide, icy blue-green eyes. To Elijah, she looked like she'd just stepped off the cover of some high-end equestrian magazine.

"Hey, Dr. Landry."

"Erin," she reminded him. "Here," she reached inside the SUV and pulled out a paper bag, "Since you're giving up your lunch hour, I picked up something for you at the Blue Goose on the way over. Burger and fries."

"Thanks!" Elijah took it gratefully. "You didn't have to do that."

"Well, I wanted to." She handed him her keys. "Listen, I'm going to take advantage of the time in town and run a few errands if that's okay with you."

"Of course."

Alone again, Elijah cranked his music back up and got to work. By the time he heard Erin's heeled boots clicking across the garage floor an hour later, he had her car down from the lift and was in Chitto's office writing up an estimate.

"Bad news or good news?" she asked, taking the seat across the desk. She had removed her ponytail, leaving her hair loose around her shoulders. Elijah was having trouble meeting her steady gaze.

"Both," he said, handing her the slip of paper. "It's not the transmission, that's the good news, but you're gonna need a new clutch and that'll take at least a week to come in. I wouldn't drive it until you've got it replaced, so we can keep it here and I can give you a ride home right now if you need one."

"That would be great."

Elijah walked her to the Camaro and opened the door for her before jogging around to the driver's side. It was strange, having another person in his car. And a long-legged, attractive female doctor at that. Elijah pulled out of the garage and turned left toward the marina at Erin's direction. They drove in silence for a few minutes. Elijah thought about flipping on the radio, but decided against it. Confined with her in the small car, he smelled the faintest hint of perfume: warm and exotic with a trace of something floral and incredibly enticing that he had never smelled before in his life.

Beside him, Erin was absently running her fingers through her hair as she slid one leg up to cross the other, and Elijah was finding it increasingly difficult to keep his eyes on the road.

"Oh, one more thing," he said, trying to pull himself back to something grounding. "I'm going to go ahead and rotate your tires for you, the tread on the back couple is a little thin."

"Okay."

He drummed his fingers on the steering wheel and cleared his throat, searching for something else to say.

"So how's parenthood treating you?"

She gave a tinkling laugh. "Life is very full at the moment. It's not a bad thing, I'm just really busy."

"I can imagine," Elijah nodded.

"Do you want kids someday?"

Elijah kept his eyes on the road ahead, but felt her gaze on his face.

"I don't know," he said, choosing to open up a little. "I'd need to find someone to have kids with first. Haven't been on a date in about four years."

"You're kidding," she gave a little laugh, "a guy as good-looking as you?"

A prickling blush worked its way up Elijah's neck and broke onto his face. He wanted to think of something witty to say back, but his mind fell completely blank and all he managed was "Well."

"Oh, right here, please." Erin pointed at a driveway on the left and Elijah swung the Camaro up the slope and into the ring of arborvitae around her house.

"Pretty place," he commented, running his eyes over the freshly painted trim and attractive shutters, each window graced with a flower box overflowing with false pink peonies.

"I like it," Erin said as she unbuckled, and Elijah was a little surprised that she didn't say *We*.

There was a white BMW parked in the open garage. Elijah nodded to it.

"So, you'll be able to use your husband's car to get around while we're waiting for the clutch?"

"Manny drives a truck," she said. "That one's mine."

"Oh," Elijah said quietly.

"I bought the SUV to have something bigger for kids," she explained as she opened her door and swung her legs out. Leaning back toward him, she placed her fingers lightly on his arm and said, "Thanks for the ride."

Elijah nodded. "Any—yeah, anytime."

Erin climbed out, closed the door, and waved. Elijah immediately turned the car around and pulled down the driveway, resisting the urge to watch her walk to the front door.

He glanced down at his arm where her fingers had been, half expecting to find her fingerprints branded into his skin, but there was nothing but a smudge of grease near his elbow. With a jerk, Elijah reached up to twist the rearview mirror so it reflected his face. There was oil still smeared across his cheek and forehead from his morning work.

"Great," he sighed, as he pulled out of the driveway and back onto the road.

His hands were clammy on the wheel and his T-shirt was damp beneath the arms, but he left the window up and let the smell of her perfume surround him as he drove back into town.

15

JANUARY 10, 1994

Sheriff Godbout held Elijah's novel in one hand and the phone in the other. He'd called the publishing house three times in the last two hours and simply couldn't get through. He let it ring for another few minutes before replacing the receiver with a frustrated click.

His day had been completely fruitless. After finding Erin's shoes in the hollow log, he and Jeremy had boated back to the Marina then drove straight out to the Leith cabin, only to find that Elijah still wasn't home. Determined to track down the man who was fast becoming their leading suspect, Jim was on his way to Elijah's office when he was sidetracked by a distressed phone call from ninety-eight-year-old Alice Nesbit. He pulled a U-turn and drove thirty minutes out to her bungalow on the sound to find that the groans of the burglar lurking in her walls was actually her radiator kicking into high gear to warm the house. On his way back to the office, Jeremy had called to let him know that Elijah had quit his job months before, leaving Jim with nowhere else to look. And now, he was wasting the rest of his day calling the number in tiny font on the inside cover of the book.

The world outside Jim's office window was disappearing into the darkness of winter's afternoon dusk, but he stayed at his desk, watching the clock. Another ten minutes passed, and he picked up the phone to dial the number again.

"Brantley House Publishing," a brisk male voice announced.

Finally! Jim sat straight up, "Yes, hello, I've been trying to get through to someone about a book that you published."

"Title?"

"*Middletide*, M-I-D-D—"

"Yep, one second." The man cut him off.

Through the phone, Jim heard the clacking of a keyboard. They must have some sort of computer database. Jim glanced at his own filing system, a cabinet with two broken drawers. He'd take it over this new World Wide Web fad any day, though. His filing cabinet would still be up and running if the power went out.

"It looks like our acquisitions editor Jeanie handled that title. I'll send you over to her office."

Without waiting for a response, the man put Jim on hold, and he waited with the phone against his shoulder as the receiver played some vague upbeat tune that he was sure would be stuck in his head long after he hung up.

"Jeanie Devin," a woman answered.

"Hey, Jeanie, this is Sheriff Godbout up in Point Orchards, Washington. If you have a minute, I'd like to ask you a few questions about one of the books that you published a few years ago."

"Okay," Jeanie said slowly, clearly confused. "Which book?"

"*Middletide*. Author by the name of Elijah Leith."

"Oh!" Jeanie's voice perked up. "Yeah, I remember it, hang on."

The music picked back up without warning and Jim tapped his heel on the floor as he waited for Jeanie to pop back on.

"Got it, still had a copy on the shelf here in my office. What were you hoping to find out?"

Jim spoke slowly. "I don't know how to ask, exactly. I guess I'm looking for some insight about the publishing process. Did anyone on your team work with Mr. Leith in developing the plot of the book?"

"I do work with our authors on story development at times, but if I remember right, the manuscript he turned in was pretty polished. There were a few rounds of edits but nothing structural; he did all that work himself and I didn't see the need for any major changes."

"Okay," Jim said, switching the receiver to the other shoulder as he picked up the book. "I don't suppose he ever mentioned if he based it on a real-life crime or anything like that?"

There was a long moment of silence on the line.

"No," she said haltingly. "No, he never mentioned where he came up with the idea and I didn't ask."

Jim felt the dead end rising up to meet him, but he pressed on doggedly.

"And then what happened, once it was published, how many copies did it sell?"

"Not many. Unfortunately, like a lot of really great books, the traction just wasn't there. Shame, too. Elijah was such a good writer. So much potential. I picked up the manuscript in a heartbeat when it landed on my desk. We didn't have a whole lot in the budget for an advance, but I remember telling him it would sell and he'd be able to earn it back plus ten times that. I don't tell authors that unless I really believe it. I felt terrible having to tell him that we were going to discontinue printing."

"What happened? Why didn't it sell?"

"Hard to say. Plenty of great books don't sell. I had a good feeling about this one, but I'm not a crystal ball. The market wants what it wants. I do remember a pretty bad review dousing enthusiasm for *Middletide* early on though. I can pull the sales file out if you want. We keep everything in there, the numbers, reviews, stuff like that."

"If it's not too much trouble."

"Let me put you on hold."

The music picked up in the earpiece and Jim was disappointed to find himself humming along. When Jeanie jumped back on the call, Jim heard the rustling of papers. Good old-fashioned files.

"Still there, Sheriff?"

"Yep."

"Okay, here it is, I found the review. A critic in the *Times* bashed the plot as implausible and said readers wouldn't be able to suspend their disbelief. Elijah was one of those clients who wanted to hear all of the feedback, good and bad, so I called him up and read it word for word. Let me tell you, that's my least favorite part of the job. I've had some pretty angry authors on the other side of this phone, but Elijah was furious. Livid. He really believed in that book, and he worked hard on it. Do you want me to read it to you?"

"Sure," Jim said.

Jeanie cleared her throat. "While the setting is unique and the voice of the narrator compelling, the pace of *Middletide* lags from start to finish and Leith asks too much of the reader's ability to suspend disbelief. Red herrings throughout the novel demand an ending with far more finesse than is delivered in the final pages. But perhaps the most difficult aspect to reconcile in this contemporary work is the plain fact that no killer, no matter how skilled, could realistically pull off this type of crime."

Jim sat up a little straighter. "Can you give me that last sentence again?"

Jeanie read the words slowly. "Perhaps the most difficult aspect to reconcile in this contemporary work is the plain fact that no killer, no matter how skilled, could realistically pull off this type of crime."

"How did he respond to that?" Jim asked, clutching the receiver tightly. "Do you remember what he said?"

Jeanie gave a short laugh. "I remember any call that ends with me being hung up on. The last thing he said before the line went dead was that it was possible. Anything was possible."

"Thanks for your time, Ms. Devin," Jim said. "You've been a big help."

Jim's morning coffee sat untouched on his desk as he scribbled away on a sheet of paper. He'd slept just five hours the night before, sandwiched between racing thoughts about Elijah's book and what Jeanie had told him over the phone. He should probably call Jeremy in here and talk it over with him. As though summoned by Jim's thoughts, Jeremy's steps sounded in the hall and the deputy appeared in the doorway of the office.

"Merry Christmas," he said, tossing a ring with two silver keys onto the desk.

Jim lifted the ring by the tag that read Point Orchards Hardware and inspected the shiny new keys.

"What's this?"

"Duplicates of Doc Landry's house keys."

"Duplicates?" The sheriff inspected them. "How? We don't have the originals."

"Stephanie over at Puget Realty called me up and said she had a pair. She heard we were investigating and wanted to help."

Jim rose from his desk, "Code for: her best friend Della told her all about it."

"She did hand them over with a request to be kept in the loop," Jeremy admitted.

Jim dropped the key ring into his pocket. "How'd she get ahold of them, though?"

"Apparently, Erin was already thinking about listing the house and downgrading to something smaller since she lived by herself. Probably too many painful memories there if you ask me. She gave Stephanie a set of keys last month."

Jim reached for his jacket. "Saves us the trouble of breaking a window. Let's go."

The temperature outside had plummeted back into the single digits, and the two men crossed the parking lot at a jog. Jim yanked the handle of the police cruiser, splintering the ice that glued the door shut, and ducked inside. On the way to Erin's house, he told Jeremy about his call to the publisher the day before.

"You think that's reason enough to murder?" Jeremy scoffed. "Because some anonymous critic in a paper claimed the crime couldn't be done?"

"I don't know what to make of it," Jim confessed, "but it's another finger pointed in the same direction, I guess."

The roads had been salted and gave the cruiser no trouble as they drove to Erin's house.

"What are we looking for?" Jeremy asked as they pulled into her driveway and parked in front of the garage.

"Her car, for one. Her purse, address book, any appointments she had written down, stuff like that. I want to know the name of anyone she met with in the last few weeks and why. Don't overlook anything without running it by me first."

"Let's do it." Jeremy unbuckled his seatbelt and Jim handed him the set of keys.

"You go ahead and start, I'll be in in a minute."

Jeremy jogged up the porch steps and vanished into the house. Jim pulled a pack of cigarettes out of the center console and flicked his lighter. He generally allowed himself one cigarette a week, and now was as good a time as any in a week he could have easily given into the temptation and smoked fifty. When the remaining warmth from the heater was gone, he climbed out of the cruiser and started toward the house.

Jeremy leaned through the front door. "Found something!"

Jim let out the smoke he was holding in his mouth. "What is it?"

"Calendar on the fridge. She has three days blocked off, December 29, 30, and 31, that just say 'M in town.'"

Jim nodded. "We should probably—"

"Call Sea-Tac Airport and make sure he left on the thirty-first?" Jeremy cut him off. "I'm on it."

Jim nodded and held up his cigarette. "Good. Let me finish this and I'll be right in."

As he smoked, he wandered to the side yard and looked out on the lawn. The hydrangea bushes alongside the railing needed pruning. Their brown heads hung ugly and limp, dead leaves still cupping tiny teaspoons of snow. Jim took a long last pull of his cigarette and released the smoke through his nose, enjoying the frozen silence of the outdoors before whatever he might have to face inside that house.

Then, so quietly that Jim might not have heard it except for the salt on the road crunching under the tires, a car downshifted to roll slowly past Erin's house. Jim dropped his cigarette and stubbed it, rounding the corner of the porch just in time to see the tail end of a sleek blue Camaro disappearing around the bend.

16

Elijah sat bolt upright in bed, illuminated by a shaft of moonlight pouring in through the window. The digital clock flashed 3:38 and he blinked at it, confused. The phone in the kitchen rang shrilly and Elijah realized with a start that the sound was what had woken him. He threw aside his blankets and made his way down the dark hall, panic flooding his veins with adrenaline. No one called with casual well-wishes at three-thirty in the morning.

"Hello?"

"Elijah?"

"Yeah."

"It's Erin Landry, I'm afraid you're going to need to get down to the clinic as soon as you can. Chitto is in pretty rough shape and he's asking for you."

"What happened? Was there an accident?"

"It's his lungs. He came in with hemoptysis a few hours ago, coughing up a good deal of blood. At this point there's not much I can do."

Elijah's legs were beginning to give way beneath him and he braced himself against the counter.

"Are you saying he's *dying*?"

Erin's reply was even and professional. "Yes. You should hurry."

Elijah hung up and ran for his bedroom, throwing on the clothes he'd laid out for work in the morning. He was behind the wheel of the Camaro less than three minutes after hanging up the phone, and he took the curves into town as fast as he dared. The small medical clinic was a twenty-minute drive across Point Orchards, and while he whipped around corners and accelerated on the straightaways, Elijah tried to make sense of what was happening. How could Chitto be dying? A few days ago, he'd come into work with another bad cold and Elijah hadn't seen him since, insisting that Chitto take the rest of the week off to rest and heal up. But it was just a cold. Just another cold.

Elijah slammed on his brakes, nearly missing the clinic driveway, and yanked the wheel to the left. He parked and glanced at the clock. 4:03. He ran through the glass doors and skidded to a stop at the sight of Erin standing in the entry hall, her hands folded in front of her, face wiped clean of emotion.

"No," he said, shaking his head as she approached.

"I'm sorry," she said.

"No!" He pushed past her and took off running down the hall. There was one open door with white fluorescent light spilling out into the hall and Elijah burst through it. Chitto lay still and gray on the bed, his eyes closed, his long braid spilling over the pillow.

Elijah sank into the chair beside the bed and let his head fall onto Chitto's unmoving chest. A single sob racked his body, and he released a sound he hadn't made since his mother died. A slender hand landed on his shoulder and Elijah stiffened.

"I don't understand," he said. "What happened?"

"He had lung cancer, Elijah."

Elijah turned to stare at her. "*What?*"

Erin pulled a stool next to him and sat to face Elijah at eye level. "He was diagnosed last fall. I'm sorry he didn't tell you. I told him he should, but he refused. He did leave you this, though."

Erin reached for a letter on the bedside table and handed it to Elijah, who held it unopened in his lap.

"I'm so sorry," she said, rising to leave.

Elijah stayed with Chitto until the sun broke the eastern horizon and two men from the reservation arrived for his body. He walked with them to the parking lot and watched numbly as they loaded his friend into the old hearse and drove away. Elijah pulled the letter out of his pocket and opened it. The garage was his now, everything signed over in his name, but Chitto didn't ask that Elijah keep it; instead he encouraged him to sell it and use the money as the means to give himself time to write again. At the bottom of the single-page letter, Chitto apologized for not telling Elijah he was dying.

> *I guess you and Doc were right about the pipe. Can't do it over and I don't regret not telling you. You've become a son to me, Elijah. The son I never had. I didn't want to spend this last year with you mourning me before I was in the ground. I'm sorry if I was wrong to hide it.*

There was no sentiment at the bottom. Chitto had simply scrawled his name. Elijah folded the letter again and tucked it back into its envelope. He drove home in a tearless state of anguish, his only friend in the world growing cold and stiff, waiting for his grave to be dug.

———

Elijah spent the morning canceling appointments and telling clients the news. He called Puget Realty at noon and put the garage up for sale, then spent the afternoon in the woods. The trail was clear, but he hacked away at random anyway, bringing the machete down on saplings and shrubs just for the feeling of slicing through them. Night came and he didn't sleep. He sat on the back-porch steps as the air turned chilly and the darkness came alive with insects. Mosquitoes buzzed in his ears and he let them bite his face and arms without swatting them away. When the dawn arrived behind morning clouds that promised rain, he climbed into his car and drove to the reservation. He tapped the brakes as he approached the border. The drizzle had started and the dirt road was already muddy.

There was only one cemetery that he knew of on the reservation, and it was deep in the woods behind the church that Nakita's father pastored. A sign that read SACRED MOUNTAIN CEMETERY pointed down the overgrown path that led past the west side of the church and straight into the forest. Elijah rolled slowly along the bumpy road that was little more than a trail. The bottom of the Camaro scraped noisily across deep potholes, and the towering fir trees on either side pressed so tightly that they swiped wet arms against his car. Finally, he pulled through into the little clearing.

The graveyard was L-shaped, the back corner disappearing around a bend in the trees. Elijah parked at the gate and climbed out, his eyes combing the grass for fresh dirt. He walked through the first section and around the corner. At the far end of the cemetery, right at the edge of the forest, he found it, a mound of rich, dark earth that rose from the grass. There was no headstone yet. Perhaps Chitto had come out here at some point in the last year and chosen this spot, tucked as far away as possible from sight, as though he wanted to be forgotten.

Elijah stood at the foot of the grave and cleared his throat. He wanted to say something, but no words came. Maybe it was more for his own sake than Chitto's, but he felt like he should honor the man with at least a few sentences. Elijah opened his mouth, but only a choked sound came out and he gave up trying, settling instead for long minutes of silence as the drizzle turned to rain that soaked his hair and clothes.

Elijah heard a car driving slowly down the road to the cemetery, but he couldn't see it through the thick patch of trees. The sound of the engine died and a door opened and closed. Was someone else from the reservation coming to mourn Chitto? A few minutes passed and no one walked around the corner. Whoever had come was visiting a different grave on the other side of the trees, and a stab of pity broke through Elijah's numbness. Was he the only one who would mourn his friend? Chitto had no family left on the reservation. His wife had died years before and they'd never had children. Most of his friends lived in Point Orchards, and of those he called friends, who, if any, were more than mere acquaintances whom he shared a pleasant word with here and there? A passing joke. A light for his pipe.

Somewhere, tucked behind photos on mantels or at the bottom of attic trunks, a few of the wooden flutes he'd carved with tender care

surely lay forgotten. Elijah stared at the churned earth with the sad realization that he had perhaps been the only one to truly know this man
who had died. The only one to truly *love* him. The first tear fell then,
lost in the rain that streamed down Elijah's face. There was nothing he
could say. Chitto wasn't there beneath the ground. All he could hope for
now was that Chitto was somewhere better than the world in which he'd
lived so meekly. Elijah turned his back on the grave and walked away.
As he rounded the bend in the forested graveyard, he looked up to find
a silver sedan parked next to his Camaro.

Elijah scanned the cemetery. On the opposite side, where two trees
formed a tangled arch over a simple tombstone, he found Nakita, her
eyes locked on him as he stood dripping in the falling rain.

She made no move toward him and stayed still as a statue as he made
his way through the graves to her. She was a hundred feet away, fifty,
twenty. It felt to Elijah like the end of a cross-country race, his body
burning with heart-pounding agony and effort as he chased down a
finish line that seemed to retreat even as he hurtled toward it.

"Is it really you?" Nakita asked when he finally came to a stop
before her.

Elijah nodded, drinking in the feeling of her eyes on him as she
searched for the boy she had known all those years ago. What a beauty
she was now . . . These past seventeen years had refined her, stripped her
of her youthful charm, leaving behind something regal, like the maple
tree in front of his cabin that budded prettily with green shoots in the
spring but demanded awe with its red splendor in the autumn.

"Kind of fitting," she said softly, looking around, "seeing you here."

Elijah glanced at the grave behind her. "I'm sorry about your husband."

Nakita gave a sad smile. "It's been three years. Sometimes it seems
like a lot longer, but every time I come here it feels like yesterday."

The rain was coming harder, but they were mostly sheltered under
the trees, tiny drops falling onto their hair and clothes as they stared
into each other's eyes.

"I'm here for Chitto," Elijah explained with a lump in his throat.
"He died yesterday. It feels wrong even saying that. I had no idea how

sick he was, and then just like that, gone. I don't know if you knew him or not."

Nakita nodded. "I met him a few times. I heard you were working at his garage in town."

Elijah nodded. "I'm selling it, actually."

He couldn't stop staring, couldn't stop running his eyes over every angle of the face that was still familiar but now belonged to a total stranger.

"You look . . ." He struggled to find the right word. "You look . . ." He gave up and let out a little embarrassed chuckle.

"So do you," Nakita said, mock seriously, her eyes dancing with laughter.

Elijah felt the grin break across his face.

"Man, you have no idea how long I've been waiting to run into you. I saw you heading into the grocery store once, but I lost my nerve. Almost got hit by a car sprinting across the street."

"Yeah?" She smiled. "One time I saw you in the Blue Goose with Chitto and I turned around and walked right back out," she confessed.

A warm spark in the center of Elijah's chest spread outward as the wall between them crumbled.

"I'm sorry," he said, shaking his head and sending raindrops flying from his hair. "I'm so sorry. I wanted to come back that summer. I meant to. I just . . . got lost for a while. I thought I was doing the best thing at the time by giving everything I had to my career. I wrote this book—"

"I read it." She cut him off with an eager nod. "It was brilliant."

He blinked at her. "You did?"

"Of course, I did."

"It wasn't brilliant," Elijah said vehemently. "It completely flopped. I gave up everything for it. I wasn't here for my dad in his last years. I wasted a decade of my life. I didn't keep my promise to you."

"I didn't really expect you to," she said simply.

Elijah felt like he'd been slapped, not by her words, but by the calm maturity with which she spoke them. He was suddenly confronted by the realization that Nakita had been much, much older as a teenager than he had.

"Did it work out?" she asked. "The life you wanted in San Francisco."

Another stab of pain shot through him.

"No."

She took a step forward, her brows drawn together as she searched his face. In the ebony rings of her eyes, Elijah saw his reflection. He looked older, so much older, than the boy he had been the last time they stood face-to-face. The sleepless night he'd endured was written in the shadows beneath his eyes, the pain of Chitto's death etched deep in the lines on his forehead. Thirty hours without a shave or shower had left him in the absolute worst shape to make a good second impression. Still, Nakita was looking at him not with disgust, but with the expression of someone who had happened upon a beloved childhood toy years later, turning it over and over, marveling at the memories it evoked.

"Are you living in the cabin by yourself?"

Elijah nodded. "You should see what I've done with the place, it's really coming along . . . I put on a new roof, a new door . . . I stocked the whole pantry . . . I've even got eggs . . ."

He didn't know what he was saying. He was a teenager again, nervous and giddy, trying to talk to the prettiest girl in school.

Nakita gave a little laugh.

"Eggs?" she said, smiling. "We're talking about eggs?"

Elijah couldn't tear his eyes from hers. Was she feeling the same butterflies that were frantically trying to escape his rib cage? Was she fighting the same magnetic pull that was threatening to yank his arms from his sides and wrap her in them?

Elijah took a deep breath and plunged recklessly ahead. "Would you maybe want to go somewhere? We could grab a drink in town, catch up a little bit?"

Nakita shook her head, the friendly familiarity in her eyes fading into something colder. "I don't think that would be a good idea."

Elijah felt the rejection like a punch to the gut. "Oh . . . I'm sorry. I didn't mean to push you or anything."

"I'm not ready, Elijah," she said, turning her back to him and facing the headstone beneath the trees. "These past few years, I've had to come to terms with facing the future without the person I planned it with.

Kailen and I . . . we had our whole lives ahead of us. We had dreams. We wanted kids. He built a house for us, me and my family. It's the biggest, most beautiful house on the rez and now I can barely stand to sleep there." She turned back to Elijah, her expression pleading, desperate for him to understand her grief. "He's still there. Not just in the house, in here." She pressed her slender hand to her heart. "I know how crazy it sounds, but I still feel faithful to him."

Resolve welled in Elijah's chest. He'd lost her once, years ago. He'd blown it. But he was here now, and so was she. Beneath her words telling him otherwise, he felt the same tug between her soul and his as strongly as he had when they were teenagers. He would be a fool to let her go again without a fight.

"Maybe the only way to move on," he said firmly, "is to take that first step toward someone else."

Nakita's composure faltered and sudden tears sprang into her eyes.

"I'm sorry," she whispered. "I can't."

She stepped around him and walked quickly across the wet grass. Elijah watched her go. She pushed through the cemetery gate and climbed into her car, leaving him standing still in the rain as she pulled away, tires splashing through puddles on the muddy road.

Elijah stayed where he was beneath the trees, replaying their conversation over and over in his mind as the downpour lightened into a gentle mist and then faded altogether, leaving the graveyard garlanded with tendrils of snaking fog that lingered between headstones and melted into shadow at the edge of the forest. In hindsight, he probably shouldn't have asked Nakita out at the foot of her husband's grave.

Drenched to the bone and more tired than he'd ever been in his life, Elijah trudged slowly back to the Camaro and drove home. He needed sleep, then he would try to make sense of what had just happened. The only thing he knew for sure was that there would be no more daydreams about a picturesque writing retreat in New England. Maine could wait. He wasn't going anywhere until he'd had a proper chance to fight for her.

17

The living room floor was covered in photographs.

Beside Elijah was an unopened bottle of champagne. It was a gift from Stephanie at Puget Realty, a closing gift. The garage was sold, the check had cleared, and he had more money in his savings account than he had ever thought possible. Still, he didn't feel like celebrating. Earlier in the day he had worked his way around Chitto's office taking down all of the photographs and memorabilia and tossing them into a cardboard box.

Chitto had used tape to hang most of the photos, but a dozen or so were framed and had been hung with nails, so Elijah had spent the afternoon patching tiny holes before he repainted the room. He shouldn't have waited until the last minute to do it; the room would still smell of fresh paint when the new buyer stepped in today, but he'd procrastinated because it would undoubtedly lead to this, a painful trip down memory lane. One at a time, he had pulled the photographs from the box and laid them around him on the floor. Chitto stood in at least half of them, Elijah's father in about half of those. In one still frame at a time, he studied a decades-long friendship between the two men, both of whom he had loved, albeit in very different ways. He had loved his dad, but the older he had grown, the more it felt like a love based purely on the biology of their relationship and nothing more. In the three and a half years since his return, Chitto had become the father he wished he'd had.

It had taken a few months for the garage to sell, but Elijah had been stubborn on one very important term and it had taken time to find a buyer who agreed to it. The name had to stay. The garage had been opened by Chitto Begay and it would remain under his name. He had heard once that every man dies twice, the second death coming when no one left on earth remembered his name, and he would do his utmost to ensure that the man buried out in that simple grave on the reservation was remembered. In the end, he turned down an executive from Seattle who proposed turning the place into a Starbucks and sold it instead to a couple who came in with a smaller offer for their mom-and-pop coffee shop, but agreed to call it Begay's Grounds.

Elijah stood to stretch his legs and glanced at the kitchen clock, surprised to find that it was a few minutes past midnight. It was December 31, the last day of the year. He added a log to the fire and poked at it with the iron until the embers glowed like rubies. In a small pot, he warmed milk and chocolate, stirring constantly to keep it from scorching, then he wrapped himself in Chitto's warm leather jacket and took his cocoa to the porch.

Feathery snowflakes were floating down from patchy clouds, but the moon had broken through, a gleaming white crescent that scraped the tips of the trees like a ghostly ship as it traced a low path across the night sky. Even warm in Chitto's coat, Elijah shivered with goose bumps lifted by the beauty of the night as he slowly drank his cocoa.

His eyes throbbed with tiredness, but he stayed on the porch, thinking about the day ahead. There was a New Year's Eve celebration in Point Orchards he'd gone to with Chitto last year, a quaint, small-town celebration at the Elks Lodge where people dressed up and played games around tables until midnight, going back and forth from their card games to the row of folding tables set against the wall, every inch covered in crockpots and casserole dishes full of meatballs and chili, cobblers and pies.

He should go again this year. Chitto would want him to. More than anything, he'd want Elijah to get out of the cabin, live a little. Last year he'd sat with Chitto and they'd played Hearts as a team, cleaning house against anyone who dared challenge them. At the end of the night, both of them stuffed to the gills with cheesy potatoes, chocolate cake, and a dozen or so other dishes made primarily of mayonnaise and meat, Chitto had walked him to his car, asking if he had a resolution for the year to come. Elijah hadn't made a New Year's resolution since his twenties and he told Chitto so. Why bother setting yourself up for disappointment if it didn't come true? His resolutions had always been writing-related and look how that had turned out. Chitto had chuckled and said a resolution wasn't a wish or something you hoped would happen to you, it was something you fought for, something you chased down and made happen through grit and hard work. Elijah hadn't bothered to ask the question in return. He didn't know if Chitto had had a resolution going into what would be his final year of life, or whether or not he'd accomplished it.

Elijah tipped the mug back, swallowing the final sip of cocoa, which had gone cold in the icy night air. He stepped back inside the cabin and put the empty mug in the sink, brushed his teeth, and climbed into bed. By the time he fell asleep, he had his resolution, and he would begin working toward it first thing in the morning.

He slept hard, waking a few minutes after nine with the kind of clarity that comes only with purpose. The snow hadn't accumulated overnight, so he took to the trail for a brisk two-mile run to start the day. He followed that with a stack of pancakes and plum preserves for breakfast and a shower, then stood in front of his open closet with a towel wrapped around his waist. He ran his eyes over the shirts on hangers. They were casual and overworn, most with grease stains from working at the garage. Not a single one was appropriate for the day he had planned. A quick detour was in order, down to Main Street, where a small store sold men's and women's clothing. He was grateful to find the doors open despite the impending holiday, and he took his time trying on dark jeans and shirts with actual collars. In the end, he chose a light gray shirt that cuffed at the forearms, accenting the broadness of his shoulders and the lean torso that had become hard and muscled from working the land. The jeans he paired with the shirt hung just right from his hips and he stared at the man in the mirror with approval. *Carelessly handsome*, as one of his brief girlfriends in San Francisco had described his looks.

Back home, he spent a few minutes running a comb through his unruly hair and a razor over his face. Then, keys in hand, he headed back out to the car, grabbing the bottle of champagne on his way out the door and setting it in the passenger seat. When he pulled out of the driveway this time, he turned right, away from Point Orchards and toward the reservation.

He passed the border sign, slowing only slightly as his tires hit the dirt. He passed Nakita's old house and the church that her father pastored, finding himself deeper into the reservation than he had ever been. The dirt road led straight toward the mountains, and Elijah glanced left and right at the houses that lined it until he came to a T in the road. Left, or right? He had nothing to go on but his gut, so he swung the Camaro to the left and kept driving.

The road narrowed and began to climb in a gently rolling set of hills that angled toward the mountains. Here, the houses were farther apart and better maintained. On his right, the snowcapped range rose up behind the forest, looming like the steady, permanent shadow of a storm. On his left, houses that were closer to his own, log cabins and dwellings that resembled small lodges, appeared here and there in the woods, smoke drifting lazily from the tops of chimneys.

Elijah drove on, looking carefully at each house as he passed. He drove past two narrow roads that led back down toward the main section of the reservation, but he stayed on the route he had chosen, even when a sign warned of a dead end ahead. Elijah followed the road as it lilted gently around a frosted foothill. On top of the hill sat a stunning house, three stories tall and sharply peaked, the front made entirely of windows that faced the mountains, gleaming pale gold in the sun that poured over the top of the ridge. This was the house. It had to be.

The road continued on, but Elijah took the driveway on the left that wound steeply around the hill. When he reached the top, he came upon three vehicles parked in front of the house: a black truck, a small red car, and a silver sedan. He recognized two of the three. His Camaro had been his divining rod, leading him to her. She had said it was the biggest and most beautiful house on the reservation, and there was no doubt about that.

Elijah parked beside Nakita's car and grabbed the bottle of champagne from the seat next to him. Steeling himself with a deep breath,
he stepped out of the Camaro and walked to her door. He reached the
stoop and knocked three times, loud enough to be heard, but not loudly
enough to startle anyone awake who might be sleeping late. Elijah
turned to stare at the mountains as he waited. He had never been this
close to them. They were right there, towering over the road, sharp and
rugged, despite the snowpack that softened their edges. On this side,
their western face, deep shadows dyed the snow glacial blue and scrag-
gly pines climbed as far as they dared like vines up the side of the ridge
before surrendering ground to the majestic row of bare peaks. What
price would an artist pay to spend a year living in this house? Stepping
outside each morning to paint these mountains in their many moods.

Someone was coming to the door and Elijah turned back around. In
the long window, the tired face of Reverend Mills appeared. He looked
quizzically at Elijah, his features both wary and perplexed. Elijah offered
a meek wave and the lock slid back with a click.

"Happy New Year's Eve, Reverend," Elijah said as the door opened.

"Come on," Nakita's father said, stepping to the side, "no point
letting the cold in."

Elijah closed the door behind him and looked around, his gaze
traveling up to the vaulted ceiling in the foyer that rose uninterrupted
through the three stories of the house.

"Wow," he breathed.

"Kailen's family owns a fifth of the Skagam Casino off I-5," the reverend said as he led Elijah down the hall.

"Ah," Elijah nodded. That explained it.

"Who was it?" Nakita called from around the corner.

"The prodigal son," her father said as he entered the kitchen with
Elijah a step behind.

Nakita turned from the pot she was stirring on the stove to stare
at him.

"What are you doing here?"

She looked impossibly lovely, her unbraided hair loose and wavy
with sleep as it fell around her face. She wore a black T-shirt over silky

pajama shorts that ended mid-thigh on her long, shapely legs. She still had the body of a runner.

Elijah held up the bottle of champagne. "I came to invite you to the New Year's Eve party at the Elks Lodge tonight."

Nakita turned a stern gaze on her father as though he might have something to do with it, but he simply shrugged and turned to leave them alone in the kitchen.

"Be nice," he called over his shoulder as he walked down the hall and Nakita rolled her eyes.

"What are you making?" Elijah asked, stepping forward to place the bottle on the counter.

Nakita turned back to the stove and flicked off the burner as she gave the pot a final stir.

"Oatmeal?" she asked, turning around.

"No thanks."

It wasn't a yes, but she hadn't thrown him out yet.

Nakita pulled a bowl from the cupboard and filled it with oatmeal. She sprinkled raisins and brown sugar over the top then turned to face him, nodding at the bar stool. Elijah took a seat. Nakita placed her bowl on the kitchen counter across from him, keeping her distance as she dug her spoon into the porridge and took a bite.

"So will you come?" he asked.

Nakita said nothing, only continued to watch him the way she might watch a jungle cat stalking her through tall grass.

"Nakita," he said softly, "I'm not the same person I was seventeen years ago."

Nakita took another bite of her oatmeal before she answered.

"I'm not either, Elijah. What makes you think we'd have anything in common now in the middle of our thirties? We were kids. It was a long time ago."

Elijah paused, eyeing her as though trying to discern her hand at a poker table. Then, he stood with a casual shrug. "Okay. If that's all it was then don't come tonight. If you can reach the end of today believing that all we had was a summer fling, then don't come. But if you felt the same pull I did at the cemetery, the same pull that I feel right now looking at you standing there in your pajamas, then at least do me the courtesy of giving us a chance." He pushed in his stool. "I know there's unfinished business between us, and if you manage to realize that by the end of the day then you can find me at the Elks Lodge at ten."

Without waiting for an answer, Elijah turned and left. He climbed into his car and drove back to his cabin without seeing the road as he turned the conversation over and over in his mind. The ball was in her court now. He'd done what he could.

The daytime hours crawled into the afternoon and faded slowly into night. Elijah spritzed himself lightly with cologne and left for the lodge at a quarter to ten, giving himself a generous 30 percent chance that she'd show up.

The lodge was full when he arrived, but Nakita was not there. Elijah played cards at several tables, but his heart wasn't in it and his eyes stayed on the door. The many smells of hot food on the tables should have tempted him to fill a plate, but he only nibbled on a few cookies, nerves and disappointment curbing his appetite. Eleven o'clock came and went, and his heart fell when the mayor stepped up to the small stage to announce the thirty-second countdown to midnight. She hadn't come. Deep down, he supposed he deserved it, but it stung nevertheless.

"Twenty-five! Twenty-four! Twenty-three!"

Elijah grabbed Chitto's jacket off the back of the chair and weaved his way through the crowd toward the door.

"Nineteen! Eighteen! Seventeen!"

All eyes were on the stage, a glass of sparkling champagne clutched in every hand.

"Twelve! Eleven! Ten!"

Elijah reached the door and stepped outside.

Nakita was leaning against his Camaro, a smile on her face. His heart leapt within his chest as they walked toward each other. Searching her eyes, he found something like forgiveness. Behind them through the open door, voices shouted, "Three! Two! One!"

She took his hands in her own.

"Happy New Year," she whispered.

18

Elijah spun a slow circle in his desk chair.

His desk chair. *His* desk. In addition to his personal resolution of reconciling with Nakita, Elijah had set a writing-related resolution in Chitto's honor. In hindsight, perhaps it hadn't been ambitious enough; he had accomplished it less than three weeks into January. He'd made the resolution that he wanted to write for a living and voilà, that's precisely what he was doing. All right, so it wasn't exactly his dream of being a world-famous novelist, but writing for the local paper was a start, and it felt like a gift, like an opportunity God had placed directly in his lap.

He'd spent the first Sunday of the year with Nakita at her father's church. It was their second second date. At first, Elijah felt keenly the eyes that followed him down the aisle. He was the only person there who wasn't Squalomah. But by the time the sermon ended and "Come Thou Fount" was played on the painfully out-of-tune organ in the corner, he found himself embraced with friendly smiles and handshakes. Nakita introduced him to several people, and one in particular, a man about Chitto's age, appraised him interestedly when Nakita told him Elijah was a writer. The man had just retired from his position at the *Point Orchards Herald* and told Elijah they were looking for a new copywriter. And, after a brief interview, Elijah found himself paid to put words on paper.

The phone on his desk rang and Elijah snatched it up eagerly.

"Right on time," he said, glancing at the clock that read 2:00.

"I'm very punctual," Nakita answered.

"How was your day?" Elijah tried to tame the stupid grin that spread across his face at the sound of her voice, but it was futile.

"It was great, I just got done at the studio. I'm covered from head to toe in paint and any artist will tell you that's the mark of a productive day."

"I can pick you up when I get off work."

"Nice try, fella, I'll meet you at the restaurant."

"When are you going to let me see it?" he asked.

"When it's done."

Elijah couldn't wait to see the painting she was working on. He had been absolutely shocked when she brought him to her studio for the first time. It was tucked in a corner of the woods beside the house that Kailen had built. He had built the studio, too, an octagonal building with windows on all sides so that Nakita could move her easel at will with access to ample mountain and forest beauty. Elijah had been exactly right about the place being perfect for an artist, but every time he laid eyes on the studio that Kailen had added to the property, it was with a pang of humility. The man he had never met was a hard one to live up to.

Inside the studio were canvases of all shapes and sizes, waiting to be taken to outdoor markets in Seattle and sold. Nakita's artistic style was unique, the lines and angles of the natural world sharp and accurate, but the colors . . . He'd been particularly drawn to a horizontal painting of the mountain ridge that she had done in hues of vivid pink and blue. It was electric and alive, like the mountains through the lens of a psychedelic trip. It wasn't all landscape work, though. Her portraits were phenomenal, too. The one that took center stage on the back wall of the hut was of her nani's deeply lined face. It was the first portrait she had done, right after her grandmother died. Now she was working on a painting for Elijah, and she was stubbornly silent as to its subject, though she promised he would love it.

"You're not even going to give me a hint?" he prodded.

"Not even a hint of a hint."

The office door slammed and Elijah glanced up to see his coworker Paul striding purposefully toward his desk. He grabbed his camera, gave a quick salute to Elijah, and turned back for the door.

"Hang on," Elijah said, putting his hand over the receiver. "Where're you going?" he called to Paul.

"Accident up on Risto Road. Bad one. I'll get pictures. If you call the sheriff's office and get something written up by tonight, we can run it tomorrow."

"On it."

He put the phone back to his ear, "Hey, can I call you back?"

"Don't worry about it, I want to get in another few hours of painting while the light's good. I'm still on for dinner at six, though."

"Okay." Elijah hung up and called the police station. The secretary told him the sheriff was still on scene at the accident and transferred Elijah through to his car phone.

"Hey, Sheriff Godbout, it's Elijah down at the *Herald*, Paul just told me about the accident on Risto Road and we'll be running something in the paper tomorrow. Do you have a minute to talk about it?"

There was a heavy sigh on the other end of the receiver, and before a word was spoken, Elijah knew that there had been a fatality.

"I guess word's bound to get out. It was Doc Landry. She slid right off a curve and rolled over."

Bile rose in Elijah's throat. He hadn't considered that it might be someone he actually knew. He didn't want to ask the question, but he had to. It was his job.

"Did she . . . did she make it out okay?"

"She's pretty shook up, probably some cracked ribs, maybe a concussion, but she'll be fine. Paramedics are with her now." Through the phone, the sheriff drew a long unsteady breath. "There wasn't anything I could do for her little girl though. She was gone by the time I got here."

The blood drained from Elijah's face and he gripped the phone so tightly it hurt. He couldn't imagine the absolute hell Erin was in at this moment, a hell from which there would be no escape for the rest of her life.

"Hello?" the sheriff asked on the other end of the line, and Elijah realized he hadn't spoken in almost a minute.

"That's terrible," he managed.

"Yes, it is."

"Thanks for taking my call."

Elijah replaced the receiver numbly. He wasn't close with Erin, but he was close enough to stop and chat for a few minutes whenever they ran into each other, close enough to see her adoration of the toddler she often had on her hip. Such a beautiful little girl, so much like her mom, with the same corn-silk hair and impossibly sweet smile.

Elijah tried to push thoughts of the accident out of his mind by working on the other mundane assignments on his desk—the upcoming spring events calendar and a recap of the Rotary Club's New Year's bake sale, but two hours later, Paul laid the freshly developed photographs on his desk and Elijah was forced to type out a description.

The photos were ugly, and Elijah couldn't look at them without imagining the noise of metal skidding across concrete, the impossibly loud collision against the Jersey barrier that had stopped the momentum, and the terrible silence afterward when Erin would have screamed her daughter's name and heard nothing.

Elijah kept the article brief and emotionless. Just the facts. That's what he was paid to do. His feelings didn't matter; he was the objective narrator. People didn't want to read about the nausea he felt while staring at the photographs. They wanted to pick up the paper, show the article to their spouse across the breakfast table, say "how awful," then turn the page and forget all about it. With a heavy heart, Elijah tucked the photographs out of sight in his desk drawer and placed the finished article on his editor's desk.

There was more work to be done, more copy that needed to be written before the paper went to print, but Elijah pushed it off. He'd rather come back tomorrow morning after a night of sleep and grind out the words before the early deadline than finish work in the mental funk he was in. What an odd job it was. How was he supposed to type up an article about the death of a beautiful little girl whose mother he knew, then flip over a blank page and write a cheerful invitation to hear a swing band from Seattle play at the lodge? The juxtaposition of life and death bounced rapidly back and forth in a constant state of flux on the pages of the newspaper, and that wasn't going to change anytime soon. Elijah was the one who had to get better at leaving work at the office, shoving the photos and stories into a mental drawer that he kept closed and locked until starting up again the next morning. At least he had a distraction planned for tonight, and a pretty good one at that.

Nakita was waiting for him at the harborside restaurant an hour north of Point Orchards. She'd picked the place and it was lovely. Hanging white lights dangled from a wooden awning upon which ivy crept in a thick arch over the open door, soft music playing within. Elijah stepped inside and found Nakita, her back to him at a small table beside the window that looked out on the sunset-tinted harbor. For a long moment, he stood in the doorway, spellbound, watching her as she gazed out the window with her chin in her hand, her shoulders revealed in the halter-style black dress. Her hair was tucked up in a French twist and there was a soft smile on her lips. Elijah still couldn't quite believe that she was sitting there . . . waiting for *him*. He was a lucky son of a gun.

He took the seat across from her and she smiled widely as he sat down.

"Hey, stranger, how was your day?" she asked.

It had become their pet name, *stranger*. That's what they were to each other, after all. The years between their two relationships spanned a generation of change, and he had to get to know her all over again. When they had been together as teenagers, they had had running in common at least. They had shared a group of friends on the team, and they had both possessed the hopeful optimism of youth. Now, in their mid-thirties, one had experienced love and both had experienced loss. They had new interests, and their time together was spent delving deep into conversation about art and homesteading and grief as they tried to line up the edges of their torn romance again. Despite their summer fling years ago, when the flames of their relationship had been fanned by physical affection, they hadn't even kissed yet this time around. Elijah understood her need for physical distance as trust was rebuilt. He was in no rush.

"It was a tough day," Elijah answered, "better now, though. You?"

"What happened?"

Elijah smiled at her frankness. She never let anything slip by.

"I had to write up an article about an accident involving someone I know. She's not quite a friend, I guess, but I know her well enough that it sucks. Her kid died in the crash."

"I'm so sorry," Nakita reached out a hand and laid it on his arm. "Who was it?"

"Erin Landry, she's the doctor in Point Orchards. You know her?"

The hand on his arm stiffened.

"I know exactly who she is."

Nakita's tone was cold and hard. Elijah stared at her, perplexed.

A waiter appeared beside their table and offered them menus and water glasses. Nakita took a long drink and scanned the menu, telling Elijah that the lobster ravioli was her favorite dish. When the waiter stepped away, Elijah laid his menu on the table.

"Have you met Erin?" he asked.

Nakita kept her eyes on the menu.

"Twice."

Elijah waited.

"Look, I don't want to speak ill of someone you're friends with, especially under the circumstances," Nakita said. "Losing a child is un-imaginable, and it can't have been fun to write about it either, so we'll just let it go."

"Nakita, what happened?" Elijah asked softly.

Nakita folded her menu in defeat.

"Six years ago, Nani had a stroke. A mild one. I took her in to see Erin. We have healers on the rez, good ones, too, but I wanted her to get a scan to see how much damage had been done. Fortunately, it was minimal, but just like any typical doctor, Erin started pushing big phar-maceuticals. She put Nani on about four different medications. I ques-tioned her about them, but she promised all the meds were safe, even though one of them is well-known for causing nightmares, sometimes even hallucinations and sleepwalking. One night, Nani did sleepwalk."

Nakita stopped speaking for a moment, and Elijah watched her struggle with the memory. "She fell and hit her head, and because one of the other medications Erin put her on was a blood thinner, she hemorrhaged. I found her the next day. If Erin hadn't put her on those drugs, she might still be here."

A single tear welled in the corner of Nakita's eye, and she swiped at it angrily.

"I was furious with Erin and I drove into town to confront her. I said I was going to sue for malpractice, but in the end, I knew it wouldn't bring Nani back and it would just mean time and money wasted in court, so I let it go. I can't say I've ever been able to forgive her, though."

Elijah reached for her hand. "I'm really sorry. Truly, I am. Erin probably thought she was helping. She always seemed like a good person to me."

Nakita turned her attention back to the menu. When she finally looked up at Elijah, she offered a smile that didn't reach her eyes.

"Let's talk about something else," she said. "Tonight's not about the past, tonight's about us."

19

Keep them closed," Nakita instructed, her hands over Elijah's eyes as she led him slowly toward the open door of her studio. His arms were outstretched, fingers feeling for the door frame. He stepped inside and she guided him forward.

"Almost there," she said. "No peeking."

They crossed the floor of the studio, and Elijah resisted the urge to peer through the cracks in her fingers as they approached the wall.

"Ready?" Nakita asked. He nodded and her fingers lifted, leaving him blinking in the bright light.

Elijah's jaw fell to his chest. Before him, on a canvas larger than life, was Chitto's smiling face. It was perfect, every crease where it should be, the roughness of his skin alive with shadow and texture. His braid was draped casually over his shoulder, and his eyes . . . they were not the flat, dead eyes of a portrait; they were completely full of life, dancing and laughing, bubbling up from a secret spring of robust joy. If it was possible, he looked more alive on canvas than he had when he was living on earth. True to Nakita's signature style, the background was an explosion of vivid color that only added to the depth of the subject, as though Chitto were backlighted by the most brilliant sunset of his long years on earth.

Elijah hadn't known what to expect, but it sure wasn't this. Secretly, he'd thought she had either been painting a portrait of him or one of herself so he could have it to hang in his cabin, but never in a million years did he think she would paint Chitto.

"How?" He marveled at it. "It looks so much like him; you said you only met him a few times."

Nakita reached behind the painting and pulled away the photograph that was taped there. It was one of the pictures from Chitto's office, a close-up of him standing with a dead fish displayed in his hands, probably taken by Elijah's dad. She must have taken it from his cabin on one of her visits.

He lifted it from her fingers. "So, you're a pickpocket now?"

She smiled. "The end justifies the means."

He turned his eyes back to the painting. "I know exactly where I'm gonna hang it."

"That's great, but"—she stepped between him and the painting—"this one isn't free, it's going to cost you something."

Elijah lifted his chin in mock negotiation. "Name your price, lady."

She stepped forward and placed her hands lightly on his forearms.

"It's going to cost you one novel. I want you to write again."

The fun dancing in Elijah's eyes faded.

"You serious?"

"As a heart attack."

Elijah dropped his eyes, shaking his head at the ground between their feet. "I don't know if I've got another one in me, Nakita."

"You do."

He looked up to search her face for sincerity and found it there, sure and steady. She was so positive, so assured, that Elijah felt the long-dormant flame of hope flicker softly to life in the dark writing room of his mind.

"Don't write it with readers in mind," she said earnestly. "Don't write it for anyone else. Write what *you* want to write. Pour your heart onto the pages and see what comes out. Write because you love it, not because you want to be famous or make a million dollars. And when it's done, you don't have to show it to another living soul if you don't want to. Well, besides me of course." She nodded to the painting. "You've gotta earn Chitto there."

"Are you going to hold him hostage until I write it?" Elijah asked playfully.

Nakita shook her head. "You can take him home right now if you want to. Just give me your word that you'll write it. Promise me."

Elijah stared at the painting. It had taken her long days, weeks, to complete it. She knew how important Chitto had been to Elijah, and getting this portrait just right had been a true labor of love. He owed her this. But *could* he write another book? It wasn't a question of willingness, it was simply that he felt like *Middletide* had scraped the bottom of the literary well in his mind; he didn't know if there was anything left down there but murky sludge. Had these three and a half years away from San Francisco been enough of a respite for that well to replenish itself? He hadn't bothered to peer into it to check.

"So?" she prompted.

"I'll try," he said, taking her hands and squeezing them gently.

Nakita nodded and turned to lift the painting from the easel. "That's good enough for me."

She carried it out to his Camaro. It was a tight fit, but together they managed to wedge it into the back seat.

"Oh, I have something else for you, don't leave yet," she called, running back toward the house. When she emerged from the door, she was carrying what looked like a small white television set in her arms. Her father was a step behind her with the other pieces, a keyboard and a large white box.

Elijah popped the trunk and stepped out. "Is that what I think it is?"

"It's brand-new, fresh off the line in Seattle," she said. "Trust me, you'll get a lot more words out on this thing than you would on your dad's typewriter."

"As long as you come with me to show me how to turn it on."

"Of course."

Nakita climbed into the passenger seat and Elijah shook her father's hand goodbye.

On the way back to his cabin, Elijah kept glancing at the painting of Chitto in the back seat.

"You're a really, really good artist, you know that?"

"I wasn't when I started," she said. "Like anything in life, the more you paint, the better you get at it."

Elijah shook his head. "No matter how much I tried, I could never paint anything like that."

"Well, no matter how much I tried, I could never have written anything like *Middletide*," Nakita countered. "The great thing is, there's only one you, Elijah. And that means no one else on earth will be able to write the book that you're going to write next. Remember that."

His spirits were lifted with hope and pride as they left the reservation behind them and drove the few miles to his cabin in companionable silence.

Elijah carried the computer in piece by piece while Nakita hammered a nail into the wall beside the woodstove and hung Chitto's portrait. In just a few minutes, the computer was up and running on the kitchen table and Elijah slid into a chair, a white page open on the screen before him with a blinking vertical dash just waiting to be pushed along by words.

"I'll leave you to it," Nakita said. "I asked my dad to come pick me up in ten minutes."

"Wait." Elijah stood and took her hands again. "Thank you."

As always, when he stood with her like this, the urge to kiss her was overwhelming, but he held himself back. They had been officially dating almost three months, but her long years of marriage to Kailen were still between them, and that was understandable. He had leaned in to kiss her when she showed up to meet him on New Year's Eve, but his attempt was met with a look of warning in her eyes and he had immediately backed away. Fair enough. She needed a little time and he could wait. He *would* wait. Until she either asked him to kiss her or made the first move herself. But as they stood face-to-face alone in his cabin, for the first time he saw something in her eyes as they flickered to his mouth. Something hungry. Still, she took a step back instead of forward.

"I'll see you later," she said, and smiled, dropping his hands.

"I'll call you tonight," he promised.

Alone in the cabin, Elijah took a seat at the table and warily eyed the machine that looked so out of place in the rustic kitchen. Truth be told, he had always been partial to his dad's orange typewriter, though the E was slightly crooked and the belt stuck from time to time. Still, it was rusting in some landfill in California and the computer was here. He'd taken his dad's typewriter with him to San Francisco and had written *Middletide* with it. On the day his editor called and read him that horrible review he had flung open his bedroom window in a fit of rage and dropped the orange typewriter to the sidewalk three stories below.

He hit a few letters at random on the computer keyboard, tasting with his fingers. The mechanical *click-clacking* was different to the insect *tap-tapping* of a typewriter, but he quickly got the hang of it. At some point during the writing of *Middletide*, he had realized that he no longer needed to look at the keys while he wrote. He had learned to touch-type without even meaning to, and as he sat at the kitchen table now, his gaze drifted to the window, and he began to type what he saw outside. From his fingertips spilled a funny little story about the three crows who were fighting over last year's dried-out corn. He reached the end of the page and realized that, different from his typewriter, he could simply delete the whole thing and start over. A fresh page without any wasted paper and the ability to edit as he went—this could be a game changer. But what on earth could he craft an entire novel out of? What story did he have to tell?

Elijah left the table and wandered out to the back porch. The woods were fragrant with the sweetness of early spring, and the blossoms on the fruit trees out front lifted high notes on the melody of breeze that swirled around the cabin. Elijah closed his eyes and breathed in the song of Almost April. There were small shoots growing in pots on windowsills inside, and soon he would have his garden back and his table full of his own harvest again.

Everything here was so cyclical, just like life itself. There were seasons of fruitful plenty, seasons of want, seasons of bad and seasons of good, seasons of grief and seasons of hope. What he'd learned these last few years was that no matter how bleak he felt life to be, there were good times coming just around the next bend, and no matter how content he felt when things were going well, there were sure to be harder times ahead. Around and around it went. The pity would be to waste the periods of bleakness rather than to use them. Just as in winter, when the ground needed to be tilled and the dead trees pruned, the hopeless seasons of life were a chance to grapple with the hard soil of his heart and let the sadness hit him like the sharp edge of a hoe, loosening and breaking apart the unyielding ground there.

Elijah's eyes flew open. That was it. That was the story. His novel would be a love letter to this land he had reclaimed, the land of his youth, the land of his redemption. It would be no mystery, no thriller that would keep readers on the edge of their seats. It wouldn't sell a million copies or be optioned for a heart-pounding film. That part didn't matter. As Nakita had said, he didn't have to show it to another living soul if he didn't want to. What he wanted to write was the story of how these last few years had pruned him down to the very root and allowed him to burst into bloom more fully than he ever would have believed. He would take liberties where he pleased, of course, but it would be autobiographical fiction. An ode to the beauty of this corner of the world, the very same corner that he had grown up wanting to leave, wrongly believing that everything he needed was somewhere else. A tribute to the wisdom Nakita had tapped into decades earlier when she nodded at a decaying log on the lakeshore and told him there were more stories inside it than he would ever find in a city.

Elijah went back inside and opened every window in the front of the house, letting in the fresh spring air. He turned the computer so that he would face Chitto's portrait as he typed, and he sat to write.

A page spilled out of him, and a second and a third as an unbridled first chapter took shape about a lost man returning to the place from which he had fled, dejected and ashamed. A lost man coming home.

20

Elijah woke with the sun and wasted no time attempting to lull his racing mind back to sleep. He kicked aside his blankets and headed straight for the kitchen. The only thing he did daily before his morning writing sessions was to make coffee. Everything else could wait.

During his long years in San Francisco, he'd always written in the afternoons. He'd dawdled away his mornings with errands or television, convinced that his mind needed time to warm up. This time around, he found himself to be most productive first thing in the day, when his mind was fresh, having had time to mull over plot and characters and sand down the fine edges during his sleep. This was also forced by necessity. In order to keep his job at the paper and make sure the cabin stayed up and running, the garden producing, and the hens laying, he needed to use the few precious hours of free daylight for chores and hard labor outdoors. There was always work to be done outside while the sun was up, but before and after, the darkness was his time to write.

He had reached the halfway point, and his morning writing sessions were becoming feverish, held back only by the speed of his fingers as his mind constantly supplied the next turn, the next scene, the next twist.

The sun rose above the trees and flooded the cabin with light. Houdini crowed for his breakfast for the dozenth time, and Elijah stood with reluctance to complete his morning chores. He threw corn into the coop and took a mental note that it needed a serious deep clean. Twelve hens now lived with Houdini and the coop was starting to stink.

Elijah was almost through watering the garden when Nakita walked around the side of the cabin.

"I didn't hear you pull up," Elijah said, turning off the hose.

"I ran here."

"I can see that." Elijah ran his eyes over the length of her body. It was warm enough to have drawn sweat, and her collarbones and shoulders glistened in the sun. She wore pink shorts and a black top that revealed just an inch of her abdomen. "You look like Easter morning," he said, pulling her in for a hug.

"Let's go for a walk." She took him by the hand and pulled him toward the woods.

In the cool shade of the forest, Nakita asked him how the book was coming.

"Really, really well. Now that I've started up again, I can't believe it took me so long," Elijah told her. "It's like this story has been in my head just knocking to get out, but I might never have actually started to write it if you hadn't forced me to. Starting was the hard part."

Nakita laughed. "Well, you're welcome. And believe it or not, I understand that feeling. Sometimes I spend hours staring at a white canvas with no idea what to paint, but once I just take the first swipe at it with the brush I can keep going."

Without any discussion, they reached the fork and took the turn to the right through the nettles. Elijah had come through with the machete earlier in the spring, razing the stinging plants to the ground, but they had regrown at a ferocious rate and were thigh-high again.

"So many writers get hung up on beginnings," Elijah continued, high-stepping through the plants, "they think they need to nail the perfect first sentence or they won't set the right tone for the book. One of the best pieces of advice I got from one of my creative writing professors was to start with the second sentence. That frees you up from feeling paralyzed that you won't get it right."

The lake appeared through the trees and Elijah walked hand in hand with Nakita toward it.

"Wanna go for a swim?" he asked, turning to her.

Nakita shook her head. Her breath was coming far too quickly, her eyes darting back and forth across his face with an intensity that didn't match their casual conversation.

"Hey, are you okay?" he asked, concerned.

"I'm nervous," she whispered.

"Why?"

Nakita lifted both of her hands to cup his face. Stepping forward, she took a deep breath and kissed him. Elijah was so surprised that his eyes stayed open as hers fell shut, but in a moment, responsiveness flooded him and he weaved his fingers through her hair to the back of her head, pulling her close as he returned her kiss.

He had kissed her a thousand times during that long-ago summer, but this was the sweetest, most longed-for kiss of his life, and he fell into it happily, dizzily. Her lips were warm and soft against his own. The unexpected surprise of it had set his heart racing at a wild clip, and when Nakita finally pulled away, he felt drunk on the feeling, his head spinning as he slowly opened his eyes.

"I want to marry you, Nakita," he said dreamily, the words falling out of his mouth before he could stop them, before he even realized they were there. But they were true. Maybe the truest words he'd ever spoken.

Sobriety came then as he watched the wave of dread crash over Nakita's face.

She stepped back rigidly, pressing her fingers to her lips as though she might be able to reabsorb the kiss through her fingertips.

Elijah reached out for her, but she broke free from his arms.

"What? What's wrong with that? Don't you want to get married again? I mean, not right now, but someday?"

Her gaze faltered and landed at her feet. In a movement so subtle that he almost missed it, she shook her head.

"Nakita?" He couldn't keep the note of pleading from his voice.

She lifted her eyes to his, sadly, and Elijah stepped forward to grip her by the shoulders.

"I want this every day. I want you, here. I want us to build a life together. I want us to walk with our children on this trail someday and take them swimming in our lake. I want to know that we have a future together and that I'm going to spend the rest of my life with you in that cabin." Desperation snuck into his voice and he wrestled it back down. "Don't you want that, too?"

Nakita said nothing and Elijah's hands dropped back to his sides.

"What are we doing here, Nakita?" He felt his heart crack at the veil of apathy that had fallen over her features.

"I don't know . . . ," she whispered.

"This is about Kailen, isn't it?" Elijah said bitterly. It was the first time he had said her husband's name out loud, and he might as well have grabbed a handful of the stinging nettles and slapped her across the face with them. Anger, hot and instant, sprang into her eyes.

"How dare you pretend you have any idea what it's like to lose a spouse when you've never been with anyone longer than a year." There was a venom in her voice that he'd never heard before. "You have no clue what it feels like to have your entire future drop out from beneath your feet without warning. You can't possibly imagine how devastating that is."

"Actually, I can," Elijah shot back. "I know what it's like to have to start over from scratch after the life you thought you were meant for doesn't pan out, remember?"

"Doesn't *pan out*? Elijah, my husband was shot in the head and died at thirty-five years old. Where do you get the nerve to compare that to your failed writing career?"

She was right, but the words still burned. He referred to his career as a failure in his own mind all the time, but to hear someone else say it out loud, to hear *her* say it out loud, brought him back to that same feeling he'd had when he'd thrown the pages from his book into the woodstove. This time, he was the one to take a step back.

"Even you," he shook his head, "even you of all people don't think I can do this. Why buy me that computer? Why demand that I try to write again? Was it nothing but lip service? Pity? What?"

"Don't make this about your writing," she said, "it's not."

Elijah wrestled his ego back down for the sake of getting at the root of the quarrel. "I'm half of this relationship, Nakita. We need to be on the same page with what we expect of each other and I'm realizing for the first time right now that we're not."

Nakita turned toward the lake, and Elijah watched her grapple with something in her mind. "I . . . I just need more time."

"No, you don't," Elijah said impatiently, reaching out for her hand again. "Look, I know it's harsh and I'm sorry, but you need to hear it. Kailen's gone. He's dead. He's not coming back. Don't you think he would want you to get married again? Don't you think he would want you to have children, to stop being a mourning widow and become a wife again? To become a mother and a grandmother? Can you tell me honestly that he would want you to be alone, grieving over him for the rest of your life?" Nakita's hand felt cold in his own, lifeless, and he squeezed it gently. "Can you?" he pleaded.

With slow finality, Nakita pulled her hand from his. "I don't know how to get rid of the faithfulness I still feel. My loyalty to him didn't come with an expiration date."

"So, what," Elijah said, panic flooding him as she slipped through his fingers like sand, "you're going to be like one of those dogs that lies at the grave of a fallen master and won't eat or drink until it dies, too? You're still young and alive, and you're telling me that you'd rather waste the years you have left wishing you were still married to him instead of being with me when I'm right here and I can promise you a future?"

"You can't promise me anything," she said, all emotion gone from her voice. "You already promised me a future once and you didn't keep your word, remember? And even if you were dependable, how could you possibly promise me that the same thing wouldn't happen to you? That you wouldn't take a wet curve too fast in your Camaro one day and I'd have to go through the same thing all over again, having to stand there with the sheriff on my doorstep telling me that you're not coming home?"

"Nakita, listen to yourself!" His voice grew louder as he tried to shout some sense into her. "Do you hear what you're saying? Literally one hundred percent of people die. Every single thing you're going to do in this life comes with a risk, but that doesn't mean it's not worth it."

"I'm sorry," she said, retreating now, stepping backward into the shadow of the trees. "I can't do it, Elijah."

She turned and ran, vanishing into the darkness of the forest, and even as Elijah shouted her name, he didn't follow. Though he could probably catch her, he knew with cold certainty that he wouldn't be able to change her mind.

21

JANUARY 11, 1994

Jeremy sat on the bed, transfixed. Downstairs, a door opened and closed and he heard Jim's boots echoing dully across the hardwood, but he stayed where he was, his eyes flying across the pages of neat hand-written scrawl.

Dear Diary,

I thought it was over. I thought I'd never feel anything toward anyone again, let alone genuine affection. My heart was shattered into a million and one pieces when I lost Anna. Two million and one when Manny left, and I sat cross-legged among the wreckage, just running my fingers through the pieces, feeling the total impossibility of ever being able to put them together again, like sitting at a table with the world's hardest puzzle laid out in front of me and not even knowing where to start. But yesterday, oh sweet yesterday, I felt at least a hundred of those pieces click back into place without even trying. Yesterday, I went on my first date since Manny and I split up.

I drove to Elijah's house, chock-full of butterflies, and told myself a hundred times on the way that I was making a mistake, that it was too soon. But when I got there and he opened the door, it just felt . . . right. It felt like coming home. He <u>made me dinner</u>, one *of the most delicious meals I've had in years, actually. Roast duck with a sauce that tasted like dates and oranges over wild rice. I don't know if it was his cooking or the candlelight, or the way his deep blue eyes stayed trained on mine as we spoke, but for the first time in forever I felt the spark of something remotely resembling love and it felt so, so good.*

Someone must've raised him right. He pulled out my chair for me, cleared my plate when I was done, and held my jacket up for me before we went on a walk afterward. His cabin is beautiful, and he showed me all around his property. He is so proud of his chickens and his garden. Manny never did anything outdoors at our house. Manny wanted all sorts of praise just for pulling a little hair out of the shower drain, but Elijah wanted to show me all of the ways he's been able to "live off the land" as he calls it and I loved seeing the pride in his eyes. Then, he looked at me with a secretive smile and asked if I wanted to see where he shot the duck we'd just eaten. I'd assumed the duck had come straight out of the deli section, but nope, he shot it on a lake way back in the woods behind his property.

Thank goodness I'd decided to dress casually and was wearing sneakers and jeans. I never could have made it back there in heels! It was a good thirty-minute walk through the woods and the sun was setting when we got there. What a beautiful place! He's so lucky to have found it. A little lake tucked back in the woods behind a row of pines that keeps it hidden from the sound. He and I skipped rocks just like kids as the sun set behind the trees.

I wish we could've stayed longer. Maybe next time we'll spend a whole day together out there, but it was dark and Elijah walked me back to my car. I know, I know, I should've let him kiss me. But I was nervous so I gave him a quick hug and drove away. Next time. One thing I know for sure is that there will definitely be a next time.

More later,
Erin

Dear Diary,

I'm in love. I'm in love, I'm in love, I'm in love. I'm in LOVE. It's crazy. It's impossible, yet here I am, flat on my face in love with Elijah Leith. I've never fallen for anyone this quickly before, never thought it was possible, but he's all I can think about and I have all the symptoms. I'm officially diagnosing myself.

The funny thing is, in many ways, he's completely wrong for me. He's right-brained and impulsive, fiery and intense. I'm left-brained, finicky and careful. But we just . . . fit somehow. He's been so patient with me as I dip my toes back into the scary waters of a new relationship. When Manny left I figured that was it. I figured I would spend the rest of my life pretty much alone. Not that I blame Manny, I don't. No marriage could survive what we went through, the guilt I've lived with since the accident. But being with Elijah has started to heal me. Being with him is slowly bringing the pieces of my heart back together.

Last night we sat on his porch under the stars and drank hot chocolate while we talked for hours. I felt sixteen again, trading stories with a brand-new boy as the hours of the night flew by. Okay, so maybe the lack of sleep is a little more of a trade-off at my age. Couldn't stop yawning as I worked through my morning appointments and opted for a thirty-minute nap at lunch, but it feels worth it. For now, I'm just going to enjoy the ride without worrying about where this is going. It's just so wonderful to not feel alone.

—Erin

Dear Diary,

I can't believe it's been a whole month since I've written! I've been busy, work of course, but busy with Elijah, too. Overall, things are going really well with him, but we did have our first fight yesterday. I know it's normal, two people in their thirties who get together are bound to have more baggage than a couple of teens would and Elijah *and I <u>both</u> have baggage. I know I've got tons. The loss of my family is a barrier between me and Elijah that I can't seem to fully break down and he's got some issues with his past that he doesn't want to talk about either. Last night we walked out to the lake again and sat there for a while, throwing bits of bread to the fish and just talking. I'll admit it, physical affection is still just not something I'm very interested in yet. It's not that I don't find him attractive, I do, I'm sure every woman in town does, and yes, I've let him kiss me several times now, but this time, with my back pressed against a tree on the shore, Elijah wanted more and I didn't. I'm just not ready and I told him so. When I turned to leave, he grabbed me by the wrist and pulled me back. I was upset, but he let go and apologized, sincerely. I know it was sincere, by now I can tell the difference. He showed up at the clinic this morning with a bouquet of flowers and asked if we could spend some time together this afternoon. I think I'm going to take him out on my boat. I've missed the feeling of the wind on the sound and that poor boat is just sitting there lonely at the marina. It probably misses the open water as much as I do.*

More soon,
Erin

"Jeremy?" Jim stomped up the stairs.

"Up here in the bedroom. Second door on the left," Jeremy called.

"Get down here, Elijah just drove by headed toward his cabin."

The sheriff appeared in the doorway.

"What is that?"

"It's her diary. I found it in her nightstand."

Jim leveled a disapproving look at Jeremy, who answered it with a defensive stare of his own.

"What? It's not just private thoughts and stuff, I think we might have something here, she's talking about Elijah."

"Well, you can keep reading it on the way; the cruiser might have spooked him and I don't want him to get far in case he decides to run."

The two men walked quickly to the car and climbed in. Jeremy retrieved the Glock from the glove compartment and nodded to the full
magazine beside it.

"Load her up?" he asked.

Jim nodded tensely as he turned left out of the driveway and hit
the gas.

"Yeah, I think you'd better."

22

Elijah poured coffee into the blue ceramic mug his father had always used and carried it to the back porch. It was still pitch-black outside, the horizon light through the woods barely visible as the sun climbed slowly behind the mountains toward the day ahead. He hadn't bothered to check the clock when he woke, but it was bound to be before five. Even now, with the computer just sitting on the table, gathering dust day after day, he couldn't seem to break his body of the habit of rising early.

It was a chilly morning and Elijah hunched over his steaming mug. He'd rather deal with the cold outside than sit at the kitchen table with the computer taunting him, forcing him to face the manuscript he'd abandoned after fifty thousand words. It's not like he had given up completely, but the well had run dry. For weeks he'd kept his behind in that chair, determined to see the story through, but in the month since Nakita had left him at the lake, he'd managed to pull fewer and fewer words out of himself until there was simply nothing left, no ideas for where to take it next.

Work had been busy enough to keep him distracted, but today was July Fourth, and not only did he have the day off, but he was going to the marina for the fireworks show without Chitto. Without Nakita. It was sure to be a day that pulled his mind in all the wrong directions.

As soon as the light behind the trees turned the vague shapes in the yard into recognizable objects, Elijah threw himself into outdoor work. There was wood that needed chopping. A lot of it. A tree had come down across the trail, and he'd rolled huge pieces of the trunk back to his woodshed. It was dense, meaty pine, the type that would burn long and slow, perfect for keeping the cabin warm all night long in the middle of winter, but the hardest kind to chop.

Elijah raised the axe again and again, splintering off pieces of each round. His shoulder began to throb when he was just halfway through the first round, but he kept going, addicted to the cracking thud of the axe head, the vibrations of the wooden handle in his palms, the tiny bursts of anger that left his body with every swift stroke. Chopping wood was therapy, pure and simple. Had his dad done this? Retreated to the shed to pour wrath into the chopping block after a fight with his mom? Come to think of it, he couldn't recall his parents ever fighting. His dad had been pretty even-tempered until she died. Elijah was the only one Jake ever fought with after she was gone, and ninety-nine times out of a hundred Elijah had been the antagonist. Not that he had been a rebellious teenager; his devotion to cross-country had kept him disciplined enough to stay out of trouble, but there was something unnatural about a man and his grown son living alone under the same roof, especially in a small cabin that felt less and less like the cozy home of Elijah's childhood and more like a claustrophobic prison as he hit his teenage years.

The sun climbed above the shed unnoticed as Elijah chopped, and he realized it was midday only when his stomach gave a painful grumble. All he'd had was coffee, hours ago. He secured the axe in the round he was working on and retreated inside for lunch, pulling off his sweaty shirt and tossing it toward the table. It landed over the computer screen like a curtain and Elijah didn't bother to move it. He put a pot of rice on the stove and pulled a jar of canned garden vegetables out of the pantry. The money from the sale of the garage sat slowly growing in his savings account, and even though Elijah could afford anything he wanted to eat, he still preferred to consume what he had grown and pulled from his own land.

As he ate from a bowl over the sink, his shoulder began to stiffen and his plans for returning to the woodshed after lunch fizzled. It was too early to get ready for the fireworks show and there was nothing pressing to do outside. For the hundredth time that week, he stared at the phone, willing it to ring. He had tried Nakita's number six times with no response in the first few days after their breakup and had been ignoring the temptation to call her since. He didn't want to be *that* guy, not knowing when to quit. What he should do was pull his shirt off the computer and force himself to put words on the page, but writing this new book had gone from feeling like a privilege, a joy even, to a painful sentence handed down by a judge, and Elijah knew exactly why. He didn't want to face her, not even on the page.

His main character had fallen in love with a woman whom Elijah might as well have named Nakita. It was her, right down to the tiny birthmark behind her left ear. He'd been stupid to let her wander into his work, and she had dug her fingers into the story until she owned it. It was too late to pull her out. She was like a garden plant that had grown too large, snaking roots into the soil around it, making it impossible to remove without taking a vital chunk of the earth with it.

Elijah dwindled the afternoon hours away in the woods. He walked the trail with the bow slung over his shoulder, stopping now and then to fire at low-hanging leaves twisting at the end of twigs or small patches of dancing sunlight on tree trunks, but nothing living. He had enough food for the next few days and fresh meat spoiled quickly. He took the trail to the lake without thinking about it and found himself blinking dazedly at the painfully bright sunlight dancing off the wind-rippled surface before he even realized where his feet had taken him. He didn't want to be here. She was all around him; in the memories, in the wind, in the beauty of this place.

In a dark pocket of shadow on the fir-covered southern bank came the stirring of ducks and Elijah crouched automatically, the bow flying into the ready position. There was no reason for him to shoot a duck. He knew that. But a sickness stirred in him here, a fever that made him want to loose an arrow and hear the shrill cry of life leaving an animal. Elijah whipped the bow to the right and fired an arrow into the hemlock tree instead, missing by mere inches the engraving he'd carved there.

His breathing was ragged, his hands trembling. He'd never felt like this before. What had Nakita done to him?

Rising unsteadily, Elijah walked to the tree and yanked the arrow free. He tucked it into the quiver he wore on his back and took off down the trail at a run. He ran all the way back to the cabin as though being chased. Even with the bowstring digging painfully into his shoulder with each swing of his arm, he didn't slow. For the first time in his life, he wanted to be as far away from the lake as possible.

He took a quick shower and changed his clothes. It was far too early to leave for the fireworks celebration, but Elijah climbed into his car anyway and peeled out of the driveway. Only three hours, five loops around town, and half a tank of gas later did he feel the anger start to dissipate. In its place, a drained emptiness left him weak and exhausted. He took a quick right on Main Street and drove slowly toward the coffee shop that had been the garage. The sign on the door announced that it was closed for the holiday, and Elijah parked the Camaro along the curb. He rolled down the window and strained to smell the familiar grease-and-tire scent that reminded him of the good times he'd shared with Chitto here, but it was long gone.

Elijah stayed in the car and let his forehead fall forward onto the steering wheel. He needed Chitto, now. He needed some calm, objective advice. Someone to tell him that he wasn't a testosterone-fueled teenager anymore and he needed to act like a man and move on. Getting dumped wasn't the end of the world.

"What should I do, Chitto?" Elijah whispered into the steering wheel. He immediately glanced up to make sure no one was walking past on the sidewalk before letting his head sink back down again. He listened, waiting for an answer, but there was nothing except the creaking groans of the Camaro's engine as it settled. He was being ridiculous and he knew it. If Chitto were here, the man would clap a hand on his shoulder and steer him toward the marina, telling him that the fireworks were worth watching, broken heart or not. Elijah rolled up the window and stepped out. It was a mile to the marina, but he needed the walk.

The streets filled with people as he moved toward the sound. There were children laughing, waving wispy clouds of cotton candy on sticks in front of them, and parents pulling wagons with bouncing toddlers inside. All around him were families. Full and complete families, and Elijah hated every single one of them for reveling in the joy that he might never have.

The wide lawn was crowded, and Elijah stayed to the outskirts, chatting here and there and exchanging fake smiles with familiar faces before he settled on the grassy slope beside the fir tree he'd taken shelter under four years before on his first venture back into the community.

His shoulder throbbed, and Elijah squeezed it, windmilling his arm a few times slowly to loosen it up. His eye caught the swish of long blond hair as it moved through the crowd in his direction. Erin Landry was coming his way, her eyes locked on him.

Elijah gave a quick glance over his shoulder to see if she was bee-lining for someone behind him, but she called out his name and Elijah stood as she approached. He hadn't run into her since her accident. Did she know he'd been the one to write about it in the paper? Should he bring it up? Tell her how sorry he was to hear about her little girl's death? He never knew how much of the quiet part to say out loud during moments like this, and he didn't want to screw up by saying too much. Maybe he should just offer his condolences.

"Hey, Doc," he said instead.

She was thinner, that was for sure, and her eyes were hollowed with the pain that no parent should have to endure, their blue-green irises far too brilliant and vivid against the pale skin that seemed stretched across her fine bone structure.

"How's your shoulder?" she asked.

"How'd you know it was bothering me?"

Erin mimicked the windmill motion he'd been doing a moment ago. "You don't do this unless you've got rotator cuff problems."

"It acts up every now and then after I chop wood, it's nothing," Elijah said. He gave a quick glance around before remembering what Paul at the office had told him. Erin's husband had left her mere weeks after the death of their daughter. Paul had speculated that Manny probably blamed her for the accident. How could you continue to live in the same house with someone you knew was responsible for the death of your child? That meant Erin was here alone, just like him.

She brushed his excuse aside. "I've got the afternoon open on Tuesday, come on in and I'll have a look at it."

"Oh, it'll be fine, I'm sure it'll feel better if I rest it for a few days."

"Still, come in Tuesday all the same," she said firmly. "I haven't forgotten that you haven't had a checkup since coming back to town. We'll run bloodwork while you're in, just to make sure everything looks good."

Elijah didn't want a checkup. The last thing he wanted was to revisit the clinic where Chitto had died and add insult to injury with a needle in his arm, but looking at Erin's face, at the new hardness in her delicate features, Elijah didn't have the heart to disagree.

"Tuesday," he nodded, "I'll swing by after work in the afternoon."

"Looking forward to it," Erin said. She gave a shallow attempt at a smile that didn't clear the haunted look in her eyes then turned on her heel and left.

Elijah sank back down to the grass with a sigh of guilt. He might be mourning the future he'd never have with Nakita, but Erin had already lost something real.

23

Elijah winced as Erin lifted his arm and rotated it in a full circle. She kept one hand on his shoulder, gently palpating the muscles as they fired in turn.

"Sorry," she said, rotating his arm a second time and reaching around to feel the muscles behind his shoulder. "I know it's uncomfortable."

"You're a monster," he replied, eyes squeezed shut as he waited for her to finish.

She laid his arm gently at his side and stepped over to her computer on the counter.

"Your rotator cuff tendon is inflamed," she said, tapping out a quick note. "It's called tendonitis, it's a common overuse injury. I could run some imaging to be sure, but I'm just about positive that's what it is."

"No, I trust you. So . . . is it a 'take two of these pills and call me in the morning' kind of fix?"

"No." She eyed him over the top of her computer. "It's a 'lay off the wood chopping for six months' kind of fix."

He had plenty of firewood stacked for the winter. At some point he was just chopping wood to blow off steam and he could find some other way to do that if he had to.

"All right," he promised, "you win, I'll retire my axe for the year."

"Good to hear." She turned to a rack on the wall that held various sizes of clear, empty vials. "Time for bloodwork."

Elijah's stomach turned over. "Do we have to? I mean, I feel pretty healthy."

Erin pulled two vials out and turned back to him. "That's the thing, you feel healthy until you don't, and sometimes by the time you don't, it's too late to do anything about it. Running labs is a great way to catch something serious while it's still in the early stages."

Elijah rolled up his sleeve. "You talked me into it."

Erin scooted her stool over to where he sat and swabbed his arm with alcohol. Elijah narrowed his eyes at the needle.

"Ready?" she asked.

He looked away, letting out a long breath as the sharp pin pierced the sensitive skin of his inner elbow.

"Tiny pinch," she said as she inserted it.

"That might work on little kids, but I can see that big fat needle, Doc."

She gave a little laugh through her nose. "Don't be a baby."

She finished filling the second vial and placed them both on the counter, peeling off her gloves.

"Well, the worst is over," she said. "Got any plans for the rest of the week?"

Elijah took the cotton ball she handed him and placed it where the needle had been.

"Not really. I might head up to the reservation. Chitto had some flutes at his place, I'd like to see them sold at the market this summer. I think he'd like that."

"What about Friday?" she asked, tossing her gloves in the trash. "Any plans Friday night?"

Elijah faltered, dumbstruck. Was she asking him out? He looked up at her, standing in the middle of the room, appraising him evenly in her crisp white coat. She was the picture of beauty and poise, and newly single, but he never, *never* would have considered the possibility of asking her for a date. And yet, she had just asked him what he was doing on Friday night. He might not be the worldliest guy out there, but he was pretty sure Friday night was still date night. And why on earth not?

The image of Nakita standing beside the lake swam into his mind but he forced it back down. What was he supposed to do? Call her a thousand times with no response? At some point he was crossing the line from persistence to disrespect. He'd been snubbed by the person he would have chosen to spend this Friday night with. Why not make a date with the most beautiful and intelligent woman in Point Orchards instead? He'd be crazy not to.

"No, no plans for Friday," he said carefully. "Did you want . . . do you have plans Friday?"

"Not yet," she said, offering a nod of encouragement.

"Would you maybe want to grab dinner somewhere?"

"Why not your place?" she suggested. "Every time I drive past your little cabin in the woods, I think about how pretty it's gotten now that the property is all cleaned up. I'd love to see the rest of it."

Elijah sat up a little straighter. He wished the way to his heart was more complicated than simple flattery, but it wasn't. It would be a delight to show her around the place he had worked so hard on.

"That would be perfect," he said, standing. For a moment, he wasn't sure if he should reach out for a handshake or go in for a hug, but Erin was still standing in the middle of the room with her hands folded in front of her, so Elijah just said, "Okay, then," gave a little wave, and left.

———

By the time Friday arrived, Elijah had stashed the computer in his closet and polished every wooden surface of the kitchen and living room until it gleamed. He'd been to the lake and back at sunrise and had the good fortune of a dead duck in his arms on the return trip, a single arrow hole in the base of its neck.

He flipped through his mother's recipe book and made a sauce that would complement the tender bird with wild rice cooked in chicken broth as a side. The kitchen smelled wonderful, and at five in the afternoon, Erin called to tell him she'd be there within half an hour.

Elijah raced to the bathroom to run a comb through his hair. After

Nakita left, he'd abandoned his morning shaving routine and his stubble had become a full-blown beard. Surprising himself, Elijah had decided to keep it. Now, when he wore his typical plaid shirts into town,
he looked vaguely like a lumberjack, minus the massive physique, of
course. He liked the feeling of hiding behind his beard, and in front
of the mirror he lightly trimmed its edges to turn his facial hair from
overgrown and running wild to deliberate and well groomed, then he
ran back to the kitchen to pull the duck out of the oven. Just in time,
too. The porch creaked as Erin walked across it, and Elijah pulled the
door open before she had a chance to knock.

"Come on in," he said, stepping aside to let her pass.

She looked lovely. Her hair was loose down her back, and she wore a
sophisticated dark green blouse over light jeans and gray sneakers.

"Well, well," she said, scanning the room, "so this is where the mysterious Elijah Leith lives."

Elijah placed the duck on a platter and tossed the oven mitts beside
it, his eyes tracking Erin as she moved through the living room, inspecting everything. He pulled a sharp knife from the drawer at his waist and
started to carve the bird.

"Who painted that?" she asked, nodding to the portrait of Chitto.

Elijah's grip on the knife tightened.

"A local artist," he said nonchalantly. It wasn't a lie.

Erin turned to face him. "I wish his death hadn't come as such a
surprise. That man loved you like a father."

Her voice was steady, clinical even, and Elijah hunched over the
duck to hide the pain that always stabbed his insides with the memory
of that day.

"I wish so, too," he said quietly. "You hungry? The duck's ready."

"It smells great," Erin smiled, following him to the table.

Elijah lit the tall candle in the middle and served up both of their
plates. He was relieved to find that the duck had turned out perfectly,
with crispy skin outside and juicy meat inside. He stole a glance at Erin's
face to see if she was enjoying it, but her features gave nothing away.

"Speaking of Chitto," she said between bites, "I have a little confes-
sion to make."

"Oh?"

"He told me you wrote a book."

Another stab of pain.

"Did he?"

Erin nodded. "I'd love to read it someday."

Elijah forced down the bite of rice in his mouth and gave her a weak smile.

"Good luck finding a copy. It barely sold and I don't have one anymore."

She was trying to be kind, but her conversational choices were killing him. He hadn't realized that this was what a first date would be like. He hadn't known that his mind was so fragile, littered with emotional land mines that blew up at the wrong word, the wrong name, the wrong sentiment. Erin was watching him closely, waiting for him to elaborate. Elijah feigned indifference as he cut another bite.

"It was just a bad review that got in the way." He shrugged.

"What did it say?" she asked.

Suddenly, everything tasted very dry. Elijah stood from the table.

"Do you want some water? Actually, I think I've got a bottle of wine in one of the cupboards, I can try to find it if you'd like some."

"No, thanks," Erin said as Elijah filled a glass with tap water and drank half at the sink before bringing it back to the table.

"What did the review say?" she asked again as Elijah took his seat.

Elijah pressed his lips together. He could recite every sentence of the review word for word if he wanted to. He'd read it at least a hundred times.

"I don't remember, exactly. Just some guy ripping apart the plot. Maybe he was having a bad day when he wrote it." Elijah gave a little chuckle, but the sound was hollow.

"That must've hurt," Erin said, tilting her head sympathetically.

Desperate for a change of topic, Elijah chugged the rest of his water and racked his brain for something new to say.

"So, anything fun planned for the rest of the summer?"

Erin's eyebrows lifted slightly.

"Well," she said as she scooped rice onto her fork, "as I'm sure you know, my life has been completely turned upside down this past year, so I'm still just trying to figure out the basics again. It's strange being on my own after so long. Manny and I were married for eight years. I still wake up expecting him to be there at the counter with a cup of coffee when I head down the stairs in the morning. But he's not."

That wasn't the worst of it, and Elijah knew it. However difficult it was to go downstairs without her husband there, at least he was still alive somewhere in the world. Somewhere in that house was the room where her daughter had slept. Did Erin have to walk past that room every day, too? Did she keep that door closed the way he kept his parents' room closed, convincing himself that someday he'd deal with their stuff? Someday she, too, would open a closed door in her house and step inside to deal with the memories. Someday she'd pull down the curtains with little giraffes or elephants on them. Someday she'd take apart that crib piece by piece. Someday it would be turned from a shrine into a gym or a little library. The room she wasn't talking about had to be a thousand times more painful than addressing the cold side of the bed that her husband had warmed for all those years.

"That's gotta be tough," he said gently.

"I wouldn't wish it on my worst enemy," she said, her bright eyes misting as she met his gaze in the candlelight.

This was impossible. She had as many land mines as he did. More. They both had far too much baggage. Try as he might, Elijah couldn't think of a single safe topic of conversation that wouldn't lead to a devastating explosion, and for a few minutes they ate in complete silence. It was so quiet in the room that Elijah could hear the flickering flame dancing on the candle wick.

"Where did the duck come from?" Erin asked, and Elijah felt a wave of relief crash over him. At last, neutral ground.

"There's actually a little lake way in back of the woods. It's beautiful back there, tucked away from the sound by a row of trees. I've been doing a little hunting and fishing around it this summer, but nothing too big. I wouldn't be able to carry a deer all the way home, but I've carried back a few trout and one or two rabbits. This is the first duck I've shot, actually."

Erin placed her fork onto her empty plate and wiped her mouth with her napkin.

"How far away is it?"

"About a mile and a quarter from the back fence."

Erin smiled as she rose from her seat.

"I feel like a walk," she said. "Take me there."

24

Sheriff Godbout flipped the lights on as the cruiser eased into speed on the curving two-lane road. The Camaro had a five-minute head start on them, and Jim kept the siren off to keep Elijah from getting spooked and making a run for it. They were less than ten minutes from the Leith cabin, and with any luck, they would find Elijah's blue car parked there when they pulled up.

"Do you want me to read it out loud?" Jeremy asked, Erin's diary open in his lap.

Jim nodded.

> *Dear Diary,*
>
> *Today is our three-month anniversary. Odd thing, celebrating an anniversary as short as this one after being married for almost a decade, but Elijah insisted we celebrate and who am I to argue? We're meeting for dinner tonight at a fancy little place on the water. It'll at least be a bit more to my taste than our last venture out, which was into the woods to hunt. I'll be honest, hunting is NOT my thing, but Elijah wanted to take me and I agreed. Gotta support the boyfriend's interests, right? Truth be told, it just creeps me out a little, the silent, lurking part, waiting for an animal to step out into a clearing so you can kill it. Elijah loves it though. He shot a*

young deer. Not even fully grown yet. As I sat there with him in the woods, watching the deer wander into range, I found myself wishing it would make a run for it and Elijah would miss with the bow, but he didn't. He sent that arrow flying right into its neck. In all fairness, Elijah is the first man I've dated who liked hunting. Manny was the sort of man to call me in to kill a spider, so maybe it's the contrast between Manny and Elijah that just makes it all so jarring, but as we walked over to the deer and I saw it lying there dead on the ground, I felt sick to my stomach. Anyway, the deer was heavy, so I had to help him carry it out of the woods. Can you imagine? Ah, the things we do for love. Well, tonight is sure to be more civilized than that, and Elijah promised I didn't have to go out hunting with him again if I didn't want to. That's an offer I'm definitely going to take him up on! More later.

—Erin

Dear Diary,

It's over. I can't believe I'm even about to write this, but I have to. I can't believe that I would allow what happened to have happened. I am no better than my mother, turning her swollen cheek away from me to hide what Dad had done to her. Elijah shoved me. Like, legitimately shoved me into the table in his kitchen. I've never been more scared in my life. I guess you never really know a person until you spend time with them, and I truly wouldn't have thought Elijah was capable of violence, but here we are. All I did was ask him about the rumor I heard about him and some local girl and he lost it. We were in his living room dancing to some of his parents' old records when I brought it up. I probably shouldn't have, but I couldn't help it, because I know exactly who the girl is. Nakita Mills. You don't forget the name of someone who accuses you of criminal negligence. She is the one who came into my office and got right in my face telling me she was going to sue me over her grandmother's death, when in reality, I probably saved her grandmother's life and gave her more time than she would have otherwise had. I was less than pleased to find out she and Elijah had been seen together so yes, I brought it up. At first, he brushed it off and kept dancing, but I just couldn't let it go. I don't know why. I probably should have dropped it, but I kept telling him to be honest with me, until he pushed me out of his arms and I fell against the table and whacked the back of my head. Not hard enough to cause a concussion or anything, but hard enough to really, really scare me. I was shocked, and I think he saw that in my eyes, because the anger when he pushed me seemed to just fall away all at once and he was at my side in a heartbeat, checking my head and saying "I'm sorry, I'm so sorry" over and over. I kept it together long enough to tell him I had to go, and I hightailed it out of there, but I knew as I drove home in tears that it was over. I love him. But I can't see him anymore. Not after this.

Dear Diary,

Christmas alone. Two words that can't even begin to describe how miserable today has been. I miss Anna. I miss Manny. As I sit here in bed with snow falling outside, snuggled in my blankets with a cup of tea on my nightstand and utter silence in the house, I even miss Elijah. It's been so tough. All of the Christmas stuff is out in the shed. I didn't bother with a tree or lights or anything like that. Truthfully, I wanted it to just be another day, just another day in a long line of lonely days and not an especially painful one, but it was. Christmas found its way in when I flipped on the TV for the news and found "It's a Wonderful Life" on instead. I don't know. They say time heals all wounds, but today it hurts worse than ever.

Dear Diary,

Yes, it's me. It's been months since I've written and I've neglected you terribly, dear diary. I'm writing today so that if I EVER feel like giving Elijah another chance, I can open to this page and

*remind myself not to. What a fool I was. We've talked a few times
throughout the spring, just keeping in touch. Every time, he ends
our calls by asking for another chance, and I finally gave in. On
Saturday, I took him out in my boat. It was such a beautiful day
and I wanted to be on the water, but I never go boating alone,
it just feels a little too risky to be out on the sound by myself, so I
invited Elijah to come with me. I don't know how I could have
been so stupid to put myself in a situation where I was pretty much
trapped in a fifteen-foot floating room with him. The entire time,
he talked about giving him a second chance and how he deserved
the opportunity to redeem himself. After an hour of this I got so sick
of it that I told him I was going to take him back to the marina.
He asked if I was seeing someone else and went on one of his rants
about the women in this town being hung up on the men in their
pasts. I'm just so embarrassed. There were a ton of people out at
the marina, and by the time we pulled in to the dock, both of our
voices were raised and he grabbed me hard by the wrist. I docked
the boat and told him to get off and we parted ways. I made it
VERY clear that whatever this was was over. I'm not proud of what
happened. I'm still shaken up about it to be honest. Unfortunately,
I still need to get my dissertation back from his place at some point.
I let him read it while we were together and I'd like it back, but I
should probably give him a while to cool down before I even ask.
Anyway, brighter days ahead and I'm not going to waste them on
him. I don't know if there's someone else out there for me, but there
might be somewhere else, some place warm where I could start fresh,
ride my bike along the ocean in the morning. Maybe I'll visit the
Mediterranean again, this time with a one-way ticket. They need
doctors everywhere, right?*

—Erin

Jeremy flipped to the next page and found it blank.

"That's it. There's nothing else."

"That's enough. She was thinking about leaving. And she had a reason to be at the cabin."

"Her dissertation?"

"Right. If he killed her, it might still be there. She didn't have it on her."

"That's not exactly rock-solid evidence of guilt."

"No," Jim agreed, "but it's a pretty good start."

Jim pressed his lips into a line as he tried to see it in his mind's eye, Elijah losing control the night Erin came for her dissertation. Della had told him about the fight at the marina, but now he had the tumultuous trail that led right up to it. It was damning to say the least, but he had to give the man a fair chance to explain himself. Elijah was innocent until proven guilty, though it was hard not to see it the other way around in a case like this. Was a diary admissible as evidence in court? Jim had no idea. He'd never needed to check before. Truth be told, he'd never had to even face the possibility of a murder trial before, and he didn't have the foggiest clue how it all worked. All he knew for sure was that his job was to hunt down answers and this was a good place to start.

"Why don't I poke around and look for it while you keep him talking and distracted," Jeremy suggested.

Jim nodded. "Almost there."

The cruiser whipped around a bend in the road and the cabin appeared up ahead on the right through the snowy forest.

"Stop!" Jeremy shouted, and Jim slammed on the brakes. "Look!"

The deputy was pointing to a patch of woods on the left. Something round and silver gleamed where a ray of sunlight broke through the clouds and caught it.

Jim hit reverse and backed up a few feet to where a forgotten and overgrown drive led into the forest. He pulled the cruiser into it, tires spinning on the fresh snow. It was an old logging road, blocked off by a rusted green gate in front of which, tucked just out of view from the road, sat a gleaming white BMW. Jim didn't pull any closer to inspect it. He didn't have to.

"Is it hers?" Jeremy asked.

"Yep," the sheriff confirmed, "that's Erin's car."

"She parked it here and walked to the cabin? Why?" Jeremy asked, perplexed.

"If I had to wager a guess, I'd say it was moved after she was killed."

"He took her keys, then."

"Probably, but even if he couldn't find them, he'd know how to hot-wire a car after working in a garage, wouldn't he?"

Jim backed slowly out of the old driveway and pulled onto the road. In front of the Leith cabin sat the shiny blue Camaro. Long-dormant butterflies leapt to life in Jim's belly, and he took a deep breath as he pulled in beside Elijah's car.

"You ready?" he asked, shifting into park and pulling the keys from the ignition.

Jeremy tucked the Glock into his holster and nodded tensely.

Jim rested his hand on his deputy's arm for a moment. "It'll be all right, just follow my lead."

Jeremy swallowed. "Okay."

Jim led the way up the porch steps, keeping to the bare patches where Elijah's boots had kicked away the snow. Behind the window, a curtain rustled, and Jim felt the crawling sensation that told him Elijah had watched them pull up.

He knocked loudly three times on the door.

"Elijah!" he called. Footsteps could be heard inside, then the sound of the deadbolt sliding back. Jeremy's breath beside him was shallow and quick, and Jim knew without looking that his deputy's hand would be resting on his holster.

The door eased open a few inches and half of Elijah's face appeared in the crack, a narrowed, wary blue eye over a dark, bearded mouth.

"Can I help you, Sheriff?" he asked slowly, his eye roving from Jim to Jeremy, down to the Glock at Jeremy's waist and back to Jim.

Jim slid his hand into the crack and gripped the wooden frame to keep Elijah from closing the door.

"I'm afraid we need to come on in and ask you a few questions. You're in a heap of trouble, son."

25

Elijah led Erin down the trail. It was the first time he had been back in the woods with anyone besides Nakita, and the contrast between the two women had never been more evident. Elijah took a deep breath of the forest air.

"Isn't it beautiful back here? There's just something about the woods at this time of day, that magical hour between afternoon and evening. Makes me wish I was a photographer so I could capture the beauty of it."

Erin shrugged as she looked around. "I guess I'm just more of a city girl at heart," she told him as they walked. "I was born in Seattle, and after I graduated, I assumed I'd take up a residency there. I never wanted to leave."

"How'd you end up here, then?" he asked her. "Point Orchards is about as far from city life as you can get."

"I ended up taking over Dr. Robertson's clinic when he retired. He was a close friend of my father's. They went to medical school together once upon a time, and my dad recommended me for the job since I'd just finished my doctorate. I liked the idea of small-town living at the time. You kind of want something different than what you know when you're younger, but truth be told I miss the noise of the city. I miss walking down the sidewalk surrounded by people and having new stores and shops to pop into all the time. And I definitely miss being able to order takeout at midnight if I want it." She gave a little laugh.

"I guess I can understand that." Elijah nodded. "I honestly don't miss San Francisco at all, though. It was tough getting used to the quiet at first when I moved back here, but if you're brought up in the woods, they'll always be home, somehow. This way, watch your step."

Elijah parted the nettles with his hands and stomped down on them as he passed, breaking their stalks and flattening a path for Erin to pass through. She was wearing jeans, so the nettles wouldn't have blistered her anyway, but Erin didn't seem like the kind of woman who should be walking through the woods in the first place, let alone bushwhacking her own trail.

He led her through the last patch of forest, until they came upon the lake, gray and silky in the evening dusk. Elijah walked to the shore and picked up a smooth rock beside the felled log.

"How many skips?" he called over his shoulder. It was a game he played with Nakita, one she almost always won.

"I don't know," Erin replied, watching him. Elijah turned to find her standing beside the tree he thought of as "ours" with Nakita. It was jarring seeing her there. She just looked so . . . out of place. *Jarring* wasn't the right word. It was *wrong*. She was the wrong woman to be with out here. She stood pale and slender beside the tree, like a houseplant, a delicate orchid that bloomed brilliantly but hated the sunlight and thrived in pots on office desks and bookshelves. Nakita was one of the trees herself, sturdy and magnificent, her roots deep in the earth.

Erin glanced down to inspect the dirt on her white sneakers and tried to wipe them clean against the trunk of the tree. The rock slipped from Elijah's fingers as he stared at her, realizing with a sinking pit in his stomach that she would never be the right woman for these woods. She would never be the right woman for him. She looked up suddenly and caught his eye.

"What?" she asked, shifting from left foot to right under the weight of his unbroken stare. Elijah blinked himself out of the daze and scooped up the rock he had dropped.

"How many skips?" he asked again. It didn't matter how much he wished he were out here with Nakita instead of Erin. Nakita had left. She was in his past now. Erin was here, right here in the present. He had berated Nakita for hanging on to Kailen when he, Elijah, was standing right in front of her, available and alive, and it was time to practice what he preached. Nakita was gone and Erin was here. Cold, hard math.

"Three?" she guessed.

"Seven," he said, turning away from her. He pulled his arm back and slung it forward, releasing the rock.

It hit the still surface of the lake and skipped six times before vanishing beneath the water. Erin said nothing, and when Elijah turned to smile at her, he found her with her back to the lake, inspecting the carving on the hemlock's trunk.

Elijah jogged over to where she stood.

Erin cast a sideways glance in his direction. "Who's N.M.?"

Elijah felt sick. She shouldn't be here, standing with him in front of this tree, in the very spot where he had shared his first and last kiss with Nakita. It felt somehow like watching a brand-new puppy eat from the bowl a beloved dog had used for the long and loyal years before it died.

He chose his words carefully. "I carved that almost nineteen years ago. Right before I left for San Francisco."

Erin said nothing. She stood still as a statue, staring at the markings.

Elijah sighed. "She was a high school girlfriend," he said, forcing his voice to be casual. "You know how it goes, back then you think your first love is going to last forever."

"Right." Erin lifted a finger to touch the E. "What's your middle name?"

"Marcus. Why?"

"We have the exact same initials," she commented, "Erin Marie Landry. That's a strange coincidence, isn't it?"

"I guess it is. Hey, come here." Elijah took her by the hand and led her away from the tree. "Watch this."

The surface of the lake had stilled after the ripples from the skipped rock spread outward into nothingness, and Elijah plucked a single fern from a cluster. He crumpled it into a ball and flicked it a few meters out into the water, where it landed softly and unfurled as it floated. For a few moments there was no movement, then the water stirred and lifted as something large moved toward the fern.

"What is it?" Erin asked in a whisper.

"Trout. Watch."

The fish broke the surface in a half jump beside the fern and flopped back down with a splash.

"That was a huge fish," Erin remarked with wide eyes.

"Right? Biggest trout in the entire sound are right here in this lake. You wouldn't believe the size of some of the fish I've seen. I think they like it here because the creek that runs through the woods feeds fresh water into the lake. Trout can live in either fresh or salt water, but they grow bigger in fresh water. Every now and then I like to bring a rod with me and fish back here, but it's a long walk back to the cabin carrying a heavy, smelly fish and all that gear. Once I spotted two fishermen back here. I don't know how they found this spot. You can only really get in at high tide, and it's pretty tucked away, but one of them must've stumbled on it accidentally. Anyway, I just sat back here and watched them fish. They got so excited when they caught one, and then they yelled at each other to keep it down because they were trespassing. It was pretty funny."

Erin gave a little laugh. "That is funny. Did they ever come back?"

"Rain or shine, every Saturday. I don't mind, though. Makes me wish I had a buddy to do stuff like that with."

They stood side by side and watched the ripples where the fish had jumped widen outward in softening circles. Elijah glanced up at the sky. Swollen clouds that had held streaks of orange only moments before were deep purple now. The sun was gone.

"We should probably head back, don't want you to roll an ankle in the dark."

"You either," she said.

"Doesn't matter if I do," Elijah joked, "I've got a brilliant doctor with me, come on."

Darkness fell beneath the canopy of the fir trees, and Elijah mentally kicked himself for not bringing a flashlight. He reached out for Erin's hand and led her down the path he knew by heart, searching for the light of his cabin windows through the trees ahead. She nearly fell twice, her sneakers catching on raised roots, and both times, Elijah caught her and helped her upright again.

She was breathing heavily by the time they reached the back fence, and Elijah kept hold of her hand as they stepped out of the forest and into the moonlit backyard. In the silvery glow, her hair seemed pure white, and he could just make out the radiant flush on her cheeks beneath eyes as luminous as the moon above. She wasn't Nakita, but she truly was breathtaking.

They climbed side by side up the back-porch steps, and Elijah held the door open. Erin looked up at him from behind long lashes as she passed, and Elijah swallowed. In just a minute or two, the inevitable moment would come. The end-of-date kiss, full of possibility. They passed his bedroom and Erin glanced inside.

"Small bed," she commented.

"Yeah," he said, "it's actually the same twin bed I had in high school. There's a king-sized one in my parents' room, but I can't bring myself to use it. Someday, maybe."

"Is that this room?" Erin paused before the closed door in the hall and reached for the knob.

It happened before he could stop her. Elijah felt his stomach lurch as she twisted the handle without permission and pushed it open.

The smell of stale, musty air flowed into the hallway from the long-unopened room, and Erin reached for the light, flicking it on.

Elijah was frozen in the hall, unable to move, unable even to breathe as he stared into his parents' room, at their unmade bed, the sheets still rumpled on the side his father always used after his mother died. A pain as sharp and piercing as a railroad spike in his chest brought him back to his senses, and he stepped into the room and led Erin out with a firm hand on the small of her back.

"I don't go in there," he said through gritted teeth, fighting a losing battle against his temper as he shut the door behind her. He tried to tell himself that it wasn't her fault. It was a mistake anyone could have made, simply wanting a tour of the cabin, unaware that he had been avoiding that room every single time he'd walked down this hall for the last four years, but who did she think she was? If he had been invited to her house and opened the door of her little girl's room, he would have expected to be thrown out on his butt and deservedly so. Instead, Erin was watching him with mild curiosity as he struggled to keep his face free of emotion.

Elijah led her to the front of the cabin and forced a yawn. Two minutes ago, he had been anticipating a good-night kiss that he now wanted nothing to do with. Every ounce of desire had drained away the second she opened that door. Erin glanced at her watch.

"I'd better get home, it's getting late."

"I'll walk you to your car," Elijah said.

What was wrong with him? Any other man would have bent over backward to keep the date going, to be alone with her for as long as possible. She was a gorgeous woman, one who was clearly in a vulnerable frame of mind after everything she'd been through; he should feel compelled to follow through with the possibility of what the evening could bring, what most men would have thought about all the way through the obligatory dinner and conversation part, but he just wanted to be alone.

Erin grabbed her purse, and together they walked to her white BMW out front. When they reached the car, Erin opened the door and turned, offering Elijah one of her brightest smiles.

"I had a great time," she said. "Next time, I'll cook for you at my place. I'll call you later this week and we can figure out what day works best."

Elijah was having trouble keeping up. Their second date would be at her house. Yes, that would be better, he wouldn't have to work around all of his painful memories there. Wait, they had a second date? Wasn't it his job to decide whether or not he'd call her again? The way she'd phrased it hadn't left him a whole lot of choice in the matter.

"Okay," he replied with a tight smile. "Thanks for coming over."

Erin didn't linger, nor did Elijah make any move toward her. She ducked into the car and quickly started the engine, closing the door behind her. Elijah stepped out of the way as she backed up and pulled to the edge of the driveway. The last thing he saw before her car vanished down the road was her blue-green eyes in the rearview mirror as she offered him a quick wave and pulled away.

Silence filled the place where the motor had been, and Elijah felt his chest deflate with relief. What a mess this date had been. Why had he agreed to host her here? He should have insisted that they go out to a restaurant. Instead he had botched the entire evening trying to keep his emotional land mines buried and failing miserably. It wasn't Erin's fault. Maybe a second date at her place would be a completely different story. In truth, he should consider himself lucky that she was giving him a second chance at all after the awkwardness he'd put on full display.

Elijah turned his back on the road and walked slowly around the side of the cabin to the woodshed. He gathered a small armful of logs and carried them inside. There was a chill in the evening air, one that belied the date on the calendar. A fire would be just the thing to stave it off. Elijah had a feeling that sleep would be late in coming, despite how exhausted he was, and it would be better to stay up deliberately. A fire somehow took the edge off how alone he felt, when the truth was, despite spending the evening with one of the most beautiful women he'd ever seen, he was lonelier than ever.

26

Elijah sat at his desk with the tip of a pencil in his mouth and a half-finished article laid out in front of him.

"Hey, Paul," he called across the room, "let me read this to you, okay?"

Paul spun around in his chair. "Sure."

Elijah read the four paragraphs he'd written about Sacred Mountain being declared a national monument and looked up to Paul for a reaction. Paul shrugged.

"Kinda flat," he said.

"I thought so," Elijah said with a sigh, placing the paper back down on his desk. "I was hoping it was just me."

"Who cares? You realize our readership can basically be counted on two hands, right?"

Elijah leaned over his desk and scratched out the first line to try again. "I just want it to be the best it can be," he muttered.

Paul spun back around in his chair. "Spoken like a novelist, not a journalist."

"If you weren't all the way across the room, I'd punch you," Elijah retorted.

"Look, why don't you get out to the reservation, interview somebody, your interviews always do well," Paul said over his shoulder. "Get away from your desk for a few hours and come back to it with fresh eyes."

Elijah tapped the end of his pencil against his chin. It wasn't a bad idea. He grabbed his bag and threw his notepad inside before slinging it over his shoulder.

"Hey," he called to Paul as he stood to leave, "if Erin calls, will you tell her I'm out for the afternoon but I'm still on for dinner tonight?"

"You're the luckiest guy in Point Orchards, you know that?" Paul called after him.

Elijah waved him off and left through the back door of the office, to where his Camaro was parked. It was raining lightly, and Elijah held his bag over his head as he unlocked the car and climbed inside.

As he pulled into the gentle flow of traffic through town, Elijah decided he'd stop at Reverend Mills's church before looking anywhere else. Hopefully he'd find Nakita's father there. That was the only person he could think of to interview, other than simply standing in the middle of the street and flagging down passing cars to ask what they thought about the national monument. Reverend Mills would either be at the church or at the house . . . where he lived with Nakita. No, Elijah chided himself, he was *not* hoping the church parking lot would be empty and he'd have an excuse to drive up to Nakita's house and run into her. At least, that's what he told himself the entire drive, but he couldn't deny the surge of disappointment that washed over him when he saw Samuel Mills's car parked beside the small church.

Elijah climbed out of the Camaro and stepped gingerly through the minefield of potholes filled with rainwater to the church stoop. He lifted his hand to knock, but before it landed, a voice called out from inside.

"Come on in, Elijah."

Elijah stepped inside and closed the door behind him.

"I saw you pull up from the window. How are you, son?"

Elijah shoved his hands into his pockets as he walked down the aisle. "Oh, you know, fair to middling." He took a seat in the front pew and placed his bag beside him.

Reverend Mills pulled his glasses off his nose. "Are you here to ask me to talk to Nakita on your behalf? Because I'm not sure—"

"No," Elijah interrupted, "not at all. She wants distance. I can respect that." *Even if I don't agree with it,* he finished in his mind. "No, I'm actually here to get an interview for the *Herald* about the Sacred Mountain Monument if you can spare a few minutes."

"Oh." Reverend Mills stepped out from around the pulpit. "Sure."

As he took a seat, Nakita's father slid his glasses back onto his nose and peered closely at Elijah's face, inspecting the tired eyes, the overgrown beard and unwashed hair.

"How are you really, Elijah?"

Elijah held his gaze for only a few seconds before his composure faltered and he looked down at the floor.

"I miss her," he said quietly. As he said it out loud, he realized just how true the words were, just how deep and open the wound was that Nakita had left behind. It was still festering, still bleeding, despite the thousands of times he had told himself it was over, that she had moved on, despite the fact that he was technically seeing someone new, information that he didn't pass along to her father.

"What happened between you two?" the reverend asked softly.

"I honestly don't know." Elijah spread his hands out in front of him as though the answer might fall into his palms. "We were happy. At least, I thought we were. I assumed she gave me a second chance because she could see a future with me, but she didn't. I feel like she's buried her future in that graveyard behind us."

Nakita's father was silent for a long minute, then he rose to grab his Bible from the pulpit.

"You didn't grow up going to Sunday school, did you, Elijah?"

Elijah was baffled by the abrupt shift in conversation, but he shook his head anyway. "Not regularly. My mom took me a few times, but my dad always said the great outdoors gave better sermons than any pastor."

The reverend chuckled. "There's some truth in that," he conceded. "You wouldn't be familiar with the story of Jacob and Rachel then, would you?"

"No."

Reverend Mills flipped the Bible open to Genesis. "Abraham's grandson Jacob fell in love with a woman named Rachel, but her father, Laban, asked for seven years of hard work before giving up his daughter to marriage. On their wedding night, Jacob pulled away Rachel's veil to find that it was her older sister Leah instead. When he confronted Laban, Laban said it was traditional to give the eldest daughter away first, and the deed was already done, but if Jacob wanted Rachel as his wife, he could earn her with another seven years of hard work."

"The original love triangle," Elijah mused. "Did he do it? Work another seven years for her?"

"Would you have?" Nakita's father asked, turning keen eyes on Elijah's face.

"I guess that depends."

"On what?" Reverend Mills pressed.

"On how much I loved her."

"Yes," he said, nodding. "That's just it. It would depend on how deep your love was, wouldn't it?"

"So, did he?"

"Of course he did. Fourteen years. Jacob worked fourteen long years for the woman he loved, seven of which were unfair by any man's standard. It's easy for us to look back now and skip over the reality of what Jacob faced after he married Leah, the decision about whether or not to go back to work for Laban. The Bible jumps right past that part in four words. 'And Jacob did so.' Jacob knew exactly what it would take to win Rachel; he'd just worked seven long and hard years for her sister, and he was faced with the choice of repeating that same work for a con man, a man he probably hated for tricking him out of his lawful wife. But to him, she was worth it."

Elijah swallowed hard. "Is this your way of telling me not to give up?"

Nakita's father closed the Bible with a thud that echoed around the empty church. "You can do what you want, Elijah. No one would blame you for moving on after you've already worked so hard for a second chance with Nakita. But life, if we're lucky, lasts a long time and someday you *will* look back on this crossroads from the distance of many years. I wouldn't want you to look back with regret, wishing you had worked those extra seven years for Rachel instead of settling for Leah."

Something that sounded like a laugh escaped through Elijah's nose, and he offered the reverend a weak smile.

"You're a pretty good pastor, you know that?"

Reverend Mills placed a hand on Elijah's back as he stood. "Not as good as the great outdoors, but I try."

"The only thing is," Elijah rubbed a hand across the back of his neck uncomfortably, "I'm kind of seeing someone else. I sort of . . . fell into it, accidently. It's not serious, but I'd have to break things off with her first. Maybe don't mention that to Nakita though."

"I won't," the reverend said. "But take my advice. Don't settle for Leah," he repeated.

Elijah shouldered his bag and rose to his feet to shake the reverend's hand.

"I don't know why you keep rooting for me," he said candidly. "I wouldn't."

Reverend Mills looked surprised. "Why wouldn't I?"

Elijah's eyebrows lifted. "Because I . . . broke her heart."

"And she broke yours. You've hurt each other. But you and I are playing for the same team now, Elijah. We both want to see Nakita happy, again."

Elijah searched his eyes. Solemn, but not hard; there was warmth and softness there, just like Nakita's. The reverend sent him off with an encouraging pat on the shoulder, and Elijah left the church without looking back.

He felt better. Much better. A weight he hadn't known he'd been carrying had been left behind in the front row of that church, and he stepped across the threshold a lighter man.

Outside, golden shafts of light had broken through the clouds, and the raindrops on his Camaro sparkled like diamonds in the bright midday sun. Only as his tires bumped over the transition from dirt to pavement across the border did Elijah realize he hadn't gotten his interview.

27

There were ten finished flutes on the coffee table in Chitto's living room. Elijah inspected them one at a time, turning them over in his hands, admiring the skill with which they had been carved. He was no woodworker, but anyone could see the great lengths Chitto had gone to in making them flawlessly smooth and detailed. Animal flutes had been his specialty, and Elijah picked up one shaped like a giraffe, its head the mouthpiece. There were evenly spaced holes running down its neck, where he placed his fingers. He blew into it and a soft note filled the small living room, haunting and ethereal. He shifted his fingers on the holes, and another note followed, deeper and sadder than the first.

Elijah stilled his breath and the music faded. That was the mark of a great flute maker, when even an unskilled flutist could play beautifully without trying, the wooden instrument practically singing by itself. He picked up a wide flute shaped like a bullfrog, its lips puckered as a mouthpiece and holes running down its belly. This one sang in happy high notes, and Elijah felt the wood vibrating under his fingers as he blew. Chitto had been right. Every man needed to create something. He could just picture his friend now, sitting on the worn leather couch with the frog flute in his hands, gently whittling away tiny shavings of wood as he smoothed out its belly. Elijah smiled down at the frog's furrowed face. Chitto was the sort of guy who would have named him and talked to him as he carved, deep in the same creative state of flow that Elijah felt on days when the words just wrote themselves.

He placed the flutes one at a time into his backpack and zipped it up. He didn't want to linger here. Everything about Chitto's house reminded him that his friend was gone. It was a simple dwelling, humble and inviting, just like Chitto had been. The second he stepped through the front door, Elijah had frozen in his tracks. Beneath the scent of dust and stale air, he could still smell Chitto here in the pipe tobacco that was probably part of the furniture on a molecular level.

Elijah closed the door behind him and gently set the backpack in the passenger seat of the Camaro before climbing in. He drove straight through the reservation, waving to a man and woman who were walking with their three children along the dirt road, and over the border. He passed his cabin and drove straight to the marina, where the farmer's market was in full swing, busy with customers who buzzed around the booths like bees in a hive.

Elijah popped his trunk and grabbed the folding table inside. At the edge of the market he set up his stand, laid out the flutes with care, and took a seat behind the table. He watched the stream of tourists working their way around the market. Many stuck to the middle of the sidewalk, eyeing the tables from afar, wary of being pulled into tents by pushy vendors eager to sell their wares. Elijah felt no such need to sell the flutes; he was here simply to see Chitto's work through, no matter how long it took.

The Point Orchards locals always showed up early and made quick work through the booths. The outsiders came later, sleeping in and then meandering down to the market after coffee or brunch. They were always easy to spot. Unfamiliar faces with sleek sunglasses wearing expensive T-shirts and bright white sneakers.

Elijah picked up a flute and turned it over in his hands, remembering that first summer he was home four years before. A woman in neat slacks and a black turtleneck had approached the booth and was looking critically at the flutes, deciding whether or not to buy one, when Chitto launched into a tale about the origin of the instruments.

It was my great-grandfather who passed down the ancient art of the mouth flute, he told her, reaching out to lay a loving hand on one. *Passed down through my grandfather, and my father before me. It's a sacred business, carving these. The wisdom of generations passed down from man to man through our tribe. Worth every penny.*

As soon as the woman paid the twenty dollars he'd asked for and left with her flute, Elijah had turned to Chitto in disbelief.

Since when are the flutes twenty dollars? I always thought they were fifteen.

They're worth whatever the customer will pay, Chitto answered sagely as he watched the woman moving through the market.

Is that true? All that stuff about your father passing down the wisdom from his father?

Chitto had snorted with laughter. *Of course not. My old man sold shoes. I might be the only one on the reservation who ever made flutes.*

Slickers, Chitto had called the tourists, and there were plenty out today. Elijah sold two flutes to a couple from Seattle who bought the giraffe and a round, mouse-shaped flute as gifts for their two children back home. A few minutes later he gave the frog flute to a little Squalomah girl who was weaving through her mother's legs as the woman sold corn at a nearby booth. The woman offered Elijah an appreciative smile as her little girl sat quietly in a corner and inspected it.

After a few hours, Elijah stood to load the remaining seven flutes into his backpack. As he folded up his table, a familiar voice called out his name, and he looked up to find Erin striding toward him from the other side of the market.

"Hey," he greeted her.

"Good morning," she said brightly. "I have something for you, I'll drop it off this afternoon if you're going to be home."

"I'm not sure when I'll be back. What is it?"

"Just something for you to read. You know how we were talking about the effects of low-dose psilocybin on elderly patients with dementia?"

You, Elijah thought. *You were talking about the effects of low-dose psilocybin on elderly patients with dementia.*

He had quickly discovered that Erin had no problem inserting herself into situations, dates, conversations, appointments. When she wanted something, she made it happen. When she wanted to talk about something, she made herself heard. It wasn't a bad quality, exactly, but Elijah was having a hard time figuring out how to gently tell someone like her that the relationship wasn't working out. Somehow, he always managed to get twisted into a conversational pretzel and ended up scheduling their next date without realizing it.

"I dug around in the attic, and I found my dissertation where I wrote all about it. It was fascinating reading through it again, and since you were asking about it, I thought you might like to read it. I'll swing it by for you later today. Two o'clock?"

Elijah glanced at his watch unnecessarily. "Sounds great."

"See you then." Erin turned on her heel with a little wave, and Elijah blew out the remaining air in his lungs. Leah. She was definitely his Leah, and it was past time to end it; he just had no idea how.

At least he would be stopping the relationship before it got too far. They'd been slow to move forward on the physical side of things. The first time he kissed her, he had leaned in right at the moment she turned her head and his lips landed on her cheekbone as she gave a chirp of surprise. He had managed to locate her lips on the next date, and they had moved forward from there, but there always seemed to be an awkwardness between them, and too often he found himself pulling back, analyzing, and comparing her to Nakita. Perhaps the problem was that his taste in women seemed to land squarely on those who were recovering from tragic marriages and weren't ready to fully move on.

Elijah slung his backpack over his shoulders, folded his table, and tucked it beneath his arm. Maybe today was the day. Maybe he'd spend the next few hours working up the courage to actually end things with her. He loaded up the Camaro and drove home, thinking about how strange it was that if someone had told him a year ago he'd be not only dating Erin Landry but considering dumping her as well, he'd have thought they were crazy. Some lessons had to be learned the hard way, and the lesson Elijah had learned this summer was that chemistry wasn't all about looks. Erin had just about as much natural beauty as it was possible for a human being to possess, but she felt far away somehow, out of reach. The feeling he was looking for existed on the other side of the coin that he called "the ache." It was the good pain, the desperate and intense longing he had felt to be closer to Nakita, always closer, even when she was wrapped in his arms.

Elijah pulled into his driveway and unbuckled his seatbelt. He hadn't known the Bible story that Reverend Mills told him, but perhaps what went unsaid in the Good Book was that Leah had been the more attractive of the two sisters on the outside, but Jacob had felt that good ache only with Rachel.

Elijah left the flutes in the Camaro. He'd return to the market to sell them next Saturday, and every Saturday until he found a home for each of the remaining flutes. Back in the cabin he gathered dirty laundry from his room and started a load, then swept and dusted the front of the house. He ate lunch and returned to his chores, washing a load of dishes and drying them with a clean hand towel, his eyes flicking back and forth from the window, where small birds were picking over the raspberry bushes behind the fence, to the kitchen clock that was approaching the two o'clock hour.

It had been a long time since he'd broken up with anyone. He couldn't even remember how long. What was he supposed to do, lie? That's what he used to do, telling girlfriends the age-old "it's not you, it's me" line. With Erin, that couldn't be further from the truth. There were times he wanted to get right in her face and scream *It is you! It's the fact that I'm ready to settle down with a woman for the rest of my life, but that woman is not you!* Even if he couldn't change Nakita's mind and he ended up alone forever, that was better than wasting his own time and Erin's in a relationship he'd never be happy with. Erin needed to move on, too. She deserved to find someone who cared for her and was willing to put in the work to help her heal and find her way back to a healthy relationship. Yes, that's how he would phrase it: she deserved better than he was able to give.

Elijah rubbed his coffee mug dry and placed it on the counter as the quick rap of Erin's knuckles sounded on the door. He shook his head to clear it, reminding himself that he was a man now, not a teenager. He could have a civilized conversation and they could part as friends. No harm, no foul, no fireworks.

"Hi," Elijah said, forcing a smile as he opened the door for her, "come on in."

"Hey, you've been cleaning," she noted with a smile as she glanced around.

"Yeah."

"Looks good. I ought to hire you by the hour, my place is a mess."

"Listen, Erin—"

"Before I forget, here." Erin interrupted him, reaching into her shoulder bag to withdraw a bound leather notebook. She held it out for him to inspect and Elijah's heart sank. It would take him weeks to get through the thick dissertation, and it was sure to be full of dense medical jargon, the polar opposite of the material that he preferred for his bedtime reading.

"Great, thanks, I'll read it when I get some free time."

"I don't want anything spilled on it in the kitchen," she said, looking around. "Sorry to be a pest, but it's my only copy, so, here, I'll put it in this drawer and you can get to it later. No rush."

"Hey, Erin?" he rubbed at the back of his neck.

Erin slipped the thick booklet into the drawer of the living room coffee table, closed it, and turned to face him.

"Yes?"

Just do it already.

"Erin?" His mouth was dry, and he licked his lips as she stared at him, waiting for him to continue. "Can you stay for a minute? We need to talk."

28

Sheriff Godbout kept his eyes on Elijah's hand as he reached up to unlock the chain. The door closed for a moment, then slowly opened to let them in.

Jim stepped around Elijah and into the cabin, outwardly steady, inwardly tight as a bowstring. Jeremy followed and Elijah closed the door behind them. The room was dim, tidy, and warm, a typical log cabin. Before he turned to face Elijah, Jim did a quick once-over, scanning every surface within reach for weapons. There was a knife block in the kitchen and a hooked fire iron by the woodstove, but Jeremy had a gun and that would be faster. Jim doubted Elijah would risk anything. Beside the faded couch in the living room, a bulging suitcase sat upright. Jim nodded to it.

"You going somewhere, Elijah?" he asked.

He was met with stony silence. Jim walked to the kitchen table, the thud of his boots on the floorboards and the metallic clank of the handcuffs on his belt overloud in the silent cabin. He pulled out a chair.

"Have a seat, son."

Elijah uncrossed his arms and walked to the kitchen table. He took a seat opposite Jim and sat stiffly, his eyes hard and bloodshot like he hadn't slept in days.

"Now, the way I figure, we have just two choices. Option A: We sit, you talk, I listen. You give me ample evidence that you had nothing to do with Erin Landry's death and we leave. Everyone's happy. Option B: You don't talk, and we're forced to assume that you were involved, leading us down a legal rabbit hole that ends with you spending the rest of your life in prison. Your choice."

"I didn't kill her," Elijah said, his eyes on the table, as sullen as a teenager in the principal's office. Jim waited for him to go on, but Elijah simply sat there, refusing to look up.

"I don't know if you appreciate the gravity of the situation, son," Jim said evenly. "All signs are pointing toward you as a murderer and there you sit, cool as the center seed of a cucumber, when a woman was killed on your property in a crime that reads pretty darn close to one I read about in a book sent anonymously to my office. A book by the name of *Middletide*."

Jim watched the ripple of shock play over Elijah's features.

"You read my book?" he asked in a voice barely louder than a whisper.

Jim nodded. "Awful lot of coincidences between the murder you wrote and Doc Landry's death."

"I had nothing to do with it!" Elijah's chair tipped backward as he shot to his feet.

Jim rose to his own feet just as quickly.

"Sit down!" he barked in his most authoritative voice, pointing to the chair on the ground, and Elijah complied, picking it up and taking a seat. Jim stayed standing, and Jeremy crossed the room to stand behind him, hands on his hips, Glock on full display. "Now look, Elijah, we know all about your relationship with Erin, and we have a pretty good reason to believe that she came back to your place looking for her dissertation, but she never got a chance to get it back, did she?"

Jim didn't miss the quick sideways glance Elijah gave toward the living room, and behind his back he lifted a finger and pointed in that direction. Jeremy stepped slowly away from the table, but Jim kept his eyes locked on Elijah's, determined to keep his attention.

"And furthermore, unless you can provide us with an airtight alibi for the evening she was killed, I have a tough time thinking of anyone else who knows the way through the dark woods to that pretty little lake back there in the middle of the night."

"I don't have one, okay?" Elijah said, his voice hard, "I don't have an alibi. Where do you think I was in the middle of the night? I was here, in my house, sleeping alone. I live here alone, remember?"

"Well, now," Jeremy said from the living room and both men turned to look at him. On his face was a smug little half smile; in his hands he held a leather-bound notebook. "What's this?" The question was rhetorical. It didn't need answering, and Jim turned back to Elijah to find defeat written across his face. When he finally spoke, his voice was pleading.

"Sheriff, listen, I know what people are saying. I know how it looks, okay? But I swear to you, I had nothing to do with this. Erin and I, we barely dated a year and a half ago, and we parted on good terms. I had no reason to kill her and she hasn't set foot in my house in over a year."

"Were you ever violent with her when you were together?"

Elijah appeared taken aback as he blinked in what looked like genuine surprise.

"What? No, I never laid a finger on her, why would you ask that?"

Jim sat back down in his chair. "Seems to me I heard something about a shouting match the two of you had down at the marina last summer."

Elijah raked a hand through his hair. "Well, yeah, okay, we did have a fight, but Erin was the one who caused a huge scene. She just started yelling at me out of nowhere. She threw me out of her boat and I left. There was nothing more to it, and honest to God, I haven't even talked to her since then."

Jim nodded slowly as Elijah spoke; then he leaned over the table and folded his hands patiently in front of him. "Take just a second and put yourself in our shoes. What are we supposed to think? That someone else killed Erin, a woman you have a rocky past with, and tried to make it look like a suicide, a suicide that's a mirror image of the one in *your* novel, on *your* property?"

"I think—" Elijah said in a small voice. "I think someone's trying to set me up."

"And who would do something like that?" Jim asked calmly. "You have enemies in Point Orchards? Anyone who would want to see you behind bars?" Jim emphasized the name of the town, trying to force Elijah to recognize the lunacy of the suggestion that anyone in a tiny town like this where everyone knew everyone would be capable of meticulously framing him for murder.

Elijah sat back in his chair, and Jim could tell he was searching for an answer, any answer.

"I don't know," he said finally. "I can't think of anyone, but that doesn't mean it's not true."

"Pardon my saying so, Elijah, but if I came home to shredded couch pillows and my dog lying on the living room floor, I'd be quicker to blame Amos than assume a raccoon broke in through the window and snuck back out again."

"Do you even have a legal right to be here?" Elijah demanded suddenly, sitting up straight. "I don't see a warrant for my arrest or even one to look through my stuff, so it might be time for you guys to leave until you can lawfully take me in."

Elijah had played the trump card, the one most people didn't know they had in their hand in situations like this. Technically, he had the right to kick them out of his house at any moment if he wanted to, and they couldn't do a thing about it until they had a warrant issued for his arrest. Jim needed "probable cause" to arrest Elijah without one, and when push came to shove, the fact that Erin's dissertation was in the cabin just didn't quite cut it.

"Fair enough," Jim said, rising to his feet and nodding to the suitcase. "But you had better unpack that bag because we *will* be back with a warrant, and if I don't find you here, you're in for a world of hurt, you understand me?"

"Yes," Elijah said through gritted teeth as he walked quickly through the kitchen and opened the front door. A gust of icy air greeted the sheriff and deputy as they stepped back onto the porch. No sooner had Jim's foot cleared the threshold than the door slammed shut behind them.

"Well? What do you think?" Jeremy whispered as they stepped side by side down the snowy steps.

"Guilty as sin," Jim muttered.

29

Elijah was sweating. He gripped the edge of the kitchen counter with clammy hands and launched into the speech he'd rehearsed. Erin stood in the living room, staring blankly at him as he broke up with her.

"I just don't know if we're right for each other," he said. "We're so different. I don't want to waste your time. You deserve someone who wants to help you rebuild your life, and I'm just not in a place where I can do that right now."

Erin said nothing, only continued to stare at him vacantly, and Elijah found himself wishing she'd be angry instead of just . . . blank. He pulled a hand through his hair in frustration.

"Look, it's not that I don't like you, I mean, look at you." He gestured with his hand up and down her body. "You're beautiful and smart, any guy in town would be lucky to date you. I'm just not in the right headspace for a relationship right now." Did he just say *headspace*?

Erin made no move, no sound. Was she just going to stand there all afternoon? At some point he was going to have to ask her to leave. Even if she had blown up in a rage and thrown something at him, that would have been better than this. It was like breaking up with a mannequin.

"What do you want me to say?" He threw up his hands. "I tried. I really tried. I'm just not there yet. I'm just not over—"

Elijah broke off mid-sentence.

186

Erin blinked at him curiously. "Over who?" she asked calmly.

Elijah's face crumpled in defeat and he stared down at the counter. "No one."

She waited, and Elijah was sure the truth of it was written all over his face.

He sighed. "It's the girl I used to see. We dated back in high school, and then when I came back I found out her husband died and I . . . I just . . . still love her. I guess I always will."

Erin made a small humming sound as she nodded.

"It's fine. Honestly, it doesn't matter," she said, moving forward to lift her purse from the counter. "There's obviously no reason for us to continue dating. I'll see you around, okay?"

"I'm sorry," Elijah said, his voice breaking over the word. He *was* sorry. Not that they were breaking up, but that he had dated her in the first place. It was bound to end, though he hadn't quite expected it to end like this, pathetic on his end, detached and aloof on hers.

He opened his arms to offer her a parting hug, but she stepped around him and out the door, leaving it ajar as she marched down the porch steps. She unlocked her car and turned around, leveling a scathing look in his direction before she climbed inside.

Elijah watched the road until her taillights vanished around the corner. Somehow, the breakup had been a hundred times worse than he had expected, and now he was going to have to walk through the grocery store and down the sidewalks of town with the unpleasant potential of running into her and reliving the awkwardness.

Elijah stepped back into the cabin and closed the door. Well, it was done. He was free.

The afternoon slid by, and he spent the hours in the kitchen, canning jam. As he stood at the stove, stirring boiling blackberries with a wooden spoon, his mind was restless, busy formulating a plan and working out the details.

When the last jar was filled and sealed, he reached for the phone and dialed the number that would get him through to the big house in the hills of the reservation. It was late afternoon. Nakita would probably be painting in her studio, but with any luck, he'd get through to the person he wanted to talk to. Nakita's father answered on the second ring, and he didn't sound surprised to hear Elijah on the other end.

"I broke up with Leah," Elijah told him, "and I'm coming for Rachel, but I need your help."

Elijah laid out his plan, and Reverend Mills agreed readily.

"I'll see you in an hour," Elijah said before he hung up.

He changed his clothes and grabbed his keys. He needed a few supplies at the store, then he'd head out to the reservation to set up.

The sun was nearing the horizon when Elijah pulled his car off the dirt road and parked beside the flat, wide field that was blooming with sunflowers. He'd noticed it on his drive out to the church the other day. It was impossible to miss, a quilt of gorgeous, deep yellow flowers all pointed at the sky. It was the perfect place.

Elijah carried the folded blanket and picnic basket to a flat spot, then returned to the car for the easel and canvas he'd bought. He laid out the food and drinks carefully, then set up the canvas facing the sunset. Low, billowing clouds sat just above the sun, their underbellies kissed with crimson light. Perfect. He glanced at his watch. They'd be here any minute.

Elijah was a bundle of nerves as he stood watching the river. To give himself something to do, he picked a handful of sunflowers, then ran across the road to wait on the bank.

Around the bend where the water swirled gently by, Elijah heard the soft sound of female laughter and his heart flew into his throat. He stepped behind a tree so that he would be hidden when the canoe came around the corner. His pulse beating quickly, he gripped the flower stems tightly in his hand.

Soon, he heard the splashing of oars as father and daughter approached, and he stepped out from behind the tree. Nakita's back was turned but the reverend spotted Elijah and dug his oar into the water, slowing the canoe.

Nakita looked around, confused.

"Will you look at that?" her father said, pointing to Elijah. Nakita turned and her mouth fell open. Elijah held out the sunflowers as her father banked the canoe and climbed out.

"What are you doing here?" she asked, rising to her feet and snatching the flowers out of his hand.

"Working for Laban," he answered, and Reverend Mills laughed.

"Oh, so you're in cahoots now?" Nakita pointed an accusatory finger first at Elijah and then at her father.

"Who knew he'd happen to be out here with a picnic laid for two? Pure coincidence," her father said with twinkling eyes as he handed Elijah the bag full of paints and brushes that he'd asked for.

"'Let's go canoeing, Nakita,'" she said, mimicking her father, "'I feel like a quick ride down the river, wanna come along?' I should have *known* he'd put you up to something like this."

"Give the boy a second, second chance," Reverend Mills said, pushing the canoe back into the water and climbing inside.

"You're *leaving*?" she called as he rowed away.

"Elijah will give you a ride home," he called over his shoulder as he paddled off.

"I'll take you home right now if you really don't want to be here, but it would be a shame to miss that sunset. I wonder what colors we'll get tonight," Elijah said, nodding to the blank canvas behind him. Nakita watched her father's boat disappear around the next bend, then she peered over Elijah's shoulder at the picnic.

"You really can't take a hint, can you?" She pushed her shoulder lightly into his as she walked past him toward the sunflower field.

"Nope," Elijah said with a grin as he followed.

He sat on the blanket and watched her paint the sunset.

"This isn't a yes, you know," she said as she dipped her brush in pale gold paint and swirled it across the canvas.

"I know," Elijah said, and she turned to look over her shoulder at him.

"It's not a no, either." She smiled.

He smiled back.

When the sun dipped below the horizon, Nakita set down her brushes and joined him on the blanket.

"One second," Elijah said, jumping up. He retrieved the small electric lantern he'd packed in his trunk and set it in the center of the blanket. It cast a warm circle of light over their meal as dusk deepened into dark purple around them. He opened the box of fried chicken that was still warm and placed a few pieces on a paper plate for Nakita.

"Potato salad?" he asked, and she shook her head, picking up a drumstick to nibble at the skin. Elijah couldn't keep the smile from his face as they ate. Could it really have been only hours ago that he broke up with Erin? It seemed like weeks ago. Months. The silence between him and Nakita wasn't one that needed to be filled with idle talk. Silence between him and Erin swelled with awkwardness until Elijah felt it would burst like a balloon if he didn't deflate it with a question or statement. Silence with Nakita was the silence of the river flowing by, peaceful and content. Even when no words were spoken between them, there was a conversation happening.

Elijah handed Nakita a glass bottle of root beer, and without hesitation she pried the top off with her teeth.

Elijah threw his head back and laughed.

"You're one in a million, you know that?"

Nakita tipped the bottle back and took a long drink.

"How's the book coming?" she asked.

"It's not."

Nakita's eyebrows lifted. "You stopped?"

Elijah lifted an apple to his mouth and took a bite.

"My muse ran away."

Nakita took another drink and turned to look at the field of flowers whose heads were now drooping toward the ground. "We'll have to do something about that."

Warm hope stirred in his chest and Elijah moved a few inches toward her on the blanket. "I want to keep writing," he said honestly. "I just need to know that my characters will have a happy ending."

Nakita's eyes left the field of flowers and settled on his face.

"Why are you still here?" she asked, setting the half-empty bottle beside her. "Honestly, Elijah, why do you keep trying to make it work between us?"

Elijah stared at her. He could write an entire manuscript about the look she was giving him at this exact moment, and yet, sitting alone with her beside a field of sunflowers, he couldn't find the words to tell her why there would never be anyone else for him.

"I just . . . can't . . . leave you alone." His voice was choked, and he dropped his gaze to the blanket where Nakita was twirling a loose thread in her fingers. He slid his hand across the fabric and gently took hers.

"Just let me be here," he said, squeezing her fingers softly. "Let me be here for you. I don't expect us to get married tomorrow or even for you to be able to let go of Kailen completely. He's a part of you, a part of your past, and you'll probably carry that pain for the rest of your life. But that doesn't mean you can't *have* a life. It doesn't mean you can't ever be happy again."

Nakita blinked away the tears that were filling her eyes, and Elijah reached up to gently swipe away the one that had spilled over and traced a quick path down her cheek.

"I do love you," she said suddenly, and her words hit him with the force of a blow that knocked the air from his lungs.

"You do?" He searched her face in the dim light.

She nodded, but her eyes were sad.

"Then let me try to win you back. That's all I ask. Just give me time. If you let me lay a foundation one brick at a time, we can build a life together."

Nakita lifted her root beer and took another sip.

"You're a great writer, Elijah, but you'd be a terrible contractor. Foundations aren't made of bricks."

Elijah laughed heartily, a belly laugh that he hadn't enjoyed since the day she left him in the woods. He looked at Nakita and found her tucking her arms to her chest to ward off the goose bumps lifted by the cool night air.

"Come on," he said, rising and offering her a hand, "let's get you home."

"Sorry," she said as he pulled her to her feet. "I wish we could stay awhile, but I'm freezing."

"It's okay," he said, rubbing his hands up and down her arms. "This was more than enough."

30

It had taken a week, a full and tedious, nail-biting week, for Jim and Jeremy to obtain the warrant for Elijah's arrest. Tracking down a circuit judge who wasn't backed up with paperwork through the end of the month had been a battle in and of itself and had required not one but three separate trips to Seattle, but now, at long last, the warrant for Elijah Leith's arrest sat in the glove box of the cruiser and Jim was on his way back out to the cabin.

Jeremy wasn't with him. Another storm was rolling into town and the temperatures had plummeted into the single digits. Freezing rain had fallen in the predawn darkness and there had already been two car accidents in town. The first was a fender bender at a stop sign, minimal damage, when a small compact car slid into a truck, but the second was more serious, a sedan that caught black ice around a curve and nailed a fence, taking down several pickets and leaving the two passengers inside with whiplash from the hard stop. He'd left Jeremy to attend to the wreck and direct traffic, reminding him to write the citation afterward. That part never seemed fair in an accident like this one. Apart from a totaled car and physical injury, the driver would receive an additional fine in the mail for "Failure to Avoid Collision." As if he wouldn't have preferred to avoid it. But that was the law, and at least Jeremy had to take the heat this time. Jim was eager to get out to the Leith cabin while it was still early, before Elijah had a chance to leave for the day, even if that meant facing the younger, stronger man alone.

Over the tops of the trees, dark gray clouds were rolling in fast and the wind was whipping the firs that lined the road back and forth in a wild dance. Jim drove as quickly as he dared. The closer he got to the Leith cabin, the more his gut tightened around the hunch that Elijah would not be there. Tiny flakes began to hit his windshield, and he flipped the wipers on as he rounded the final curve before his destination.

Up ahead, the cabin came into view with dark windows and a smoke-less chimney. Jim slammed his palms into the steering wheel and swore loudly. There was no blue Camaro parked out front. Elijah was gone.

He yanked the wheel to the right and peeled into the driveway, kicking up gravel in a wide arc behind him. Jim unbuckled and jumped out of the cruiser, leaving the door open as he ran up the porch steps.

"Elijah!" he shouted, banging on the door. "You better open this door if you're in there!"

There was no sound from within. Jim pressed his ear to the wooden door but couldn't hear anything over the sound of the wind howling through the forest around him. He threw his fist against the door one more time.

"Elijah!" he shouted at the top of his lungs.

Jim took two steps back and braced himself. It had been a long time since he had taken a door down, but he still remembered how. He kicked hard, and his boot caught the wood just below the doorknob. The door gave a groan of protest, but it didn't open. Jim kicked it again, but it held firm. Flooded with adrenaline and frustration, Jim kicked it a third time, but it still didn't budge. Jim scanned the front of the cabin. There were two windows; he could shatter the glass and crawl in. Jim stepped forward, realizing he hadn't even tried the doorknob. To his surprise, it turned easily and the door popped open, Elijah had left it unlocked.

The kitchen was cold and dark. Jim flipped the light on and glanced around. The suitcase that had been propped beside the couch during his last visit here was gone. Elijah had made a run for it. Jim swore again as he left the cabin and ran back to the cruiser.

He slid into the driver's seat and reached for the glove box. Beneath the warrant was Erin's diary. He flipped it open, scanning the entries as quickly as he could until he found what he was looking for.

> *All I did was ask him about the rumor I heard about him and some local girl and he lost it. We were in his living room dancing to some of his parents' old records when I brought it up. I probably shouldn't have, but I couldn't help it, because I know exactly who the girl is. Nakita Mills.*

Nakita was a Squalomah name. If Elijah was with her, he was somewhere on the reservation. Jim flipped on the lights and pulled out onto the road. The snow was coming harder now, and he didn't have time to waste. He flew around the curves, the wind hissing through the cracks between the windows and doors as though trying to find a way into the car.

"Come on, come on, come on," he muttered, applying the brake as a car pulled out of a driveway ahead of him. He turned the siren on for a moment, and the car pulled to the shoulder, letting Jim whiz past. He bumped over the border and onto the dirt road of the reservation. The constant winter cycle of freeze and thaw had done a number on the road, and it was littered with potholes that Jim bounced through too quickly, scraping the bottom of the cruiser. He looked left and right at the houses that rose up along the road. At the first one that had light behind its windows, he stopped and jumped out.

He ran to the door and rapped three times. A young Squalomah woman with a baby bundled to her chest answered his knock. There was fear in her eyes, and Jim realized what he must look like, a crazed policeman with cruiser lights blaring behind him, standing unexpectedly at her door in the middle of a storm.

"I'm sorry to startle you, ma'am," Jim apologized. "I'm looking for the house where Nakita Mills lives. Can you tell me how to get there?"

The young woman's baby started to cry, and she bounced it gently in the wrap as she thought.

"My husband went to see Reverend Mills once. He'll know where it is."

The young woman retreated into the house, closing the door behind her. Jim waited on the stoop, his arms folded tightly across his chest as the wind continued to blow in over the mountains. Though it was approaching midmorning, the sky grew darker as charcoal clouds, pregnant with snow, rolled across the heavens like a scroll.

After a long minute, a young man opened the door halfway and gave Jim brief directions, pointing toward the mountain and telling him to take a left where the dirt road hit a T. From there he would follow the road that was cut into the lower ridge until he reached a house that looked like a ski lodge. Jim thanked him and climbed back into the cruiser.

He drove deeper into the reservation than he'd been in a long time. He'd been out to the mountains before, but it was a few years back. A hunting accident. As he drove, Jim snatched the diary up from the passenger seat and read the name again. *Nakita Mills*. Of course! Now he knew why the name had sounded familiar when Jeremy first read it. He'd already been to her house, just once, to deliver the news of her husband's death.

He remembered now, arriving at the trailhead to find the frantic young man hunched over the body of his friend, tears streaming down his face. He remembered calling for the ambulance. He remembered how slowly he'd driven this exact stretch of road in the dark of night, dreading what lay ahead. He had turned left at the T and followed the rolling hills right up to the house that stood like a beacon, ablaze, every light on though it was nearly midnight. There was a woman inside, pacing and wringing her hands, wondering where her husband was. Jim swallowed dryly at the recollection of walking up to the door and knocking. It had flown open in seconds, and he had watched the relief on the beautiful young widow's face fade into glassy-eyed horror as he bowed his head and told her the news. He might have forgotten her name, but he would never forget the look on her face as her future fell out from under her. The only solace Jim had felt that night as he climbed into bed in the early-morning hours was that she was young and strong and might find a way to start over with someone new. And now it seemed that she had found someone, a man on the run with a warrant out for his arrest.

Jim reached the T and turned left. The cruiser climbed with the road, ever nearer the mountains as the tiny snowflakes continued to fall in gusting swirls. The world outside his car grew even darker as the road angled east and the shadow of the mountain fell across it. Higher and higher he climbed, passing houses that grew in stature until he came upon the one he was looking for. And there, parked beside three other cars, was the blue Camaro.

Jim switched off the lights and eased the car to a stop beside Elijah's. He snatched the warrant and climbed out of the cruiser, reaching down to make sure his handcuffs were at the ready on his belt.

The house's many windows mirrored the rolling clouds that scraped over the mountain ridge, giving nothing away as Jim stepped up to the door and knocked. He heard footsteps coming down stairs and took a step back, bracing himself. Nakita answered the door and stood facing the sheriff. In her eyes he saw the flash of recognition, then the fear of what his presence meant this time around.

"I'm not sure if you remember me, ma'am—"

"I'll never forget your face as long as I live," she interrupted.

Jim nodded tersely. "I'm here for Elijah."

"I know."

"Then you'd better step aside and let me do my job."

For a moment, she looked like she might slam the door in his face, but to Jim's surprise she opened it wide and moved back for him to enter.

He followed her down the hall and into the kitchen, where Elijah sat at the counter with an older Squalomah man who must have been Nakita's father, their heads bent in conversation.

"Elijah," Nakita said, and something in her voice made his head snap to attention. His eyes traveled past where she stood and landed directly on Jim, who took two steps forward into the kitchen.

"Elijah," he said, holding out the warrant, "you're under arrest for the murder of Erin Landry."

Not one of them looked surprised.

Elijah rose slowly to his feet.

"You've got the wrong guy, Sheriff."

"Funny, the warrant has your name on it," Jim said with no trace of humor.

"Just listen to me. We heard her husband was in town, we think—"

"I don't care what you think, you're under arrest."

"Will you just listen—"

"Manny flew out on the thirty-first," Jim cut him off again, "three days before she died. We called the airport and checked. Now, I'm going to tell you this just one more time. You're under arrest, let's go."

"You remember what I said," Nakita's father murmured quietly, and Elijah nodded, his eyes on the warrant. He crossed the kitchen and stopped right in front of Jim, bringing them face-to-face.

In his eyes, Jim found the desperation and anger that he expected to be there, but there was something else, too, something that made the sheriff pause for a moment as he pulled the handcuffs from his belt. It was the look he might expect from an innocent sheep the moment before its throat was slit. It was sincerity, a belief that truth would win out in the end and everything would be resolved. For the first time since reading Erin's diary, Jim wondered if he had the right guy.

Pushing the doubt from his mind, he stepped behind Elijah and handcuffed his wrists. The kitchen was dead silent except for the metal-lic clicks as the cuffs slid into their locks.

"Let's go," Jim said.

Nakita and her father followed them down the hall without speak-ing, and when Jim glanced over his shoulder, he found silent tears run-ning down Nakita's face, her father's arm around her shoulders.

"Stay put," he said to father and daughter, leaving them in the light of the doorway as he steered Elijah out into the storm. The wind was raging now, and Jim flinched at the sound of a fir bough crashing to the ground somewhere in the woods. He opened the back door of the cruiser and spun Elijah around so that he faced the house.

"I love you!" Elijah shouted suddenly over Jim's shoulder at Nakita as the sheriff pushed him down into the cruiser. "I love you, Na—"

Jim slammed the door and Elijah's voice was cut off. He avoided looking at the father and daughter who stood in the doorway of the massive house as he started the cruiser and pulled away. It would be the second time he had left that woman crying on her doorstep.

31

Elijah propped the trunk of the Camaro open and pulled out the two folding chairs inside. He placed them side by side in front of Begay's Grounds and took a seat, balancing the huge bowl of candy he'd brought on his knees. The sidewalk to his left and right was filled with adults setting up chairs, while kids ran around in costumes, but there was no sign of Nakita.

Two twin boys dressed as Thing One and Thing Two darted behind Elijah's chair, and Thing Two's plastic candy basket whacked the Camaro's bumper.

"Watch the car!" Elijah chided.

"You're starting to sound like a grumpy old man."

Elijah turned to find Nakita taking a seat in the second folding chair.

"Sorry I'm late," she said, grinning at Elijah as she took his hand. "I was completely lost in a painting and I looked up at the clock. I thought I'd been in there for forty-five minutes, but three hours had gone by and it was starting to get dark out."

Elijah nodded. "I get that. Sometimes, writing is like being in a trance, and you suddenly stop and look up, surprised that you're sitting in your own house and not actually living in the world of the story."

Nakita laughed. "Jarring, isn't it . . ."

"It really is, especially when you realize that the world you've been living in for the last several hours isn't even a real place."

Nakita gave him a long appraising look.

"I promised myself I wasn't going to ask until you said something about it, but are you writing again?"

"A little bit here and there. It's tough to pick the story back up after so much time off, but I'm giving myself time in the chair to see if the words come."

"They will," she said confidently. "And if you need extra motivation, just think how horrible it would be to die mid-manuscript. You wouldn't want me to have to finish writing it for you, trust me."

"You can be kinda dark, you know that?" Elijah said, laughing.

Nakita smiled and looked around. "I haven't been in town for Halloween in years. My mom and dad used to take me here to trick-or-treat when I was little. One year, I think I was about ten, I had my dad wrap me entirely in tinfoil for a costume. I could barely walk from house to house."

"What were you supposed to be?"

Nakita laughed. "A baked potato."

Elijah snorted.

"I've never actually seen the parade though," she said.

"It's great, I remember walking in it when I was a kid." Elijah chuckled at the memory. "It's sort of a reverse parade, all the kids dress up and walk down the street with their trick-or-treat bags, and the parents on the sidelines throw candy to them."

Nakita held her hands out and Elijah dumped several pieces of candy into her palms. She opened a Kit Kat and popped it into her mouth. A handful of volunteers in reflective vests were trying to corral the children at the end of the street and failing miserably. Tiny monsters, witches, and pumpkins were darting in and out between them as they shouted vainly and waved their arms.

"What they need is a firehose," Nakita said seriously. "Blast those kids into line."

"You're going to be a swell mother someday," Elijah said, only half-kidding.

From the end of the street, someone hit the button on a boom box, and "Monster Mash" began to play. In a wave, the children rushed forward. Elijah and Nakita stood and tossed candy onto the pavement, laughing when it was scooped up by tiny, quick fingers. Elijah handed the bowl to Nakita and wrapped his arm around her shoulders as she threw handfuls of candy into the street. It was the little moments, the ordinary moments, moments like these, that made their relationship special, and he savored the sound of her joyful laugh as she threw the last of the candy to the toddlers in the back.

Through the wave of kids, Elijah felt eyes on him from the other side of the street and looked up to find Erin there, staring at him with narrowed eyes.

Elijah's arm fell from around Nakita's shoulders and he looked away.

"Ready?" he asked, turning to fold up his chair.

"Ready?" Nakita laughed. "What do you mean, ready? I just got here."

In his peripheral vision, Elijah could see Erin crossing the street, headed their way. *No!*

"I mean, you know, the earlier you leave, the less traffic you have to fight on the way out, want me to fold up your chair for you?" He knew he was talking far too quickly, but he couldn't stop. He couldn't avoid what was about to happen.

"Elijah, what's going on?" Nakita asked.

Too late.

"Long time no see," Erin said, stepping between them and facing Elijah with a bright smile.

Over Erin's shoulder, Elijah watched Nakita's back stiffen as she recognized the doctor.

"Having fun?" Erin asked, her voice high and saccharine.

"Yep," Elijah muttered. "We were just leaving, actually."

"Oh, that's too bad, I was hoping you'd introduce me to your new girlfriend, but wait," she turned to meet Nakita's seething gaze, "we've already met, haven't we?"

Elijah's hold on the situation was slipping through his fingers like sand, but there was nothing he could do to stop it.

"Nakita, right?" Erin asked. "Nakita Mills? That makes sense, I should have known Elijah would throw me over for the girl whose initials were carved in that tree."

A shadow of confusion crossed Nakita's face as her eyes flicked from Erin to Elijah then back to Erin.

"What are you talking about?"

"Oh." Erin's eyebrows lifted. "Didn't Elijah tell you? We dated for a while this summer."

Nakita laughed as though Erin had told a ridiculous joke and turned to Elijah, waiting for him to dispute her words. Elijah felt like he might throw up. He couldn't look at her. He couldn't look at either of them. He stared down at the sidewalk, hot with shame.

Erin spoke slowly, deliberately. "I'm sorry, I assumed you knew."

The damage was done. The wedge she had driven between them could not be removed, and as though she knew it, Erin shrugged her shoulders and walked into the street with a casual spring in her step, disappearing into the crowd.

When Elijah looked up, Nakita's eyes were cold. She stayed just long enough for him to see the pain he had caused before turning and fleeing through the stream of people on the sidewalk.

"Wait!" he shouted, running after her, but she was already around the corner of the next building.

Elijah dodged parents and small children as he followed her, ducking off the main road and onto a darkened side street where her silver sedan was parked.

Nakita had the door open when Elijah gripped her shoulder and turned her to face him.

"Nakita, stop! Will you just let me explain?"

"*Her?!*" Nakita yelled, slamming the door. "Of all people, Elijah, you chose the one person I can't stand in Point Orchards to date after we broke up. I *hate* that woman, and you knew that. What's wrong with you?!"

There were at least a dozen people within earshot, but Elijah no longer cared what anyone thought except the woman who stood before him.

"You broke my heart!" he shouted. "You broke it, Nakita. *I* was broken. And yes, Erin asked me out and we had a few dates, but that's it, I swear to you. There was nothing real between us, nothing! We didn't have a single thing in common. I knew it wouldn't work when I took her out to the lake and saw her standing next to our tree. It was just so wrong seeing her there. I knew then that you were the only woman I could ever commit to. Can't you understand that?"

"You took her to our lake?" Nakita's voice was small.

"I—We—We went out there once. But we were never serious about each other. Honest to God. She's just . . . I don't know if it's because of what happened to her kid or what, but she's still just kind of emotionally frozen."

Nakita's mouth was hard, her brow lined with the pain of his betrayal.

"Why didn't you tell me?"

"Because I didn't want *this* to happen, for you to find out and leave again. I swear to you, Nakita, if I could take it back, I would. I just thought you were done with me and I was depressed and lonely, okay? I missed you and . . . and . . . Erin was, well she was just there."

For one horrifying moment, Elijah thought he might break down and cry right in the middle of the street, drop to his knees and beg her to stay as children in ridiculous Halloween costumes peered at the spectacle. Instead, he reached for Nakita and gathered her into his arms, holding her tenderly even as her body stayed rigid with protest.

"Please, don't leave me again," he pleaded into her hair. "I'm not strong enough."

Her body softened as the air left her lungs in a long sigh.

"I'm not leaving," she said quietly. "I've made my choice and we're in this together, through thick and thin."

He could have cried again, this time out of pure relief.

"I'm so sorry," he whispered. "You have no idea how sorry. I should have told you."

"Yes, you should have. Is there anything else you're not telling me?"

"No." Elijah pulled away to meet her eyes in the darkened street. He shook his head vehemently. "Nothing. I'll never hide anything from you again, I promise."

Nakita nodded.

"Elijah." She took his hands. "I don't want you to ever see Erin again."

"Point Orchards is a tiny town, I'm bound to run into her now and then."

"I understand that," Nakita said with a nod, "but you need to understand that I hold that woman responsible for the death of someone I loved. I know it's wrong for me to hate her and I'll try to get past that, but I'm nowhere close to forgiving her for what she did. Seeing her tonight, the way she just stood there rubbing in the fact that you two dated, I—I could have killed her."

"Hey," Elijah said, tipping her chin with his finger, "I won't ever be alone with her again, okay? You have no reason to worry. I'm yours, Nakita."

"Promise me."

"I promise."

Nakita leaned forward and kissed him on the mouth. Elijah pulled her close, wrapping her tightly in his arms.

"I'm yours," he said again. "Only yours."

He let her go reluctantly, and Nakita climbed into her sedan and pulled away, leaving Elijah standing alone in the middle of the street. Slowly, the world around him came back into focus. Children riding the wave of Halloween sugar were still hollering in the streets, and behind the buildings, the boom box set up for the parade was playing Michael Jackson's *Thriller*. A group of giggling teenagers ran past with rolls of toilet paper in their hands. Elijah blew out a long breath and walked slowly back to Main Street. Up until a few minutes ago he had felt sorry for Erin Landry, but after tonight Nakita would not be the only person in town who hated her. The promise he had just made would be an easy one to keep.

32

The computer blinked brightly to life, and Elijah placed his mug of coffee next to it with a contented sigh. He slid into his chair and cracked his knuckles. It was four-thirty in the morning. It was time to write. He'd fed three small logs into the woodstove while his coffee was brewing, and the kitchen grew warm and fragrant as he typed.

When he had first arrived back at the cabin and discovered that the well wasn't working, Elijah had turned on the taps to find rusty spurts of water. Undrinkable. He'd hired a handyman to fix the electric pump, and the man advised him to let the faucets run for a while afterward to flush out the rust and gunk until the water ran clear.

Writing was like that. If he let an unfinished manuscript sit for too long, he came back to it stale, typing out rusty, unusable paragraphs in forced and choppy blocks. But as he kept at it, continuing to write day after day, the pump came slowly back to life and the story flowed clear from his fingers once again. November had seen a little progress in the form of two chapters, but now, with December only half-gone, he had already added another twenty thousand words to the manuscript this month alone.

For the next ninety minutes, the kitchen was filled with the uninterrupted sound of clacking keys. There was a lot of good, hard work that went into writing a book, but this time around, Elijah was discovering that there was magic to it as well. Before he'd started drafting *Middletide*, he'd plotted the book extensively until he knew exactly how long each chapter was going to be, which arc each character would follow, and where each scene would land. This time around, he let his words run unrestrained across the page, often shocked at the twists and turns that presented themselves as he wrote. It was like he wasn't writing the book at all, but rather reading it as it emerged from somewhere in his brain he didn't quite have conscious access to.

Houdini crowed outside, breaking through the sound of click-clacking in the kitchen, and Elijah glanced up, surprised to find daylight pouring in through the windows. He turned to the woodstove and found nothing but glowing embers remaining. How long had he been writing? Elijah did a double take at the clock. Four hours had passed since he sat down with his coffee and it was well past time for his morning chores.

The kitchen window was frosted at the corners and the world outside was sugar-coated with frozen dew. Elijah stood and stretched, intending to retrieve his flannel coat from his closet, but on his way down the hall, he stopped short and turned, facing the closed door of his parents' bedroom. His breath was shallow as he reached for the knob and pushed the door open. He hadn't realized he was ready, but a force was driving him inside, telling him it was time.

Elijah stepped tenderly over the wood floor as though a creak might disturb some long-dormant spirit within. Standing in the middle of the room, he turned in a slow circle. He looked at everything and let the memories hit him. His mother's dresser sat in the corner, a beautiful porcelain pitcher and wash basin on top. It was one of her treasures, though he'd never once seen her use it to wash her face. Beside the dresser was the bed with its two nightstands, his father's stacked with books, his mother's empty except for the clock that blinked a red 12:00. Undoubtedly the time had stopped when the electric company cut the power after his dad died. On the wall above the bed hung a landscape painting of a stormy sea, steely blue waves crashing into rocks between which was a wind-blown ship, tipping precariously to the starboard side. Elijah stared at the painting. He had been fascinated by it as a child, climbing on his parents' bed to look at it with his nose nearly touching the canvas, imagining himself as the captain of that ship, rain-soaked behind the wheel, searching for the harbor light as his vessel was battered by the waves.

Elijah walked to the closet. Inside, the piggy bank shaped like a gorilla with a slot for coins on the crown of its head sat crouched in the corner beside a row of his mother's shoes. At eye level, a dozen of her dresses hung straight and limp on their hangers. He could stand here for hours, pulling each dress down and touching the fabric, remembering the feel of it as he was embraced by his mother's warm arms. There was an entire childhood's worth of memories in those dresses, and Elijah ran his hand across them with a lump in his throat.

At the back of the closet, he found what he was looking for lying in a heap on the floor where his father had tossed it. It was a jacket, light denim on the outside, silver buttons down the front, and lined with sheep's wool on the inside. He lifted it and held it to his nose. Whenever he pictured his dad, it was always in this jacket. It was the all-purpose garment his father had worn into town, around the property for chores, even to cross-country meets late in the fall when the air was cold. Elijah could remember sprinting toward various finishing chutes, his eyes scanning the crowd of spectators for this very jacket, for the look of approval or disappointment in the eyes of the man who wore it, depending on how well the race was going.

Elijah slid his arms into the sleeves, surprised to find that the jacket fit him perfectly. He had imagined that it would fall past his wrists, like he was still a boy trying to fit into his father's clothes. He turned to the mirror that hung on the closet door, and for a moment, he saw his father staring back at him.

He had the same beard and the same build. Like his father, Elijah's square shoulders fell away to narrow hips, and his straight posture seemed always braced for a punch, but from the nose up, he was his mother's son. Her dark hair and bright eyes would live on in him until age stole their luster.

What would his dad make of him now? Would he be proud that Elijah had managed to survive here alone? Disappointed that he hadn't

become the writer he claimed he would be? Would he finally acknowledge that the man in the mirror was in fact a man and no longer a boy?
Though he couldn't pinpoint when, Elijah had, somewhere along the
road, undeniably made it to manhood.

As he left the closet, his eye snagged on something familiar in
the stack of books on his father's nightstand. There, among the thin,
cream-colored Louis L'Amour books, was a spine that he recognized.
Elijah moved the top two books to the side, and there it was, right in
the middle of the stack. His father had bought a copy of his book. Elijah
stared down at the cover. From his throat came a sound that was half
laugh, half sob. He hadn't bothered to send a copy of *Middletide* to his
dad. When he'd called home to announce that he'd finished writing it,
his dad had made a comment, asking if Elijah had finally "gotten this
writing thing out of his system." When Elijah had fired back with some
defensive retort, his dad had backpedaled, saying he wasn't trying to be
unsupportive, he just wanted to see Elijah with a consistent income that
could put food on the table for a family someday. After that phone call,
Elijah had never mentioned his book to his dad again. Never thought
the old man would bother reading it. And yet, here it was.

Elijah left the book and walked out of the bedroom in his father's
jacket, leaving the door cracked behind him to bookmark the accomplishment of venturing inside.

In the backyard, the morning sun was pastel. Houdini and the
hens were ruffled balls in their nests, feathers fluffed in the cold. Elijah
coaxed them out with feed and pulled seven warm eggs from the coop.
He would need to keep the fire going all day for warmth, so he gathered
an armful of logs and laid them on the back porch.

Back inside, fire blazing in the woodstove, Elijah whisked four eggs
in a bowl and poured them into a pan. As his breakfast cooked, he sat
at the computer, reading what he'd written that morning and picking
right back up where he left off.

He ate his eggs without tasting them. The sprint to the finish line
was becoming feverish, and he stayed where he was at the kitchen table,
only leaving his work to stoke the fire when the warmth began to ebb.
The word count on the bottom of the page ticked past eighty thousand

and he kept going, the climax of the story unfolding page after page. A knock on the front door broke him out of his trance and he rose to find Nakita on the porch.

"You're early," he said and smiled, letting her in.

"No, I'm not."

Elijah glanced at the clock in the kitchen. It was three in the afternoon. He felt like he had checked the time not half an hour before and it had been eleven in the morning. Another four hours of writing had gone by and he'd fallen into the time warp of storytelling.

Nakita was eyeing him curiously.

"You've been writing," she observed.

"How can you tell?"

"You have that glassy-eyed stare like you just woke up. That's how you always look after a good session at the computer."

"You don't miss a thing," he noted. "I've been writing all day. Actually, I didn't realize until right this minute that I'm starving."

"Sit down, let me make you something."

Elijah sat back at the table, intending to give his eyes a break from the screen, but his fingers crept toward the keyboard, and before he could stop himself, he was typing again, immersed in the story as Nakita put bacon and lettuce sandwiches together in the kitchen.

She sat and handed him his plate, peeping over his shoulder at the page.

"Thanks," he said gratefully, taking a bite.

"This bread looks homemade," she commented.

Elijah swallowed. "Is that a good thing or a bad thing?"

Nakita laughed. "Good thing. Did you make it?"

Elijah nodded. "I'm still learning. Yeast is no joke, but every loaf has been a little better than the last one."

"Full of surprises," Nakita said affectionately. "So, how's the book coming?"

"Pretty good," he mumbled with his mouth full. "I might actually finish this thing today. I'm pretty close."

"Are you serious?" She looked elated.

Elijah nodded. "I'll print it as soon as I'm finished and get it to you, but be honest about it. I alternate back and forth between thinking it's genius and thinking it's garbage. Maybe you can decide."

"You know I'll give you my real opinion," she promised. "But right now, I'm just glad you did it."

Elijah finished his sandwich and Nakita handed him the second half of hers.

"Here." She laughed. "You need it more than I do."

Elijah took it gratefully, and Nakita carried their plates to the sink.

"I'll leave you to it," she said.

"You don't have to go."

Nakita offered him a knowing smile. "Right now, that manuscript is your girlfriend. And rightfully so. At some point I'd like to know what it's about, though."

Elijah gave her a long look that was half-wary, half-eager.

"It's about whether or not you can ever truly come home."

"And?" she pressed.

"I guess you'll have to read it to find out."

Nakita walked over to run her fingers gently through his hair before she turned to leave, stepping outside and closing the door quietly behind her. Elijah placed his fingers back on the keyboard, grateful for a full belly and a woman who was understanding of his passion.

He sat at the kitchen table as darkness fell outside, his body still, his fingers flying across the keys. Dinnertime came and went, and the fire died in the hearth. As the clock announced the beginning of a brand-new day, Elijah typed the most beautiful two words in the English language: The End.

It was finished. As soon as the library opened, he would print it out and deliver it to Nakita's house.

Elijah slid the keyboard to the side, placed his arms on the table, and lowered his head onto them. Exhausted, he fell asleep where he sat.

33

Elijah lay on his back on the stiff canvas cot. His cell was dark. The single fluorescent light on the ceiling buzzed so loudly that he had asked the deputy to shut it off. There wasn't much to look at anyway; the cell was all squared angles, everything over-straight and blocky. Square room, square sink, rectangle cot, rectangle mirror, straight bars, straight fluorescent bulb. The only thing in the room that had any curvature at all was the stainless-steel toilet that protruded from the wall beside the sink.

The Point Orchards Jail wasn't much of a jail at all, just an extension off the back of the police station. Down a long hallway with a sharp right turn cutting it off from sight, the room opened up and split into two cells. The other cell was vacant, and Elijah found himself lonelier than he'd ever been in his life. A man could be forgotten back here.

He rolled onto his side and pulled the thin blanket up around his shoulders. He had barely slept since his arrest, and when he did, his dreams were feverish and patchy. Whenever he managed to slip into sleep, he saw Erin's lifeless body swinging from a frozen rope, her glassy eyes fixed on his. Over and over, the image threw him back into consciousness while outside, the storm continued to rage. Wind rattled the tiny window at the top of his cell, howling against it like a mournful dog.

It was eerie, all alone behind the station, and Elijah found himself tossing and turning as he struggled with the question every occupant of this room must have asked themselves at one point or another. How did it come to this?

Footsteps approached down the hall, and Elijah sat up as the deputy appeared around the corner. Elijah squeezed his eyes shut, willing Jeremy to bring him good news. There was a set of keys in his hand, and Elijah jumped to his feet as the deputy stuck them in the lock.

"Bail's been posted," he said. "Let's go."

Jeremy held Elijah by the arm and led him down the hall toward the station as Elijah flooded him with questions.

"How? I don't understand. Who paid it?"

Jeremy didn't answer, but led him into the sheriff's office, where Jim Godbout stood behind his desk, looking worn down and frazzled.

"Seems you've had a stroke of good fortune, son," the sheriff said, stepping around his desk. "Samuel Mills and his daughter have posted the fifty thousand for you."

Elijah didn't know how to feel. On the one hand, he was sick to his stomach at the thought of how much money Nakita's family had just paid for his freedom, but on the other, he was desperate to be out of that godforsaken cell.

"So, you mean I can just go? I'm free to leave?"

"Not exactly," the sheriff said, holding up a black cuff with a blinking red light on the side. "You'll be wearing this until your trial. It's an ankle monitor. You step more than two hundred and fifty feet outside of your house and you land yourself right back here. You understand?"

Elijah nodded.

The sheriff had him put a leg up on the chair and slipped the cuff over his ankle. It snapped shut with a loud click and Elijah flinched. He put his leg back on the floor and Jim took a step closer, bringing them eye to eye.

"I mean it, Elijah," he said quietly. "You set one foot outside the boundary and I'll throw you back in that cell and not lose one second of sleep over it."

The sheriff cuffed Elijah's hands behind his back and led him into the lobby, where Nakita sat on the bench beside the front door. Her eyes were rimmed in red. When she caught sight of Elijah, she rose to her feet and attempted a smile.

Elijah couldn't tear his eyes away from her; even as he was led to the front desk and his paperwork was processed, he kept his eyes locked on Nakita's.

The sheriff and deputy each took an arm as they led Elijah past Nakita and through the front doors. It was dark out, and Elijah wasn't sure if it was early morning or late afternoon. This time of year, the daylight hours were short, and his time in the cell had left him with no idea how much time had passed.

When they reached the cruiser, Jeremy put a hand on top of his head and pushed him into the back seat. As the door closed, Elijah searched the parking lot for Nakita's silver sedan and watched her duck inside, flipping her headlights on as she waited to follow him home.

The sheriff and deputy climbed inside the car and started it up. The radio came to life, playing soft, classical music, and Elijah almost laughed. What a contrast. Here he was, being driven home to await his trial for murder while a chipper Vivaldi piece played over the radio and the sheriff drummed his fingers in time on the steering wheel. Elijah was in the darkest, most desperate trouble of his life, but it was just another day on the job for the two men in the front seats.

The cruiser drove slowly through Point Orchards, and Elijah marveled at just how much snow had fallen while he was in jail. The entire town was coated in a thick blanket of white, pretty as a gingerbread village, and down at the marina, the boats were floating in a sea of broken ice.

The open vents on the dashboard filled the car with warm air, and Elijah leaned his head against the window, allowing his eyes to fall shut. He was dead tired.

The next thing he heard was the slamming of a car door and he woke with a start as the sheriff stepped around to open the back door. He was home.

Elijah stood still in the driveway while Jim unlocked his cuffs. The sheriff turned Elijah to face him.

"Two hundred and fifty feet," he repeated.

Elijah nodded.

The cruiser backed out of the driveway just as Nakita pulled in. She jumped out of the car and ran to him, wrapping her arms around his waist.

"It's freezing," he said, "let's go in."

The cabin was so cold inside that Elijah could see his breath. He started a fire and knelt close to the woodstove, holding his hands out for warmth.

"The chickens!" He remembered.

"They're fine," Nakita said. "I ran an extension cord out to the heat lamp. I've been driving down to feed them."

Elijah stood and embraced her again.

"I don't know what I'd do without you." He pulled back to meet her eyes. "I have some money left from the garage. I can pay you back for bail."

Nakita shook her head. "You might need that for a lawyer or something."

She was right. Somehow, being back in his cabin for a few minutes had tricked him into forgetting that he was still in the middle of this mess, and the worst was yet to come.

"Why don't you get some rest," she suggested. "I'll make some food and you can eat when you wake up."

"I'll rest on the couch out here," he said. "I don't want to be alone."

Nakita nodded and led him by the hand to the couch. Elijah lay down, and she tucked a blanket around him as tenderly as his mother used to do. For a few minutes, as she moved around the kitchen, Elijah watched her, comforted by the sounds of pots and pans and the chopping of vegetables. When his eyes were too heavy to keep open, he let them fall shut and drifted to sleep.

The rich smell of stew greeted him before he opened his eyes, and Elijah sat up to find a steaming bowl in front of him on the coffee table. Nakita was watching him from his father's recliner, an empty bowl in her lap.

"How long was I out?"

"Couple of hours."

Elijah took a spoonful of stew. It was delicious, a hearty broth full of tender vegetables and meat that melted in his mouth. He wasn't sure where the meat had come from.

"Venison," she answered his unasked question. "I thawed some from the freezer."

Elijah ate ravenously, certain he'd lost a few pounds during his stay in the cell. When he was finished, Nakita carried his bowl to the sink. She washed the dishes, glancing over her shoulder when he came to stand behind her.

They needed to talk about it. There was so much to say, but he had no idea where to start.

"I didn't do it, Nakita."

"Elijah," she turned around to face him. "I know you didn't. You don't have to prove your innocence to me."

"I'm going to have to prove it to a whole courtroom full of people."

"We'll get you a lawyer. Leave that to me. I've already been looking. There's no one in Point Orchards, but there are plenty in Seattle. We'll find you the best there is."

"Nakita," Elijah stared into her eyes, "I'm going to need you. Whoever did this, they read my book and they're using it to frame me. I don't know how many people in Point Orchards know about *Middletide*; maybe Dad spread it around town that I'd written a mystery novel. But someone knew about it and saw the opportunity to kill Erin and have me take the fall for it. I just keep thinking that they must've messed up somewhere. There's got to be some evidence, something I can use to prove I'm not guilty, but I can't even leave the cabin to try to figure it out."

"I'll be your eyes," Nakita promised. Her hands were warm and wet from the dishes as she took his. "Whatever you need me to do, just tell me."

Elijah pulled her close and held her for a long minute in the quiet kitchen.

"I'm going to find a way out of this mess," he whispered into her hair. "I won't let anyone take away our second chance."

34

In the log house at the base of the mountains, the phone rang. Nakita raced down the stairs to answer it, but her father beat her there.

"For you," he said, handing her the receiver as she ran into the kitchen.

"Hello?" she answered breathlessly.

"Nakita Mills?"

"Yes, this is Nakita."

"This is Cindy Gresham at Madison House Publishing in Seattle. Do you have a minute to talk about the manuscript you submitted?"

Nakita gripped the phone with tight fingers, her heart leaping in her chest. "Yes."

"I'll cut right to the chase, Ms. Mills. We loved it and we'd like to publish it."

Nakita threw a silent fist pump in the kitchen, her smile so wide it hurt.

"That's so wonderful to hear," she burst out, and her father's head popped around the corner curiously. Nakita turned to him, her eyes dancing with joy as she mimed reading a book with her hands and pointed to the receiver where Cindy was delivering more good news.

"We're hoping to contract Elijah for a two-book deal; there's strong material for a sequel and we'd like to support him as he pursues that."

"That's unbelievable, I can't wait to tell him!"

"We'd love to meet with him and have him sign the contract at his earliest convenience. Can he make it down to Seattle sometime next week?"

"I'm sure he can. I'll get back to you."

Nakita hung up the phone and danced her way across the kitchen to give her father a hug.

"That was the publishing house I sent his book to," she explained. "They're going to publish it!"

"Have you told Elijah that you sent it in?"

"Of course not! He'll be shocked."

"Give him a call."

"Actually," Nakita spun toward the phone, "I've got a better idea. I need to call Cindy back."

"Ready?"

Nakita slammed the trunk of the sedan and climbed into the driver's seat beside Elijah, who was buckling his seatbelt.

"I still don't know why we need to go all the way to the city," Elijah said. "There are plenty of lunch places around here."

"It's not the destination, it's the journey," Nakita quipped. "You haven't been to Seattle since you moved home. It's a beautiful drive. Maybe being in the city will energize you. I seem to recall you telling me once that there are experiences you can only have in a city, not a small town."

"Yeah, well, I was wrong about a lot of stuff when I was eighteen," Elijah said with a laugh.

Nakita looked left and right for cars and pulled onto the road. In ninety minutes, they'd be in Seattle and she would no longer be bursting at the seams with the wonderful secret she had been dying to share with him. She flipped on the radio and dialed into a station playing classic rock.

She took the turn for the interstate and eased the sedan into the flow of traffic on I-5.

She hadn't been lying, it really *was* a beautiful drive. Rich green forest pressed in around the paved corridor of the freeway, and far ahead, the tip of Mount Rainier rose like a steeple on the horizon. Elijah sang along with the radio as they drove, and Nakita smiled happily at the off-key sound of his voice. It was going to be a wonderful day.

The flow of traffic grew thick and snarled as they neared the city.

"I definitely don't miss city driving," Elijah commented as they inched forward with the bumper-to-bumper jam.

The silver sedan dipped into a freeway tunnel that glowed red with brake lights, and Nakita glanced at her watch. They were going to be late. She drummed her fingers on the steering wheel impatiently.

"What's the holdup?" she murmured under her breath, craning her neck to check for an accident up ahead.

"Hey, it's the journey, not the destination," Elijah reminded her as he leaned over to kiss her cheek.

"Right."

Slowly but surely, they made it through the tunnel and emerged into the heart of the city. Nakita took the exit that Cindy had specified and turned left at the light. They drove past Pike Street and into a quaint neighborhood full of modern brick apartments over ground-level storefronts.

"This is the place," Nakita said, pulling forward to parallel park the sedan in front of a cozy Italian restaurant.

"Cute," Elijah commented, peering through the window. "How'd you find this place?"

"I didn't," she said, climbing out and closing the door. "Cindy recommended it."

"Cindy who?"

Nakita took his hand as they walked to the front door. "You'll see."

Nakita scanned the restaurant. Sitting at a table against the back wall was a woman with a graying bob, sipping a glass of water. In front of her on the tabletop was a stack of papers. Nakita took Elijah's hand and led him across the room.

"Nakita?" the woman asked, standing and offering her hand.

"Yes. Cindy?"

The woman nodded and turned to Elijah.

"And you must be Elijah Leith." She took his hand and shook it vigorously. "I can't tell you how much we loved your book."

Nakita risked a sideways glance. Elijah's face was lined with bewilderment as Cindy pumped his hand up and down.

"Uh . . . Thanks. Sorry," he said, "I'm a little confused, who are you?"

"Cindy Gresham," she said, "Madison House Publishing."

Elijah's jaw fell open and he turned to Nakita.

"I sent it in," she said with a smile, and watched the shock on his face turn into the radiant delight of a child on Christmas morning.

"You mean," he said, turning back to Cindy, "you want to publish it?"

Cindy nodded to the contract on the table. "Not just this manuscript; we'd like to support you for your next book as well. You've got a bright future as an author, Elijah."

Elijah's eyes misted over. He cleared his throat and pulled out a chair.

"I think I need to sit down."

Cindy signaled for the waiter and asked him to bring a bottle of champagne to the table.

As Cindy spoke about Elijah's manuscript, pouring out compliments about his writing, Elijah kept looking back and forth from her to Nakita with eyes full of disbelief.

When they'd finished eating and their plates had been cleared, Elijah signed the contract.

"Man, that's a great sound," he said as the pen scratched across the paper. He slid it back to Cindy, who offered him another handshake.

"We'll be in touch over the next few weeks." She smiled as she stood to leave. "For now, you two make sure and celebrate. This is a huge accomplishment, Elijah."

Nakita waited until Cindy had stepped out the door before squealing with delight and gripping Elijah's shoulders.

"You have no idea how hard that was to keep to myself all week!"

Elijah was staring at her with something like awe in his eyes.

"I don't know what to say," he whispered. "I don't know how to thank you. I never would have even written this book if it wasn't for you, let alone attempted to have it published. I just . . . I don't know what to say."

Nakita lifted her glass and touched it to his. "How about cheers?"

When the bottle was empty, they left the restaurant and decided on a walk through the neighborhood. Nakita felt like she was floating along the sidewalk, giddy with champagne and the success of her surprise.

"I just want to stop everyone we're walking past and tell them the news," she said to Elijah as they stepped into the Pike Street Market.

She stopped at a booth to stare at a row of foggy-eyed fish, and when she turned around, Elijah was holding out a bouquet of purple irises from another vendor. She took them and held them to her nose, inhaling the fresh green scent.

"I don't think anyone in my entire life has ever done something like this for me," Elijah said, shoving his hands in his pockets. "I just can't believe you did that. I can't believe you care so much about my writing that you chased down a publisher for it."

"I'd do anything for you," she said. "That's just how I am, when I make my mind up about someone or something, I'm all in." She gave a little laugh. "I remember one time about five years into my marriage with Kailen, I was out running and I had this whole scene play out in my head of how I'd fight someone to the death if it meant saving his life. Only when I got home did I realize how worked up I'd gotten over this imaginary scenario, and he laughed at me when I told him about it. I'm not sure most girls are like that, but when I say I'd do anything for the person I love, I literally mean I'd do anything."

Elijah smiled, but his eyes were serious. "I would, too."

Nakita took another long sniff of her flowers and held out her free hand to Elijah.

"So, what now?" she asked. "Will you quit your job at the paper now that you're officially a paid author?"

"I think so. Maybe I'll wait for the first check to clear just to be safe, then clean out my desk and bring everything home. I can always do freelance work in the meantime if this falls through."

"This isn't *Middletide*." Nakita gave his hand a reassuring squeeze. "This time it's really happening. You've done it."

Elijah beamed down at her. "I wish I could explain how good it feels. I feel invincible, like I can't lose."

Nakita's chest swelled with the happiness she heard in his voice, and she pulled her hand free to slide it around his waist.

"Let's go home."

35

From where he stood washing dishes, Elijah caught the shadow that crossed the front window. Wiping his wet hands on a dish towel, he stood behind the door and waited for the knock. As he let the lawyer in, Elijah looked him up and down the way he had the first two. This man was the third in what had so far been a disappointing first round of interviews. He looked about the same as the others—dark suit, clean shoes, neatly styled graying hair. Another of Chitto's *slickers* if he ever saw one.

The lawyer was looking him up and down, too, his eyes lingering on Elijah's left ankle, where the monitor bulged beneath the cuff of his pants.

"Come on in," Elijah beckoned. "Thanks for agreeing to meet with me, I appreciate it."

"I'm Kenneth Burke," the man said, reaching out to shake his hand. "Happy to be here."

Happy? Was he really *happy* to be here alone in a cabin in the woods with a man suspected of murder? Just another day on the job for a defense attorney.

"Let's sit at the table," Elijah said, leading him to the chair beside the computer.

Kenneth placed his briefcase on the ground and sat, looking around.

"Nice place. I've been wanting to get a second home up here, but my wife wants one in Hawaii, so we're torn."

"Oh." Elijah nodded.

The lawyer cleared his throat and lifted his briefcase onto the table.

"Now, I went over the details of the crime with Nakita Mills on the phone," Kenneth said, opening the case and pulling out the papers inside. "I won't lie to you, Elijah, it doesn't look good, but I'm happy to represent you if you wish. I've got a great record as a defense attorney, one of the best in Seattle, as I'm sure she told you."

Elijah didn't know what to say. Nakita had been searching for a lawyer for two weeks. Paying out of pocket for them to commute to Point Orchards and meet with him, but he already had a bad feeling about this guy. He seemed arrogant. Cocky. The last thing he wanted was to be defended in court by someone with an ego that could turn the jury off, but he owed it to Nakita to at least give him a chance.

"Where should I start?" he asked.

"First, why don't you go ahead and tell me your side of the story. I've already heard the cold, hard facts, but I want you to tell me in your own words about your past relationship with the victim and what happened that night."

Elijah sighed. By now, it felt like he was performing a soliloquy for a play, but he charged ahead with the story, brief and to the point. Yes, Erin Landry was an old girlfriend of his. No, he had never been violent with her. Yes, they had had a public fight where they yelled at each other in front of witnesses. No, he didn't kill her. Yes, the murder was similar to one he wrote about in his book. No, he had no idea who would want to frame him for such a heinous crime.

Kenneth nodded and scribbled on a piece of paper as Elijah went over the timeline of what had happened since Erin's death.

"I shouldn't have run to Nakita's house, I know that, but I just panicked. I knew what people were whispering about in town and I just couldn't stay here, knowing at some point the sheriff would show up and cart me off to jail. I knew it was coming, I just didn't want to be alone when the other shoe dropped."

"Understandable," Kenneth said with a nod as he continued to write. "I think a jury can be persuaded to believe that."

Elijah gave a smile that was half grimace. "The ironic thing is that all

I ever wanted was for people to read my book. I just never thought in a million years someone would use it against me."

"Well, we can be optimistic that there are enough discrepancies between the crime scene in your novel and the one in real life to convince a jury that it was purely coincidence, but we'll have our work cut out for us. Alibi?"

"I don't have one. I was here, asleep."

Kenneth scribbled another note. "And do you happen to know where Miss Mills was on the night it happened?"

It took a moment for Elijah to grasp what the man was asking him. "Are you asking me if the woman I love is guilty of murder?"

Kenneth sat back in his chair and looked at Elijah appraisingly for a long moment. "I'm asking if Nakita Mills, who is in fact your current girlfriend *and* a person who filed a formal complaint against the victim in her line of work, has an alibi for the night of the crime."

Elijah's hands clenched into fists beneath the table. "Mr. Burke, you don't know me from Adam, but I hope at the very least you can see how offensive that question is."

Kenneth laid his pen carefully on the paper and folded his hands. "Elijah," he said, leaning forward an inch. "It's my job to convince a jury of *your* innocence. Do you understand what I'm saying?"

Elijah opened his mouth, but Kenneth held up his hand and made a noise to stop him from speaking. "Say no more about it. I'm only responsible for what I *know*, if you catch my drift. Sometimes the best thing a defendant can do in a case like this is simply keep their mouth shut and leave plenty of room for doubt to be planted in the minds of the jury."

Elijah was flabbergasted. The first two lawyers he'd met with had been incompetent and admitted point-blank that they didn't think they could build a convincing case for his innocence, but this guy, this smug hotshot in his perfectly pressed two-piece suit, was basically telling him that he'd fight to get Elijah off the hook by sinking it into Nakita instead. Elijah wanted to scream, to grab Kenneth by the shoulders and slap the knowing smirk off his face. Instead, he rose calmly to his feet and held out his hand.

"Thank you for your time, Mr. Burke, but I don't think I'll be needing your representation."

Kenneth took the offered hand and shook it quickly. "You'll give me a call if you change your mind. I really do have the best record in Seattle, you can look it up."

Elijah followed him to the porch and closed the door behind him.

"What a jerk," he muttered under his breath as he reached for the phone and dialed the big house on the reservation.

Samuel Mills answered.

"How'd it go?"

"It could have been better. Is Nakita around?"

"I'll go and grab her. Hang in there, Elijah, we'll figure something out."

Elijah leaned against the counter, his shoulders slumped as he waited for Nakita's voice to come through the receiver.

"Any luck?" she asked eagerly.

"No. He was worse than the other two."

A heavy sigh on the other end of the line told him she was just as frustrated as he was.

"Can you come over?" Elijah asked.

"Yeah. I'll bring my dad. We'll figure this out, I promise."

Elijah hung up the phone and sat on the porch to wait. The fruit trees lining the front fence were naked, the grass beneath them dormant and dull. Winter was the year's ugliest season, and it was bitterly cold out, but Elijah couldn't spend one more second inside the house alone. Before his arrest, he had been relatively content in his own company in the cabin, but now, with no option to leave, it felt more and more like that dark, hard jail cell than home. He looked down at his shoes, fighting the urge to sprint toward the woods and just keep going until his legs were on fire, rip off the ankle monitor and chuck it into the lake to be rid of the thing.

Nakita and her father pulled in twenty minutes later and followed Elijah inside, where he told them about his meeting with Kenneth Burke.

"I mean, the arrogance, sitting there implying that he could set me free if we proved you were guilty."

"Forget about him. We'll just keep looking," Nakita said evenly, though she looked rattled as they took their seats at the table. "We won't give up until we find someone willing to fight for you because they understand what a huge mistake this is."

"Nakita, the trial starts in two weeks and we're wasting our time looking for a unicorn," Elijah said, shaking his head. "I mean, come on. You have to know how bad this looks; how guilty *I* look. If I didn't know any better, I'd probably think I did it, too."

Samuel Mills rose to his feet and came around to stand behind Elijah, placing a fatherly hand on his shoulder. "It does look dark. But you know the truth, Elijah, and the truth shall set you free."

Elijah turned to look at him, finding his steady eyes full of compassion.

"You really believe I didn't do it?"

The reverend's black eyes did not waver. "Beyond the shadow of a doubt."

Nakita stood.

"Then will you do it? Represent him at the trial?" she asked, her eyes trained on her father.

"What?" Elijah turned to her, but Nakita's gaze remained fixed on Samuel's face.

"I know you didn't graduate, but you took three years. Can you?"

"It's been thirty years since I studied law—"

"Can you?" she pressed. "Are you allowed to?"

It was a long moment before Samuel spoke. "I'm allowed to, yes."

"Then will you," she insisted.

Elijah closed his eyes as he waited for Samuel to decline, but the hand on his shoulder didn't flinch or recoil. Instead, it gave a reassuring squeeze.

"If God will grant me the right words to say, I'd be honored to defend him."

"Daddy," Nakita said, her voice choked as she came around the table to hug her father.

"Elijah, get me a notebook and pen," Samuel instructed, rising to his feet.

"I'll put on a pot of coffee," Nakita said, striding eagerly into the kitchen.

The heaviness of the impending trial weighing down on Elijah lifted a fraction of an inch as the three of them bustled around the cabin. Samuel Mills wasn't the hotshot city lawyer with twenty years of experience, but at least the three of them would build his case under the assumption that he was innocent, and that meant far more to Elijah than having a snazzy defense attorney with a great record. For the first time since his arrest, he felt the small, far-off whisper of hope.

36

Elijah sat bolt upright in bed. Sweat was beading on his forehead and his chest heaved with quick breaths as the dream faded into blurry unreality and he regained his bearings. He was in his dark bedroom, alone, not in the forest with Erin, following her through the woods to where two nooses hung side by side from the hemlock tree. One for each of them.

Elijah turned to the clock on his nightstand. It was five in the morning. At least he'd managed to rest for a few hours. He'd fallen asleep around one o'clock, when his racing mind finally caved in to exhaustion. He should try to get a few more hours of sleep, but the pounding of his heart would not slow as he lay with his eyes fixed on the ceiling. As scary as the dream had been, reality was worse.

Elijah climbed out of bed and walked to the kitchen. Early-morning moonlight poured in through the window and Elijah filled a glass with water at the sink. As he drank, he stared at the silver moon floating just above the treetops. Had Erin seen the moon on the night she died? Out there in the woods, was it still and quiet or had her screams for help vanished into the wind as her murderer tightened the rope around her neck?

For the thousandth time since he'd heard of Erin's death, Elijah tried to picture the man who had killed her, but the image was dark and undefined, the mystery man's identity evading his grasp. It could be anyone. It could be literally any citizen of Point Orchards. Or the reservation. Or Washington State. Or anywhere else. One thing he knew for sure was that whoever killed Erin had done a flawless job of dumping the crime onto Elijah's shoulders. What he didn't know was why. How could any living person hate him enough to frame him for murder?

Staring into the night world outside the window, Elijah felt the hair on the back of his neck rise. Had the murderer staked out his cabin in the dark, watching through the windows, learning his patterns and studying his behavior to plan and execute a crime tailor-fit to incriminate the man who lived inside?

Elijah took another drink and dove into his memories again, racking his brain for something, anything he could have done to create such a terrible unknown enemy. Since he came back to town, all he had done was work at the garage, sell produce at the market, and write for the paper. He'd come into contact with plenty of people in those three jobs, almost everyone in town at one point or another. But who had he hurt?

For a mere fraction of a second, an image flashed across Elijah's mind, an image so fleeting and forgotten that he almost didn't recognize it.

"No," he whispered, his eyes widening in the dark as he caught the memory and pulled it back to the forefront of his mind. "No," he repeated, shaking his head as he ran to turn on the lights.

He raced to the coat closet and threw it open, reaching up to pull down boxes from the top shelf. In one of them was the contents of his desk at the *Point Orchards Herald*, cleaned out and stored the day after he had cashed the paycheck for his advance. He found the box he was after and took it to the living room, overturning it and dumping everything right on the floor. Elijah knelt over the pile and began sorting through the newspaper clippings and photographs with his fingers.

At the very bottom of the pile was the photograph he was looking for, and he held it up to the light, his heart thudding wildly in his chest. His memory hadn't lied to him; there it was in full color in a five-by-eight photograph. Elijah stood and stepped over the mess as he walked to the phone. It was five-thirty. They'd probably be up. Maybe not, but this was worth waking them for.

"Hello?" the groggy voice of Reverend Mills answered on the third ring.

"It's me. I'm sorry to be calling so early, but can you and Nakita come down here?"

"What's going on?"

"I need you to see something. I think I know who's trying to frame me."

37

It was a perfect summer morning, all pale blues and golds and greens, but Erin did not lift her head to enjoy it as she walked to the marina. The day had one objective. Just one, and then her work would be over.

She passed the white gatehouse, holding up the card on a lanyard that permitted her access to the private dock where the expensive boats were housed. Inside the booth, the attendant sat behind a newspaper, a half-finished Danish in a plastic wrapper in front of him. He barely glanced up at her access card and waved a lazy hand for her to pass through.

Smile, she reminded herself. *Dazzle him. Make him remember that he saw you here this morning.*

"How are you, Frank?" she asked, reading his name tag.

Frank's eyes appeared from behind the newspaper again, and Erin slowly swiped her wave of blond hair back over her shoulder.

"Doing well, how 'bout yourself?"

"Lovely morning to be out on the water," she chirped brightly.

"It sure is," Frank said, folding his paper.

"I'm going to take Elijah Leith out in my boat today. If you see him, can you point him in the right direction?"

"Sure thing, ma'am."

Erin wiggled her fingers at Frank as she passed the booth, but the smile fell from her face the second she was out of his eyeline.

Her boat sat at the very end of a row of small luxury crafts, and she boarded it with the practiced balance of a sailor, trying not to breathe in the familiar scent of salt and leather. She used to love that smell. She used to love this boat. There was a time when she took it out on the sound every weekend, but tucked away in the storage space beneath the seat was a toddler-sized life jacket and far too many memories to reckon with. This would be her last time sailing the boat, and she was fine with that.

She sat still as a statue, scanning the marina, pleased to see the docks filling with people at this peak morning hour. It was early enough that fishermen would still be out, and late enough that pleasure-boaters would have finished their Saturday brunch and wandered down to the marina for some time on the water. There would be plenty of bystanders only too eager to spread the news of a shouting match between the town's doctor and the mysterious man who lived by himself in the woods. Erin tucked her purse beneath the bench and took the driver's seat. She pinched the key in her hand, twisting it back and forth between her index and middle fingers as she watched the marina parking lot.

A lean, shiny blue car slid behind the first row of vehicles, and Erin tracked it as it parked. Elijah climbed out and looked around. He didn't see Erin below the railing where she sat at the helm of her boat, fighting down the repulsion she always felt when he stepped into her line of sight. It never dulled, her rage at his effortless way of walking through the world like nothing bad had ever happened to him.

She closed her eyes and pulled a long breath in through her nose as she straightened her shoulders, reaching up to make sure her long hair was flipped attractively to the side.

Elijah passed the white booth, and Frank leaned out the window, pointing down to the dock where she sat. Elijah followed the wooden boardwalk down the hill and onto the water, offering a small wave as he approached.

"Hey!" she said, smiling brightly. "Thanks for meeting me here. I was just about to take the boat out; any chance you wanna come for a ride?"

"Oh, I— I can't. I've got a ton of stuff to do today."

Erin nodded, her sunny disposition falling into practiced disappointment.

"So, you said I left something at your house?" Elijah asked, his eagerness to leave evident in his tense stance.

"Oh, right! Here," she said, retrieving her purse from under the bench and pulling out a blue glass bottle of cologne. Elijah leaned down and lifted it from her fingers.

"Oh . . ." He turned it over in his hand, confused. "Yeah, this is mine. When did I leave it there?"

She shrugged. "Beats me."

You didn't. I took it from your house when I used the bathroom.

Elijah stared down at the bottle as he tried to retrieve a memory that didn't exist, while Erin kept her eyes on the boat's hood, right on the spot where the sun's reflection was gleaming against the shiny white paint. The brightness made her eyes water, but she let them fill, resisting the urge to blink.

"Well, I should probably get back home," Elijah said, taking a backward step. "I've got a lot of editing to do. Thanks, though." He held up the bottle appreciatively as he turned to leave.

"Elijah," Erin said softly, tearing her burning eyes from the hood and looking up at him. She blinked then, and two tears spilled in twin paths down her cheeks.

"Hey, are you okay?" he asked, stooping down on the dock to face her, his forehead lined with genuine concern.

Erin shook her head and lifted her finger to gently wipe away one of the tears.

"Do you have a second to talk?" she asked in her most vulnerable tone.

Elijah stood to full height and stole a quick glance over his shoulder.

"I don't know if we should. There's a lot of people here, and I don't want anything getting back to Nakita that sounds less than innocent."

Erin nodded sadly. "I understand. Really, I do. Please don't think I'm being unfair, but after all I've been through, I still feel like you and I didn't really reach a point of closure. I know you've moved on, and I'm happy for you, but I still have questions that need answering."

Elijah took another quick glance over his shoulder as he ducked down beside the boat again.

"Like what?" he asked just above a whisper.

Erin opened her mouth to speak, then lowered her head and shook it. "You're right. This should be a private conversation. I can come over sometime to talk about it."

"No." Elijah's voice was clipped and impatient. "No, we can talk about it now."

He took another quick scan of the marina and climbed down into her boat. "Let's just pull out of the harbor so we can have some privacy, okay?"

Erin smiled sweetly as she twisted the key and started the engine. "That's a great idea."

She pulled the boat smoothly around the docks and into the open mouth of the harbor. The little craft lilted up and down with the surges of water rushing in through the black-rock jetties on either side. She looked over her shoulder to find Elijah hunched in the back seat, his denim collar pulled up to hide half his face. What a fool. He was far more likely to be remembered like that, clearly trying to disguise himself, than if he'd simply offered a passing wave to other boaters, who would greet him and then forget him.

The little boat shot out past the jetties, and Erin gently guided it left where the murky, oil-slick water of the marina gave way to clean sapphire depths. She drove parallel to the shore for half a mile, nodding to the handful of other boats she passed, waving and smiling whenever she saw a male driver alone. Her hair blew wildly behind her. Any other day she'd have put it up in a ponytail, but not today. Men wouldn't forget seeing her long blond hair whip by on this perfect summer morning.

Up ahead, a little cove dimpled the shoreline, tucked far enough back to be shadowed by the forest around it. Erin pulled the boat inside and cut the engine. Two ducks near the shore squawked in protest as they flapped noisily across the water and took flight to seek solitude elsewhere.

Erin turned to face Elijah and found regret already written on his face.

"What's wrong?" she asked.

"We shouldn't be out here alone. I'll answer any questions you have, but let's just try to make it quick, okay?"

Erin left the front of the boat and took a seat beside him in the back.

"Elijah," she said calmly, "do you have any idea what it's like to have everything taken from you unfairly?"

Elijah blinked at the unexpected words. "Well, no, I mean, not in the way that you have, but I've seen loss. Plenty of it. And I wasn't trying to add to your hurt by breaking up with you. I just didn't think it was fair to keep stringing you along. I meant it when I said you deserved someone who is willing to put in the time with you."

Erin sighed and glanced around. They were wasting time back here, tucked out of sight where no one could overhear their conversation.

"Well, thanks," she said, turning back to Elijah, "I appreciate that. And you're right, I guess we probably don't want to be spotted out here by ourselves, let me get you back to the marina."

The relief was written across Elijah's face as he nodded at her, like someone who had been handed down a much lighter sentence than he'd expected.

Erin smiled as she started the boat and pulled out of the cove. He had no idea what was coming.

The boat slowed to approach the jetties and Erin guided it expertly into the harbor, waiting until they were mere feet from the dock before speaking again.

"Do you love her?" she asked over her shoulder.

Elijah was quiet in the back seat for a long moment, and as she pulled the boat to a stop Erin turned to face him.

"I said, do you love her?" she repeated a little louder.

"Yes."

"So, you always loved her then, you were just leading me on?" Erin added another few decibels to her voice, speaking loudly enough to attract a few stares.

"What? No. I mean, yes I've always loved her, but I wasn't trying to lead you on."

Elijah rose to his feet, and Erin pointed a finger at his chest.

"How dare you!" she accused, shouting now. "How dare you take advantage of me like that when you knew I was in a vulnerable place in my life!" She edged deliberately backward until she felt the rim of the boat behind her, then threw her arms out as though she was about to lose her balance and fall over the side.

Elijah did what she expected him to, reached out to grab her wrist in an effort to keep her on board.

"Erin, stop. We're fine, everything's fine," he hissed through gritted teeth. "You're causing a scene."

"Let go of me!" she shouted, wrenching her arm back far more dramatically than was necessary to free his grip. "Don't you ever lay a finger on me again!" She screamed the words into his stunned face. "I'll call the cops, do you hear me? I'll call the police if you ever touch me again!"

Elijah's expression was a perfect blend of bewilderment and desperation as he scrambled backward out of her boat and onto the dock, where at least a dozen bystanders were frozen in their tracks, watching the fight unfold.

"Get out!" she screamed. "Go!"

He turned and ran, pushing his way past the small crowd that had gathered along the railing.

The most difficult part of the whole charade was this moment. It was so hard to keep the smile of triumph from her face as she watched him sprinting toward his car, but the eyes of the witnesses were still on her, and faking a rasping sob, Erin started her boat again and roared back out of the harbor into the open expanse of sparkling blue water.

She had done it! There was so little goodness left in her life, so few moments of joy, but this one topped them all. She was high on the success of her plan, and she relished picturing him now, trying to catch his breath behind the wheel of the Camaro as he pulled out of the parking lot, humiliated and confused and, most of all, completely unaware that she had just created a moment out of thin air that would seal his fate.

Erin sank into the driver's seat with a contented sigh. Everything was falling into place. Later today she would pack up Anna's most precious treasures, and as soon as she could talk Manny into flying out to meet with her, they would be safely in his hands and she could get on with it.

She drove leisurely past the fishing boats that were dredging their nets back and forth for seafood, and drifted out to where the water and sky were only separated by the tiny green islands dimpling the horizon, before pulling the key from the ignition. In the back seat, Elijah had left the bottle of cologne lying on its side. Erin picked it up and held it out over the lapping water.

Still smiling, she loosened her grip and it slipped from her fingers, hitting the surface of the sound with a little splash. She watched it sink. A spot of sunlight glinted faintly off the glass until it was swallowed by the darkness.

38

From Nakita and her father came identical deer-in-the-headlights stares and neither spoke as Elijah held up the photograph.

"This was taken on the day her daughter died; it's a picture of her wreck that I used to write up the article in the paper. See that back right axle? You can see what's left of her tire hanging off in shreds. That's what caused the accident. Her back tire blew going around the curve. It was her tire!"

Nakita and Samuel shared a confused look.

"Elijah, you're not making any sense. What does that have to do with her murder?" Nakita asked.

"Erin brought her car in while I was working at Chitto's garage to have it serviced. While she was there, I told her I was going to rotate her tires. I mentioned that they looked worn, but I didn't tell her that she needed new ones. I didn't feel good about sending her back out on them, but that's what I did. It was only a year later that she had this accident that killed her little girl and I—I think . . ."

"You think she blamed you for her daughter's death," Samuel finished Elijah's thought, reaching for the photograph and inspecting it closely.

"Exactly." Elijah nodded, swallowing down the lump in his throat. "I should have told her to change her tires that day, but I didn't. I had no idea one would blow out and cause an accident. I'm not a crystal ball.

I never dreamed something like this would happen." His voice faltered and Elijah closed his eyes.

Nakita stepped forward and put her hands on his shoulders. "It's not your fault. It's just something that happened."

"She was so different after the accident," Elijah said quietly. "The life was just gone from her eyes. There was no personality anymore. Before the accident she was so friendly and happy. This is why she asked me out, to get close enough to me to figure out how to frame me. I knew something was off. I knew she didn't really like me. That's why she picked that fight with me at the marina, too, so we'd be heard arguing in public and people would suspect me after she died. It all makes sense. It was the ultimate revenge. She got even with me for killing her daughter *and* she got her escape from a life that was just too hard to bear after losing her family."

"So, you're saying her murder made to look like a suicide was actually a suicide made to look like a murder that was made to look like a suicide." Samuel's brow was lined with concentration as he unpacked the scenario.

"That's right," Elijah said. "Who else could it have been? She spent time with me. She learned my habits *and* she had the motive to do it."

"Do you honestly think losing her daughter would drive her to do something like this?"

Nakita still looked disbelieving, and Elijah turned to Samuel, the only parent in the room.

"Yes. There is no grief deeper than losing a child," Samuel confirmed with a sad nod. "Nothing more terrible."

"Okay let's say she did it, there's still one major problem," Nakita said. "We have to prove it in court."

"I know. I haven't figured out that part yet," Elijah admitted. "Erin was so much smarter than me, and if I'm right about this, then she had been planning it for a very long time. She was methodical and calculated and I'm guessing she left zero loose ends."

"If this is how it happened, then there's bound to be a way to prove it. If the three of us put our heads together, we'll find a way to crack it open," Nakita said firmly. "There's no such thing as a perfect murder."

39

Elijah took his seat behind the defense table, feeling keenly the hundreds of eyes boring into his back.

The courtroom smelled like old wood and far too many brands of perfume. Most of the women were gussied up in print dresses and heavily spritzed to witness his fight for innocence. The room buzzed with conversation, and Elijah couldn't help but hear it. His name bounced back and forth like a Ping-Pong ball around the room. A wave of nausea washed over him as he listened to the various snippets, realizing with a jolt that most of the conversations didn't center around whether or not he was guilty but whether he would receive life imprisonment or the death sentence.

"All rise," the bailiff called over the voices, "the Honorable Judge Gary Whalen presiding."

The sound of creaking wood filled the courtroom as the two hundred spectators who had managed to cram themselves into the small space stood from their benches. Outside, another hundred or so were bundled in coats and scarves, waiting around the steps or listening at windows that had been cracked open to bring fresh air into the packed room.

Elijah stood, too, his bare arm brushing the sleeve of Samuel Mills's shirt. He watched the door of the judge's office open, and a man in a long black cloak stepped out and climbed the stairs to take his seat.

For the first time in his life, Elijah felt the disorientation of an out-of-body experience. The present moment felt no more real to him than watching *Perry Mason* or *Matlock* on TV. He should be able to look up and see stage lights and cameras, rather than a blank ceiling with a spinning fan.

Across the aisle was the prosecutor, a carbon copy of the three Seattle lawyers Elijah had met with, and Elijah watched him through the corner of his eye, wondering when he was going to look over at the defense table, at the man he was trying to throw in prison for the rest of his days.

The judge took his seat and everyone in the courtroom followed suit. The prosecutor went back to the papers laid out in front of him, arranging them into neat piles. Past his table were the twelve faces of the jury, and they did nothing *but* watch Elijah. After the first few minutes, he avoided looking in their direction. It might seem shifty. It might imply guilt. Half of them were looking at him with curiosity, the other half with disgust. One woman appeared terrified that he might leap right out of his chair and string her up from the ceiling fan at any moment. For a system that was supposed to operate under the assumption of innocence, the twelve faces in that booth proclaimed the opposite loud and clear.

Judge Whalen beckoned the prosecutor forward to make his opening statement and the murmurs in the rows behind Elijah faded into a silence so heavy that Elijah heard the prosecutor's knee pop as he stood up.

"Ladies and gentlemen of the jury," he began, "the case I present to you today is a horrific one, not just in its gruesome details, but in its injustice to a beautiful and intelligent young doctor whom many in this town knew and loved. I will prove beyond the shadow of a doubt that her life was cut short in a brutal and calculated manner by the man you see sitting behind that table right there."

The prosecutor swung his arm to point, and Elijah flinched.

"Steady," Reverend Mills said under his breath.

"You will listen," the prosecutor went on, "as I present not only incriminating physical evidence, but ample means and motive as well, proving that Elijah Leith, the violent ex-lover of Erin Landry, led her into the woods on his property on the night of January second and hung her by the neck until dead. You will learn that he tried, and failed, to make her death look like a suicide and that he made far too many mistakes in the process. You will hear about how he evaded law enforcement afterward, and you will consider the fact that an innocent man has nothing to run from. No crime is perfect, ladies and gentlemen, and this crime is far, far from it. I believe that when this trial is over and you step into the chamber to make your decision, you will bring the hammer of justice down for a pillar of the community who did not deserve to die, and you *will* find the defendant, Elijah Leith, guilty of murder in the first degree. Thank you."

The prosecutor took his seat, and Elijah felt the angry flush running from his neck to his ears. He wanted to stand up and scream for the jury not to listen to the pile of nonsense they had just been fed, to leap across the table and slam his fist over and over into the face of the man who had just spooned them those lies, but that would hardly showcase his innocence. The judge called for the opening statement of the defense, and Samuel Mills rose, clearing his throat as he stepped out from behind the table.

"Good morning. Like many of you, I knew of Elijah Leith as the man who lived alone in a cabin in the woods. A writer. This is a small town, rumors spread, and by now most all of you know that Erin Landry's death looked an awful lot like the one Elijah wrote about in his book. That's convenient. Far too convenient. The case we're bringing to you tells a different story than the one the prosecutor laid out, but has an explanation for every single scrap of evidence that points in Elijah's direction. Our story is one about a woman driven out of her mind by grief and a longing for retaliation against the man she believed responsible for the death of her daughter. Our story is one of suicide made to look like murder."

The reverend paused as the ripples of shock moved through the crowd in audible gasps and unhappy whispers. Elijah bowed his head over his hands. These were not the sounds of a crowd that was on his side. It would be an uphill battle for his freedom.

"We are going to take you back not only to the night Erin Landry died, but to the months leading up to it, when she meticulously planned her suicide to look exactly like the version the prosecutor laid out for you. All I ask of you when you walk into that chamber at the end of this trial is to leave your emotions at the door and take the evidence inside. Another word for evidence is truth, and as we uncover the truth of Erin Landry's death together, you will find that Elijah Leith is not only innocent of murder, but the target of a broken woman, driven to psychosis by her blinding and understandable grief. Thank you."

Samuel Mills returned to his seat. Elijah risked a sideways glance at the jury and found stony faces unconvinced by the reverend's statement.

"The prosecution calls Kevin McGinty to the stand."

Elijah watched as a man he didn't recognize made his way to the front of the room. He wore dark-rimmed glasses over a straight nose, and though he was young, the perpetual slump in his thin shoulders told Elijah he was someone who spent all day at a desk. He reached the witness stand and took a seat, straightening the thin tie he wore over a white button-down shirt.

"Mr. McGinty, will you please tell this court what you do for a living?" the prosecutor asked, stepping up to the stand.

"Yes sir," he answered in a small voice. "I'm a DNA forensics specialist at Dynatec Laboratories in Seattle."

"In layman's terms, Mr. McGinty, what is your work in the sphere of criminal cases? And please do speak loudly."

Kevin McGinty touched the center of his glasses with a finger. "In layman's terms," he said only a little louder, "I analyze physical evidence such as blood and hair left at crime scenes for DNA, and I run it through our system to match it to suspects who are in a medical database."

"That's right." The prosecutor nodded. "And how accurate are the matches between the DNA left at crime scenes and the names in the database?"

"I'd say ninety-nine point nine percent. We're obligated to leave a small margin of error in any relatively new technology, but so far we don't believe we've had even one mismatch."

"Now, in this particular case, you were sent a single shoe and a small sample of blood collected from under the victim's fingernails." The prosecutor turned away from the witness stand and strode to his desk to snatch up a photograph. "We've got a picture of the shoe right here." He held the picture up to the jury and walked slowly along the row before carrying it to the witness stand and laying it on the railing. "This is a boot that belonged to Erin Landry and was found near her body. Do you recognize it?"

"Yes, sir, that's the boot that was sent to us for DNA extraction."

"That's right. Now, for those in the courtroom that can't see this photograph, can you explain what sort of evidence this boot has on it?"

"There's linear blood spatter in a diagonal line across the toe. Six drops."

"And were you able to match the DNA from the blood found on her shoes and under her fingernails to anyone in the Washington State medical database?"

"Yes, sir, we were."

"Can you kindly indicate for the jury who that DNA belonged to."

Elijah felt the breath leave his body as Kevin McGinty turned to look at him.

"The blood belonged to Elijah Leith, the defendant."

Another ripple of whispers ran through the crowd, this one loud enough for the judge to slam down his gavel and demand order.

The prosecutor plucked the photograph from the railing and folded it in his hands.

"Thank you, Mr. McGinty, that will be all." He turned to look down his nose at the defense table and nodded smugly. "Your witness, Mr. Mills."

Samuel scooted his chair back an inch, but Elijah clapped a hand onto his arm and leaned over to whisper a few sentences into his ear. Samuel nodded and stood, clearing his throat as he approached the witness stand.

"Mr. McGinty, you say that you match DNA found at crime scenes to a medical database. Can you explain what that is? Where do the names in that database come from?"

"Yes, it's pretty simple. When a patient at a hospital in the state of Washington has their blood drawn, in addition to it being tested for various levels and deficiencies for medical purposes, their DNA is entered into a database for future forensic purposes, not just for the identification of criminals, but victims as well. This has been helpful for identification in cases where a John or Jane Doe is disfigured or unclaimed by family postmortem. If their DNA matches anyone in the database, we now know exactly who they are."

"So, what you're saying is that a doctor who draws blood is responsible for entering that information in the database."

"Well, it would be the lab technician's job to enter it in the database, but the technician would receive the sample from a doctor, yes."

Reverend Mills nodded. "So, when my client, Elijah Leith, went in for a visit at Dr. Landry's clinic and she insisted on drawing two vials of blood, we can presume that that was when his information was entered into the database?"

Kevin McGinty shifted slightly in his chair. "Yes, I think that's a reasonable assumption."

"And how much blood is necessary to obtain a sample of DNA?"

"Not much really, no more than a drop or two."

"Then, is it possible, in your opinion, for one of those vials to be sent in for routine bloodwork and database collection and the other to be withheld for a separate purpose, such as to falsify blood spatter on a pair of shoes and under fingernails?"

A rash of loud murmurs sparked around the room and the prosecutor shot to his feet.

"Objection!" he shouted. "Judge Whalen, this is pure speculation."

Samuel Mills turned his dark eyes to the judge. "I only asked if it was possible, Your Honor, not probable."

The judge nodded at Kevin McGinty, who licked his lips and cast a quick glance at the jury, all of whom were leaning forward in their seats.

"Yes. I guess it's possible."

40

Elijah sat on the canvas cot, his arms resting on his knees, his head in his hands. He was back in the cold cell for the duration of the trial. The clock that hung outside ticked the minutes away, the steady mechanisms echoing faintly up and down the hall sixty times a minute, but from the angle of his cell, Elijah could not read the time. If he had to wager a guess based on absolutely nothing but the headache that throbbed around his bloodshot eyes, it was two in the morning.

He had given up the hope of a decent night's sleep and sat hunched on the cot thinking about Erin. Her ghost was with him in the cell, sitting across a mental chessboard, and Elijah was studying the pieces on her side, wondering what her next move would be. How could he counter it when she had locked his king into checkmate months ago? Every path to freedom had been blocked before he even understood that he was playing the game. He was in the fight of his life against a dead woman who had slammed and locked every possible door of escape.

Elijah lifted his head at the sound of footsteps in the hall.

"You shouldn't be here," he said, rising to his feet as Nakita appeared silhouetted against the fluorescent light of the main office. "You should be home getting some sleep."

Nakita shook her head as she reached through the bars to take his hand. "I couldn't sleep, thinking about you all alone down here."

"How'd you get in?"

"Jeremy's on an air mattress out front."

Elijah managed a dry chuckle. "I'm hardly a flight risk all locked up back here."

Nakita smiled sadly and ran her thumb along his knuckles.

"Any news?" Elijah asked hopefully.

"Nothing," she said quietly. "It seems like every scrap of evidence points right back to you. I just can't seem to find a chink in the armor."

Elijah swallowed hard. "We're running out of time, Nakita."

"I know." Her chin dipped and her hair fell in a dark wave around her shoulders. Elijah reached through the bars to take a lock of it in his fingers, and Nakita tilted her head until her cheek rested in his palm.

"I just want this to be over," she whispered.

"Your father's doing a good job in the courtroom," Elijah murmured. "He could still make a career out of this if he wanted to."

"He doesn't. Trust me."

A moment of silence passed and then Elijah cleared his throat.

"I need you to do something for me."

"Anything."

"Go to the cabin. The manuscript for my book is on the kitchen table. Can you write down a note on the front page? I want it dedicated to my dad. I want to make sure that gets done in case I don't . . . make it back there. I'm not sure if it's being stuck in here or going through the trial or what, but I've been thinking about him a lot. I screwed up, Nakita. I should have come home to see him. I shouldn't have wasted all those years being angry at him for his drinking. He was just trying to cope. Trying to survive. He wasn't doing it to hurt me."

Nakita's gaze fell to the floor, and Elijah watched her throat bob with emotion.

"What is it?" he asked.

"Elijah . . . Cindy called."

Elijah didn't want to ask the question, but the words fell out.

"They're dropping me because of the trial, aren't they?" he said numbly.

Nakita gave a sad nod of confirmation.

It was Elijah's turn to swallow down the lump in his throat. He felt the warning of tears behind his eyes and forced an obvious yawn.

"I should probably rest."

She nodded again. "At least try to get some sleep tonight. You don't want to look like a zombie in court tomorrow."

"I will," he lied. "You too."

"I'll see you tomorrow." Nakita kissed him through the bars and walked quickly back down the hall.

Elijah stood gripping the bars of his cell after she turned the corner. He heard a muffled conversation between Nakita and Jeremy in faint voices, and to his surprise, Jeremy appeared in the hall just a few minutes later, carrying a mug in his hand.

"So, uh," he stammered as he approached Elijah and held out the mug, "Nakita mentioned you were up thinking about everything so I'm bringing you the Jeremy Hart 'lights out special.' Here."

Elijah peered into the swirling liquid that was brown with just a hint of something viscous and blue.

"What is it?"

"Hot chocolate with a spoonful of NyQuil."

Elijah laughed and took the mug. "It sounds horrible. I'll give it a shot."

Jeremy stood still and watched Elijah throw back the contents of the mug. When he was finished, he grimaced.

"I also call it the 'choo-choo to dreamland express,'" the deputy said with a completely straight face, and Elijah laughed again as he wiped his mouth on his sleeve.

"You missed out on a career in marketing, Jeremy."

"I like doing this, though," the deputy said, missing the joke. "My dad always said real men were the ones who answered when the call of duty came. I like to think I have."

Elijah passed the empty mug back through the bars, and Jeremy took it but made no move to leave.

"I'll admit, that was quite the little rabbit trail Reverend Mills took us down with that DNA database stuff today. I didn't see that coming. Honestly, it rattled me a little bit, mostly because Erin was a doctor, so of all people, she *would* have had access to your blood. It's starting to make me rethink the whole case."

Elijah nodded. The deputy was starting to doubt. If only the jury would follow. It was clear that Jeremy wanted to talk about the case, but at the same time, he had carried them onto thin conversational ice. If Elijah said the wrong thing or pushed back too hard, he'd land himself in hot water. He opted for a question instead of an answer.

"How well did you know Erin?"

Jeremy's eyebrows lifted. "Well, I didn't, really. I've never been sick enough to go to her clinic, but she was always friendly around town, I guess. I didn't really know what her life was like until we found the diary."

Elijah's mouth popped open, but he closed it quickly, praying that the deputy would be willing to keep talking. "That's good detective work," he said, appealing to the young man's ego. "Were you the one that found it?"

"Yep. It was in her nightstand when we searched her place."

"You read the whole thing right then and there?"

"Well, there wasn't a whole lot to it. Dozen entries, maybe less, mostly about her relationship with you."

Elijah needed a copy of that diary. He needed a way to untangle the false threads that Erin had woven on those pages. He opted for a little white lie in the hopes it might work.

"That's one of the things that surprised me about this whole trial situation," he told Jeremy. "Even someone's personal diary can have copies of it printed up and handed over as evidence. I think Reverend Mills asked the sheriff for a copy. I haven't had a chance to see it yet, but I probably will in the morning."

Jeremy tilted his head thoughtfully. "Well, I . . . I mean I've got the diary here. I guess it wouldn't hurt to show it to you since you'll be looking over the pages in the morning."

Elijah kept his face casual. "Only if you wouldn't mind. Actually, I'm bored stiff back here, it would be nice to have something to read."

Jeremy looked at Elijah for a long, assessing moment, then he nodded and walked back down the hall, returning a minute later with a green journal in his hands.

"I'd better sit back here with you as you read it, though. I don't wanna come back to find pages flushed down the toilet."

Elijah wanted to laugh, but the deputy was stone serious.

He kept his face wiped clean of emotion as he read through Erin's entries. One after the other, they were full of mistruths about their relationship, about him, even about herself. The diary belonged to a happy-go-lucky girl. A girl in love. A girl whose relationship was going sour, and in the end, a girl afraid for her life. This diary did not belong to the icy and calculating woman he'd known. It belonged to someone who didn't exist, and that made perfect sense. That was a part of her plan. She hadn't written this for self-reflection; she had written it in the knowledge that it wouldn't be missed by whoever came to search her house. She'd created it to make Elijah look like a monster. Another piece of her chess game locked into place, and Elijah could almost hear the echoing sound of her laugh as she'd closed the journal for the final time and placed it somewhere it was sure to be found.

"Hmm," he said, flipping the pages back and forth, "that's interesting."

"What?" Jeremy asked, leaning closer.

"There's a spot at the top of every page for a date, but Erin never entered one. I would think most people who keep a diary mention when they're writing an entry, but if you were falsifying information in there, you wouldn't want to put dates, would you? Let's say she claimed that I shoved her on October eleventh but in court I could prove I had an alibi and wasn't with her that day?"

Jeremy reached through the bars and took the diary from Elijah's hand.

"You're right," he said, checking each page. "Not a single date."

Elijah drew a deep breath and plunged forward recklessly.

"Jeremy, I know things look bad, and I'm not gonna sit here and beg you to believe I didn't do this, but I could put my hand on a Bible right now and swear to you that there isn't a word of truth in that diary."

"But you did have a relationship with her."

Elijah nodded. "Yeah, I did."

"And she wrote in here about the fight you had on the docks. That happened. Plenty of people heard it and saw her throw you out of her boat."

"Because she *wanted* people to see it. It was another piece of evidence she was putting in place, I just didn't know it at the time. Think about it, Jeremy, someone as calm and collected as a doctor coming completely unhinged in front of dozens of people in public? That's not like her. She screamed for me to get off the boat and that she'd call you guys if I ever threatened her again, but did anyone on the docks actually hear me threaten her? No. They just assumed I had because of what she said."

Jeremy was staring down at the diary in his hands uncertainly.

"But— your book," he said firmly. "*Middletide*. You wrote about a murder just like this one. You probably researched long and hard to learn how to make a murder look like a suicide."

"And then what," Elijah spread his hands out in front of him. "I committed a murder just like one I'd already written? On my own property, where she was sure to be found and I'd be the main suspect? If I wanted to kill her, wouldn't I have at least done it in a way that wouldn't automatically incriminate me? Do you honestly think I'd leave her body there for you to find, on my property, in a crime exactly like the one in my book? I'd be the world's dumbest criminal."

Elijah watched Jeremy closely. The wheels were turning in the deputy's mind as he rubbed his fingers absently over the cover of the diary.

"The sheriff said you'd say that. That you'd try to outsmart everyone with the exact story you're telling me right now. Saying it couldn't be you because it was a perfect framing of your book and you'd have never done it that way."

Elijah reached out to wrap his hands around the steel bars. "Jeremy, you don't have to believe me. You're not the judge. You're not on the jury. But man to man, can't you see how it's at least possible that Erin planned this all along?"

Jeremy scratched at his stubble. "I'll admit that I can see *how*, but the real question is why. What did she have against you?"

Elijah's head fell forward and he told Jeremy about the car accident and Anna's death.

"I never would have put two and two together if I hadn't worked at the paper, but the photo landed on my desk and I saw the shredded tire for myself. I guess a mother never really gets over the death of her child. Especially if she knows exactly who to blame for it. At the end of the day, I can't deny the fact that at least some of the fault is on my shoulders. If I'd just made her change her tires, I don't think it would have happened. I'd give anything to go back to that day and do things over. If I could do that, I don't think I'd be here right now."

Through the bars, Jeremy's hand landed on Elijah's shoulder and Elijah looked up in surprise.

"I don't know why," the deputy said quietly, "but I want to believe you."

Elijah looked into Jeremy's brown eyes and found sympathy for the first time from anyone outside of Nakita's family. The deputy was about his age, maybe a little younger, and sure, this whole mess had pitted them against each other as enemies from the start, but in some other life, under completely different circumstances, he liked to think they could have been friends.

"Thanks," he said, and he meant it. The NyQuil was starting to kick in, and Elijah's eyelids drooped heavily between blinks.

"You should try to sleep." The deputy withdrew his hand. "Tomorrow's a big day. Oh, before I forget, we do have a little reading material if you want it."

"That would be nice."

"Mostly procedural stuff, though. Actually, the only novel we have in the place is yours."

Elijah's eyes flew open. "What did you say?"

"I said we have your book, you know, from when it was sent in to the station anonymously, remember? You want me to bring it back here?"

Elijah's brain wrapped itself around Jeremy's words, squeezing them until the answer popped through. *Of course! How had he missed it before?*

There it was. The chink in the armor. There was a way to win this chess game, just one way, but it meant finding a pawn, a single, innocent pawn in Erin's game that was still out there somewhere. The only problem was that Elijah had no idea where to look.

"Elijah?" Jeremy asked again. "You want the book?"

"No," Elijah replied, lying down on the cot and pulling the blanket up around his shoulders, "but thank you for asking."

41

Elijah settled into his chair behind the defense table. The room was even more crowded than it had been on the first day of the trial, and he had been steered by the sheriff and deputy through a mob of spectators outside that was at least twice the size it had been the day before. Every single one of them had been angling for a look at the man with the beard who kept his chin tucked as they led him inside.

Rumors of the case Elijah and his defense team were presenting must have spread like wildfire. The possibility of Erin's death swinging the metronome from suicide to murder and back to suicide was far and away the biggest news in the history of the small town, and what most folks had assumed would be a straightforward murder conviction now had sizzling drama. Still, the insults whispered under breaths and the dirty glances in his direction told Elijah that an impromptu poll of the crowd would see him favored for a guilty sentence.

The courtroom buzzed with impatience as the door to Judge Whalen's chamber remained shut five minutes past the hour. Elijah and Samuel sat side by side without speaking. Behind them, soft footsteps approached and wood groaned. Elijah pulled in a breath through his nose and smiled at the hint of vanilla and rain.

He didn't have to turn around to know that Nakita had slid onto the bench behind him.

Elijah glanced up at the bailiff, whose hard eyes were fixed on the defense team.

"Any luck?" he asked without moving his lips.

"Not yet," Nakita whispered back.

Elijah's shoulders fell an inch, and Reverend Mills offered him an encouraging nudge with his elbow.

"He's out there somewhere, Elijah," Nakita whispered. "I'll find him."

The bench creaked as she stood to leave, and Elijah listened to her footsteps as they faded from the courtroom.

The door to the judge's chamber opened, and Elijah rose with everyone else as Judge Whalen took a seat and scanned the room behind his half-moon glasses. He took a long drink from his glass of water and invited the prosecution to pick up the case where it had left off the day before.

The prosecutor shot eagerly to his feet and called for Sheriff Jim Godbout to take the stand.

All eyes were on the lined face of the sheriff as he took the witness stand and stated his name for the record.

"Sheriff Godbout, when you arrived at the crime scene on the morning of January third, how did you get there?"

"By boat. There's an inlet between two pines that flows from a lake on Elijah Leith's property."

"Now, here," the prosecutor laid a piece of paper in front of the sheriff, "is a tide chart for the night of January the second, when Dr. Landry was killed. The coroner places her death at roughly three in the morning, can you please tell the courtroom what the tide was like at three in the morning?"

"The tide was out," Jim said without looking at the chart.

"Yes." The prosecutor turned and carried the chart back to his desk. "It was low tide. Now, I've been out to this little lake, and I made the mistake of heading out without checking the tide chart first. I had to wait until the water rose enough for me to get the boat through. Which means, at low tide, when Erin Landry was killed, it's very unlikely that whoever killed her came with her by boat. Now, please tell us who lives on the other side of those woods, Sheriff Godbout."

"That would be Elijah Leith."

"Elijah Leith," the prosecutor repeated as he grabbed a paperback book from his desk.

Elijah's heart sank.

"The author of this book right here. *Middletide*." He passed the jury slowly, showing them the cover, his finger resting on the noose that hung from a tree in the center. "A story about a woman who is murdered in a crime meant to look like a suicide, a crime in which the tide plays a major role, a crime that reads awfully close to the killing of Erin Landry. *Middletide* is a book that flopped, ladies and gentlemen, because a critic wrote that the crime was not believable."

The room had settled into a tense silence as the prosecutor walked a slow circle around the open area between the jury and the witness stand. Elijah felt the tiny pulses of wind beating down on him from the ceiling fan, and for a split second, he considered running, just turning and bolting out the back door as fast and as far as he could, until he reclaimed his freedom or a bullet found the back of his head. Either way, he'd be out of this stifling courtroom that smelled like musty perfume, out from under the stare of hundreds of condemning eyes.

The prosecutor placed the book back on his table and returned to the witness stand.

"One more question, Sheriff Godbout. When you confronted Elijah at his cabin and he told you to obtain a warrant for his arrest if you wanted to take him in, what was your response?"

"I told him to stay put. I told him not to run."

"And when you returned with the warrant?"

"He was gone. I tracked him down at his girlfriend's house on the reservation."

"He fled arrest?"

"Yes."

"And on the way out to his cabin, you found a vehicle hidden in the nearby woods. A white BMW. Now, this almost goes without saying, but for the record, can you tell us who this car belonged to?"

"It belonged to Erin Landry."

More murmurs echoed around the courtroom, and Elijah closed his eyes, willing the day to be over. Being trapped alone in his tiny cell was miserable, but it was a thousand times better than having to sit here silently while a suited stranger convinced hundreds of people that he was a cold-blooded killer.

The prosecutor turned to the jury and held up a hand to count on his fingers.

"Let's see now, Elijah's blood on her shoes, a crime he knew good and well how to commit, access to the area from his property, near which her car was found, and fleeing arrest. There's one more piece to this puzzle, but I'll hold off on that one until I call my next witness. Thank you, Sheriff, no further questions."

As he strode back to his chair, the prosecutor nodded to Samuel Mills.

"Your witness."

Samuel stood slowly and Elijah looked up at him. What could he possibly ask the sheriff? How could he spin this in their favor? It looked terrible because Erin had designed it to look terrible. They had been pigeonholed. All Samuel could do was make the sheriff repeat the same information through the lens of her death being a suicide, but the more times they went over it, the less plausible it would seem. Samuel must have been on the same wavelength as Elijah, because he cleared his throat and sat back down.

"No questions."

"Well, no questions," the prosecutor repeated, standing again and stepping out from behind his table. "I sure am getting a lot of exercise today," he said to a few chuckles in the back of the room. "The prosecution calls Frank Gibson to the stand."

Elijah leaned to his right and muttered under his breath.

"We're getting clobbered."

"It's not over, son," Samuel whispered back. "Have faith."

A portly man in a white jacket a size too small made his way to the front of the room. He looked vaguely familiar, but Elijah couldn't place him.

"Mr. Gibson, please tell the courtroom what it is that you do for a living."

"I work down at the marina, manning the access booth to the luxury boats."

The prosecutor nodded. "Now, I know you see a lot of faces come and go, but Erin Landry had a hard face to forget, didn't she, Frank?"

Frank nodded, and a woman in the back gave a stiff cough. Elijah noticed the wedding band on Frank's third finger and wondered if the cougher was Frank's wife.

"Now, I want you to think back, Frank. Think back to this past summer. On the morning of July 10, Erin Landry took her boat out on the water, did she speak to you as she passed the booth?"

Frank nodded.

"What did she say?" the prosecutor prompted.

"Uh, she said good morning, and she said it was a nice day to be out on the water. And she told me she was taking Elijah Leith out on her boat and that if I saw him I should point him in the right direction."

"And did you see Mr. Leith that morning?"

"Yessir."

"That's right, you did. Because Erin Landry *did* take Elijah Leith out on her boat that morning, and something happened when they returned to the marina. Can you please tell the courtroom what that was?"

"They had a fight."

"Frank, will you please elaborate? What was said between the defendant and Dr. Landry?"

"They were standing in her boat, and I heard shouting, so I leaned out the window and I saw Erin pull her arm free. Elijah had her by the wrist, but she yanked her arm away and yelled that she'd call the cops if he ever touched her again. I was this close to heading down there and teaching him a lesson, but he jumped right out of her boat and left. When he passed my booth, he looked pretty mad."

The prosecutor turned to the jury and held up his index finger.

"There it is, folks; the final piece of the puzzle. Violence. Erin Landry and Elijah Leith had a public fight where he displayed an inclination toward violence. Violence toward a woman. Violence toward someone smaller than he was. Now, we all know that violence in public almost always foretells of worse violence in private, and I'd like to leave you for today with one word to chew on, a word that comes into play a whole lot in cases like this."

The prosecutor turned his back to the jury and, for the first time, looked Elijah straight in the eyes as he spoke.

"Escalation."

42

Elijah sat up at the sound of boots in the hall. Dawn light was spilling over the edge of the high window. It was about time for Jeremy to bring him his oatmeal and banana. Elijah stood to greet the deputy, but the sheriff appeared around the corner instead, breakfast tray in hand.

"Thanks," Elijah said stiffly as Jim slid the tray through the slot. Jim nodded and stayed standing on the other side of the bars as Elijah placed his breakfast on the cot and sat beside it.

"Is there something you need?" Elijah asked.

The sheriff hesitated, his hands on his hips.

"I just wanted to see how you're holding up through all this."

Elijah didn't look at him. He picked up the banana and started to peel it.

"Do you care? You think I killed her, so what does it matter?"

"It's the jury's job to decide if you're guilty or innocent, not mine."

"Great, thanks," Elijah retorted. "You walk all over my house and property, arrest me in front of my girlfriend and throw me in jail, and now you want to have a nice chat about how the fate of my future is in the hands of twelve people who couldn't care less whether I live or die."

"Elijah, I'm just doing my job."

He sounded resigned. Sad, even, and a stab of shame cut through Elijah's anger. He looked up and offered a slight nod.

"I know. You had a part to play in this game, and you've played it exactly how she wanted you to. I can't fault you for that."

The sheriff rested an arm on the cell door and pulled off his hat. "The God's honest truth is that I don't know what to believe anymore. I just keep turning this thing over in my head, trying to see it how I pictured it happening that night, and now I can't seem to make it work."

Elijah's oatmeal was growing cold, but it was the furthest thing from his mind. The sheriff was on the fence about his guilt, and if *he* was, maybe others were as well.

"What do you mean?" he asked.

The sheriff ran his thumb absently across the steel bars. "Something felt off the day I found her shoes in that log. It was too easy. I knew they'd be there. And I knew there'd be blood on them, probably your blood. You couldn't have done a better job of placing evidence if you were *trying* to get caught."

Elijah's eyes stayed locked on the sheriff's face. "But the idea of Erin setting it all up herself," he interjected, "you still think that's far-fetched, don't you?"

Jim closed his eyes.

"I don't know. Yes, I guess it's pretty far-fetched, but so is the alternative, and I can't think of any other options besides those two."

The sheriff opened his eyes and stared intently at Elijah, as though he could peer through the younger man's eyes and into his mind for the answer he sought.

"I guess what it boils down to is that I think you're smarter than that."

Their eyes stayed locked for a long moment, pale green in the lined face of the lawman at the door and vivid blue in the younger face of the captive on the cot, each seeking truth from the other.

"I am," Elijah said quietly. "I'm not saying I'm smarter than Erin, but she messed up somewhere, Sheriff. I just don't know if I can prove it before the trial gets turned over to the jury."

The sheriff didn't ask him what he meant and Elijah didn't elaborate. Technically, they weren't supposed to be talking about the case anyway.

"Eat up," Jim said, breaking the silence. "I'll walk you over there in half an hour."

Elijah ate his cold oatmeal and banana, deep in thought. As he scooped up the last of the oats with his spoon, he stared into the empty bowl with a dry mouth. Would this be the last meal he ate before a guilty conviction? If Nakita couldn't find the one person who could prove his innocence, then their window to fight this thing would slam shut after the final witnesses were called today.

The sheriff returned to unlock the cell, and Elijah was surprised that Jim did not cuff him as he led him across the street to the courthouse. The crowd was even larger than it had been the day before, and among the warmly dressed bodies were chunky black cameras and boom mics. White and red news vans from stations as far away as Portland were lined up and down the street. The press had caught wind of the trial, and they had showed up by the dozens to report the final day, shoving their way to the front of the throng to shout questions at Elijah and thrust their microphones into his face.

"Elijah, can you tell us why you didn't bury the body?"

"Mr. Leith, are you expecting a not-guilty verdict?"

"Elijah, do you have any comment about *Middletide* going back into print because of the trial?"

Elijah swiveled to face the reporter who held her microphone hopefully under his nose. He stared at her, bewildered, as a ray of sunshiny hope broke through the shell of desperation he'd been living in. Before he could open his mouth to ask her about it, the sheriff pulled him away toward the courthouse.

"Back off," Jim commanded, holding his arm out stiffly to give Elijah a wider berth up the stairs. "He's got nothing to say to you. Go on home."

"Thanks," Elijah breathed as the courtroom doors closed behind them.

Jim hesitated, and Elijah wondered if he had more to say, but he merely nodded toward the defense table and Elijah left him.

"Good luck," the sheriff called out behind him after a beat.

Beside the table, Samuel stood deep in conversation with Nakita.

From the looks on their faces, Elijah knew she still hadn't found the person they were after.

"Nothing?" he asked, taking his seat.

"I'm starting to think she went somewhere besides Seattle," Nakita said. "If she thought far enough ahead, then she would have known we'd be trying to track him down. This was the one loose end she had to leave untied, so she would have made it as hard as possible to find."

Elijah took his seat and folded his arms on the table. Seattle was a maze, a city you could lose yourself in easily, looking for anyone or anything. That's what Erin had wanted, for them to waste the little time they had left scurrying pointlessly around the city because they assumed that's where she had done it. Meanwhile, the clock was ticking the minutes away to his guilty sentence.

He turned to Nakita and her father.

"Try Yacolt," he said with a sudden flash of inspiration.

"Yacolt?" Nakita scoffed. Yacolt was the tiny community just north of the reservation, a town with a population of less than a thousand. Elijah had driven through it on his way to the fancy restaurant where he and Nakita had dined the night she told him Erin was responsible for her grandmother's death. He tried to pull an image of the "blink-and-you-miss-it" town into his mind, but he couldn't remember if Yacolt had a church, or a post office, or even a stoplight for that matter. But it was a relatively short drive, and it was the only real town within miles of Point Orchards. It would have been the perfect place for Erin to put the final piece of her plan into action.

"I know it's a long shot. But you've been running around Seattle for two days and I think that's what she wanted."

Nakita turned to her father and Samuel nodded. "It's worth the drive."

Nakita grabbed her purse and left without another word, taking with her the basket that held all of Elijah's eggs.

The bailiff announced the "all rise," and Judge Whalen stepped slowly up to his stand, looking every bit as tired as he had the day before. In a town where not much ever happened, these tedious all-day trial dates were surely not something he was used to. The jury, too, filed in with slumped shoulders and shadowed eyes, and Elijah realized he wasn't the only one who was losing sleep over his case.

The only person in the room who looked well rested was the prosecutor, who shot to his feet and cheerfully called Deputy Jeremy Hart to the stand.

Jeremy settled into the witness chair, and Elijah tried to catch his eye, but Jeremy was looking anywhere but at the defense table. As the prosecutor stepped up for questioning, Elijah noticed a journal tucked under the man's arm. It had a simple green cover, and Elijah's heart sank as he recognized it.

"Deputy Hart, on the morning of January 11, you and the sheriff entered the home of Dr. Erin Landry, is that correct?"

"Yes."

"And upstairs in her bedroom you found a diary." The prosecutor turned to face the courtroom and held the journal out. "This diary. Correct?"

"Yes, that's correct."

"I've marked a few passages here," he said, opening to a dog-eared page and laying the diary in front of Jeremy. "Will you please read aloud this one in the words of Erin Landry herself, marked in green."

Jeremy's eyes darted for an instant to where Elijah sat, just long enough for Elijah to see the apologetic flicker in his gaze.

"'He asked if I was seeing someone else and went on one of his rants about the women in this town being hung up on the men in their pasts. I'm just so embarrassed. There were a ton of people out at the marina, and by the time we pulled in to the dock, both of our voices were raised and he grabbed me hard by the wrist. I docked the boat and told him to get off and we parted ways. I made it very clear that whatever this was was over. I'm not proud of what happened. I'm still shaken up about it to be honest.'"

Loud whispers broke across the courtroom benches behind him, and Elijah's head began to swim with the realization that everyone in the crowd was buying it. Everyone believed the lies Erin had written. This was unjust. It was unfair. It was just flat out *wrong*. It had been one thing to sit in his cell and read the words he knew were untrue, but for them to be read aloud here, with everyone in the room listening and swallowing them down as truth exactly the way Erin intended, it was just too much to bear.

"That's a lie!" Elijah burst out, leaping to his feet and shocking the room into gasping silence. "She's a liar! It didn't happen like that!"

Judge Whalen's gavel came down in three sharp whacks.

"That's your one warning, Mr. Leith!" he shouted, his finger pointed straight at Elijah. "One more outburst like that and I'll hold you in contempt of court, do you understand me?"

Elijah sank back into his chair amid the hushed murmurs of discontent behind him.

"May I continue, Your Honor?" the prosecutor asked, still perfectly calm and collected.

"You may."

"And this earlier passage right here, please, also marked in green."

Jeremy's face appeared pained as he turned back to Erin's diary and read the second passage.

"'He pushed me out of his arms and I fell against the table and whacked the back of my head. Not hard enough to cause a concussion or anything, but hard enough to really, really scare me. I was shocked, and I think he saw that in my eyes, because the anger when he pushed me seemed to just fall away all at once and he was at my side in a heartbeat, checking my head and saying "I'm sorry, I'm so sorry" over and over.'"

Judge Whalen had lost control of the crowd. Accusations were no longer whispered beneath breaths but shouted in the open all around the room. Elijah's face was in his hands as the words *murderer* and *monster* landed on his back like blows. In the front of the room, just loudly enough to be heard, the prosecutor announced that he had no further questions.

Erin had won. It might as well have been her in the witness stand, exhumed from the grave, telling the town that Elijah was the one who had killed her. How could they argue with what she had said in her own words? The diary was her trump card and the prosecutor had played it at the perfect moment. The final few grains of sand were slipping into the bottom half of the hourglass. It didn't matter that Elijah knew he was innocent; they had run out of time to prove it.

Samuel Mills rose to his feet and walked slowly to the witness stand. Judge Whalen was still calling for order and, inch by inch, regaining it. When the room was quiet enough for the judge to be heard, he told Samuel to proceed with his cross-examination.

"Deputy Hart," Reverend Mills began. "Will you please tell the court the date of that final diary entry."

Jeremy sat up a little straighter. "I can't. There isn't one."

"No," Samuel said, turning to the jury, "there isn't. There isn't a single dated entry in the diary, because Erin Landry didn't want anyone to have the ability to check her story against a calendar."

He turned back to the witness stand. "Deputy, I won't ask you to read any more from that diary. There's only one question I can ask you, and it's the very basic question of credibility. The words are on the page. There's no undoing that now. The story has been passed from pen to paper. But from mind to pen, we can never know how much truth is in the words of a woman who was full of despair and longing for someone to pay for the hurt she had suffered. This whole courtroom already knows the answer, but in your opinion, is it possible that Erin Landry was lying in her diary?"

"Yes." Jeremy's answer was swift and firm, but it could not undo the damage that Elijah felt all around him in the courtroom. There was no one left to testify. No witnesses left to call. The only case he had presented was the leanest suggestion of suicide to save his own skin. There had been no way to prove that she killed herself to frame him. No one had told the truth. The jury had decided already; it was written in the hard lines of their faces as they watched Jeremy rise to step down from the witness stand.

The judge turned his face to the jury and opened his mouth to speak just as the back door of the courtroom flew open with a bang. Every head turned, including Elijah's. Nakita stood with sunlight pouring in around her. A man stood behind her shoulder like a shadow, and Elijah's heart leapt in his chest as they stepped into the room and he recognized the white-and-blue insignia of the man's uniform.

"Praise God," Samuel breathed, turning to face the judge.

"Your Honor, may I have a word with my daughter?"

The judge nodded.

Nakita rushed to Samuel, and they spoke in whispers with their foreheads almost touching. Elijah stared at the skinny middle-aged postman, with a thick head of white hair and a drooping mustache, who stood awkwardly in the middle of the aisle. He had never been happier to see a complete stranger in his life.

"With permission, Your Honor, the defense has one last witness," Samuel Mills said loudly. "We call Martin Shaw to the stand."

The postman took the stand amid confusion in the courtroom. Not one spectator in the room recognized him or knew why he was there.

Samuel turned to face the crowd, not the witness, as he spoke.

"On the tenth of January, seven days after the death of Erin Landry, a package arrived on the sheriff's desk. Inside that package was a copy of Elijah Leith's book and a note encouraging the sheriff to investigate Elijah as a suspect in Erin's death based on the content of his novel. On the outside of that package was no return address. Just postage." He turned to face Martin Shaw.

"Mr. Shaw, at your post office in Yacolt, is it possible for someone to drop off a package with instructions to have it delivered at a later date?"

Martin Shaw nodded. "Yes. It happens all the time. We time-delay packages so that they'll arrive on people's birthdays and anniversaries, things like that."

"My daughter, Nakita, asked you today if you remembered a package sent from your facility to the Point Orchards Police Department with instructions for delivery on January 10. Do you?"

"I do. A woman came in when we opened on the Friday before New Year's and asked for her package to be delivered there on the tenth of January."

Samuel strode for the defense table, where Nakita had placed a framed portrait of Erin, taken from the wall of her clinic office. He lifted the frame and carried it to the jury, giving each and every one of the twelve jurors a close look into the face of Erin Landry before he carried it to the stand and laid it on the railing.

"Mr. Shaw, beyond any shadow of a doubt, was this woman, Erin Landry, the one who asked you to send that package?"

The room was soundless, the tension unbearable, and Elijah was certain he would lose the man's answer in the sound of blood rushing past his ears, but when Martin Shaw spoke, his voice rang out clear and sharp, cutting through the breathless silence like an axe.

"That's her."

43

The jury was out for exactly nineteen minutes. During that stretch, Elijah laid his head on the desk and, for the first time in his adult life, breathed a prayer of thanks.

All around the courtroom, hushed voices were discussing the shocking twist delivered by the final witness, but for the first time since the trial started, Elijah had no trouble tuning them out. Their chatter was no more distinct than the steady hum of the Camaro's engine as he basked in the cleansing wave of relief.

In just a few minutes, it would be over. Martin Shaw had identified Erin as the person who mailed his book to the sheriff, and in that moment, with those two simple words from a man he had never met, the hideous, ever-building tension he had felt since the news of Erin's death had started to drain away. But he knew the anxious adrenaline pulsing through his veins wouldn't clear altogether until he heard the words *not guilty*.

The desk was cold against his forehead and Elijah opened his eyes, bringing the grain of the wood into focus. It was dense and intricately swirled beneath a thick layer of varnish, probably oak, long and slow burning. Samuel placed a gentle hand on his back, but Elijah's forehead stayed pressed against the desk. He no longer cared what the people behind him thought. They could judge him all they wanted now; it was over.

The postman from Yacolt slipped quietly out of the witness stand and walked over to Nakita to ask for a ride back to work. As she led him through the room full of strangers, Elijah smiled. Martin Shaw would certainly have a story to tell his wife over dinner tonight.

Elijah finally lifted his head when the door to the jury chamber opened with a creak. He watched the twelve people as they climbed into the jury box with downcast faces. Judge Whalen lightly tapped the gavel.

"Please rise for the reading of the verdict."

Elijah stood with everyone else as the man at the far end of the jury box, the one Elijah recognized as the owner of the grocery store across the street from Chitto's garage, turned to face the courtroom and cleared his throat.

"We the jury find the defendant, Elijah Leith, not guilty of murder in the first degree."

Even though Elijah had sat just feet from the witness stand as Martin Shaw proved his innocence, he had still expected the verdict to fall with the commotion of a bomb dropped into the courtroom. That's the way it happened in the movies. But as his freedom was announced, there was only a collective sigh that seemed to carry all the air in the room out with it.

Judge Whalen turned to Elijah.

"Mr. Leith, I'd like to apologize on behalf of the court for your time spent in detainment. You're free to go."

Elijah turned around. Every eye in the courtroom was on him. Every one of them now knew what he had known all along, that he, Elijah Leith, was the victim of this crime, not the offender.

Though he was tempted to linger over the faces of the townsfolk who had wrongly turned against him, Elijah looked over their heads to the back of the room, where the sheriff and deputy stood side by side. He lifted his chin and met Jim Godbout's eyes. The ghost of a smile crossed the sheriff's lined face, and he nodded slowly to Elijah before turning and pushing his way through the back doors.

Nakita was parked in front of the cabin when Elijah arrived home, and he embraced her wordlessly in the driveway, clinging tightly to her slender frame. The sun was bright above and the snow was half-melted, some still sitting in patches around the yard and pushed at angles into the corners of the building. Elijah held Nakita's warm body for long minutes, breathing in the smell of her, fighting back the awareness of how narrow his escape had been, how close he had come to never being able to hold her like this again.

"Thank you," he whispered into her hair. "Thank you."

When he finally pulled back, he lifted his hands to cup her face.

"Did you ever doubt me?" he asked, his eyes deeply shadowed. "Did you ever wonder if I was guilty?"

"Yes," she said, holding his gaze. "For maybe twenty seconds after I first heard the news."

Elijah couldn't have explained why, but he laughed. Her honesty was as dependable as the sun rising in the east, and it was the thing he loved most about her. She would always be real with him.

"I'll light a fire and make us something to eat," she said with a smile. "You must be starving." She kissed the inside of the hand still cupping her face and turned away, walking toward the porch.

"I'll be back in a bit," he called after her.

Elijah ran past his cabin and straight into the woods, just for the pleasure of being free to do so. As he ran, he reached out to touch the dormant berry bushes and brush his fingers over the top of a cluster of ferns. These woods were his future. His life would be green and full of light, not the dark, concrete existence of a prisoner. Not the life Erin died believing she had condemned him to.

His legs carried him forward without forethought, and Elijah found himself running farther and farther down the trail. It cut a bare ribbon through the snow-kissed forest, and when Elijah reached the nettles, he plunged through the dead stalks, breathing hard. He startled two deer, who leapt in graceful bounds into the deep part of the woods, but his eyes were on the lake ahead.

He ran straight to the hemlock tree and stopped beneath its boughs. He was sweating under his jeans and jacket and his breath came in heavy rasps. He looked up into the branches of the tree, searching. He had assumed there would be some lingering sign of what had happened here, some broken twig where Erin had climbed or some small threads of the rope she had used, but he found nothing. There was nothing left of her, and Elijah would not let what she had done ruin this beautiful place. He would not allow her to haunt his woods. This place belonged to him, and to Nakita, not Erin. In time, forgiveness would take root and even now, he could feel his resentment folding under the weight of pity. More than anything else, he was sorry for her.

Someday, beneath the carving he had etched at seventeen, he would engrave the initials of his children. He would swim in this lake with his family, pick berries with his kids in the forest, and continue to learn the endless lessons of the land alongside the people he loved most.

Elijah placed his hand against the bark of the hemlock and lowered his head.

"I don't—"

He stopped, his words choked with emotion.

"I don't know if I can forgive you, but I hope—"

His voice caught again, and Elijah swallowed back the guilt that rose like bile in his throat. Through misty eyes, he turned to stare at the frosty lake, where white tendrils of vapor were rising from a surface as still and perfect as glass.

"I hope wherever you are, that you're together. That you're with her again."

Elijah watched the fog lifting from the lake as the sweat cooled beneath his clothes. Slowly but surely the chill crept in, and soon a steady shiver ran the length of skin between his shoulder blades.

Turning his back on the lake, Elijah caught sight of distant woodsmoke puffing merrily above the eastern treetops. He smiled as he turned and ran back into the woods. Back to the woman who was waiting for him on the other side.

Epilogue

Twinkling white lights were the only decoration in the old church on the reservation. It was all she had wanted, for the room to glow like it was full of fireflies. The tiny bulbs shone against the rustic wooden benches and looped around the altar, where a single lit candle illuminated the open Bible in Reverend Samuel Mills's hands. Nakita had asked Elijah for a night wedding, and the darkness outside the windows only added to the enchanting glow inside the church.

She had wed Kailen in the traditional ceremony of the Squalomah; outside in broad daylight, everyone on the reservation dressed in colorful garb as vows were exchanged and a feast partaken between traditional dances. Her nani had sat in the place of honor, rising to give a speech about the sacred bond between two halves that Mother Earth had destined to form a whole before the beginning of time, but Nakita no longer believed that ancient myth. Life was messy. Unpredictable. And marriage, while still a sacred union, was far more practical. It was an agreement between two people who woke up and chose to face whatever life brought them together day after day. This marriage was not a match made by an earth goddess an eon ago, but a relationship that had been tested and stretched, nearly broken and reforged stronger in the end. Nakita had surrendered her belief in the destiny of Mother Earth to the will of her father's God, the one whose book he was holding in his hands.

"'Love is patient,'" Samuel read aloud. "'Love is kind. It does not envy, it does not boast.'"

Nakita basked in the wonder of Elijah's gaze and smiled softly at her groom from behind her veil as the words of Paul the Apostle fell around them.

"'Love is not proud,'" her father read on. "'It does not dishonor others, it is not self-seeking, it is not easily angered, it keeps no record of wrongs. Love does not delight in evil but rejoices with the truth.'"

Her father lifted his face from the text and looked from Nakita to Elijah as he finished the passage from memory.

"It always protects, always trusts, always hopes, always perseveres. Love never fails."

Nakita watched as her father placed the Bible on the altar and nodded to the three young men who stood at the back of the church, the only witnesses to the ceremony. They raised the flutes that Elijah had given them, Chitto's flutes, and began to play, filling the empty church with the haunting spirit sound that was half music, half whispering wind.

Nakita recited vows that were straightforward and true, telling Elijah that she was honored to accept his hand and work alongside him for the rest of their lives in a bond as unbreakable as stone, through whatever joy or sorrow life brought them. She listened as Elijah recited vows that were tender and loving, promising her the adoration that she deserved and the loyalty she had earned as the only woman he had ever loved; the only one he ever would love.

She closed her eyes as he lifted her veil and let it fall back over her hair. Her father reached for her hand and placed it into Elijah's, stepping back as her groom pulled her close, kissing her in the glowing light, with the sound of Chitto's flutes swirling around them.

They walked slowly hand in hand down the aisle, husband and wife. Nakita looked up at the man who was gazing at her, his chest swollen with pride as he opened the door and she stepped through.

When the door closed behind them and they were alone in the warm, still night, Nakita turned to face him. The muted flute song in its final refrain faded away and was replaced by the gentle chirping of frogs and crickets alongside the riverbed.

Elijah bent his head to kiss her again, this time deep and lingering, his hands gently cupping her face.

"I was thinking," he murmured between kisses, "why not come back here? To this church. We can renew our vows every year. Every five. Every hundred."

Nakita pulled away and smiled happily up at him, her black eyes reflecting the star-filled sky above.

"I'll be here."

He returned her smile with one of his own, full of love and intention. "So will I."

THE END.

Acknowledgments

I would like to acknowledge the extraordinary wealth of stories that have shaped my writing. Without those many imaginative pioneers putting their pens to paper, this page and all those before it would not exist.

A thousand thanks to my editor, Lindsay Sagnette, who is one of the brightest human beings to grace the publishing industry, or any other industry, for that matter, and whose sharp eye and guiding hand brought my story to life in a way I never dared believe possible.

To my agent, Jane Dystel, for taking a chance on a manuscript with a made-up word for a title and a fast-talking scatterbrain for an author. I am forever grateful.

To the entire team at Atria, who gathered behind this book and launched it into the world with an amount of energy and enthusiasm that writers only dream about.

To Tina Muir, the voice of encouragement and support in my life. Thank you for fifteen years of stubbornly refusing to give up on me.

To my husband, best friend, and diaper-changer-in-arms, who supported this ridiculous dream of mine long before it brought in a cent. Michael, you are a saint.

And finally, to my children, Charlotte and Emerson, who were immensely disappointed to find out that the book Mommy wrote contained no pictures.

About the Author

Sarah Crouch is known for her accolades in the world of athletics as a professional marathoner and four-time Olympic Trials qualifier. She was raised in the Pacific Northwest, and currently lives in the South with her husband and two children.